Edna

Why does Cathie Giffor[...] feel compelled to tend [...] lying in the grounds of [...] estate? For Piers Denham, a handsome aristocrat, has chosen to fight against his own kind and serve as a captain under Cromwell. Doubly an enemy, he is now at the mercy of Cathie and her beautiful widowed cousin Rachel, who has fled from Exeter to seek refuge with the Giffords.

Why should such a man cause Cathie to doubt her loyalty to the King's cause? Anyway why should she resent so fiercely the fact that Rachel Devereux seems more welcome at Piers' bedside than Cathie herself?

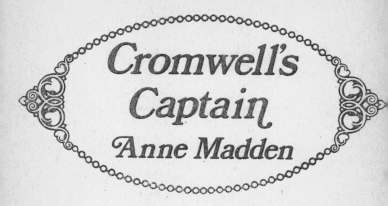

Cromwell's Captain
Anne Madden

MILLS & BOON LIMITED
London · Sydney · Toronto

First published in Great Britain 1980
by Mills & Boon Limited, 15–16 Brook's Mews,
London W1Y 1LF

ISBN 0 263 73230 4

Set in Plantin 9 on 10pt

Made and printed in Great Britain by
C. Nicholls & Company Ltd.,
The Philips Park Press, Manchester

CHAPTER
ONE

IT was during the afternoon that they heard the sound of shots being fired—a sudden burst, followed by a spattering in reply. Then a brief silence.

'What was that?' Mary, hand at her throat, had risen, her needlework slipping from her lap to the floor. 'Can you see anything, John?'

The latter was already halfway to the window, but had no time to answer her before they heard the second volley.

'It's coming from the bridge!' Cathie exclaimed, joining her brother. They could not see the bridge from the windows of the winter-parlour. 'If we went out——'

'*No*!' Mary's tone was forceful. 'You must not. I forbid it!'

They looked at their sister-in-law in undecided silence. Then, with a quick glance at John, Cathie nodded.

'Very well, Mary. But I wish we knew——'

The door opened. A young woman entered the room with a rustle of wine-red silken skirts. Slightly younger than Mary, she was darkly beautiful, her green eyes, almond-shaped, long-lashed, brilliant with excitement.

'So you heard it too! Can Fairfax have sent an advance guard into the valley?'

'I shouldn't think so, Rachel.' John was frowning slightly, deliberating. 'He would scarcely bring his army *this* way.'

'He has already advanced beyond Crediton; and the Royalists are only on the other side of the Cornish border. They may even have crossed it by now, if Lord Hopton intends to force a battle.'

Mary, who was expecting her first child within a few weeks, sank back into her chair, her face whitening. Her husband, Sir James Gifford, was with Hopton's troops. She bent forward awkwardly to retrieve her needlework, but Cathie went to her aid, handing it to her with a quick, reassuring smile.

'Now that Lord Hopton is back at the head of the army, things will be better,' she said stoutly. 'Didn't James tell us he was the best leader we had in the west? Better, even, than Sir Richard Grenville, who he said was always quarrelling and causing trouble with the others, before being deprived of his command.'

'And ten times better than Lord Goring, who from all accounts was always drunk,' John observed, returning to his post at the window.

Rachel Devereux shrugged. 'Drunk or not, he had a way with him. Can you see anything?'

She went to stand beside John, and he gave her a swift, sideways glance that was not lost on Cathie, watching them with that feeling of helpless resentment the sight of them together always gave her. Even now, when anything might happen at any minute, John could not help but show how completely he was beneath Rachel's spell: a spell she had cast upon him ever since her arrival at Fern Place in the previous autumn, fleeing from Exeter before the Parliamentarian advance upon the city.

Her arrival had been as dramatic and unexpected as her own turbulent personality. Not for her the exhausting journey seated pillion-wise behind the groom; she and her maid, Grace, had been carried all the way in a fine gilded coach, with an armed escort provided by her good friend, Lord George Randolph, whose father was one of the King's counsellors. Cathie suspected he must be a very good friend indeed, and had said as much to John, expecting him to share her amusement, but to her surprise he had curtly bidden her to hold her tongue.

Her surprise had rapidly given way to wrathful indignation as she had watched him with Rachel, his eyes adoring her, his boyish face radiant whenever she turned to him.

At twenty-two Rachel was nearly three years his senior, used to commanding attention, accepting homage as her due, experienced and completely self-interested. In the ordinary course of events their paths would never have crossed, but circumstances had brought them together and Rachel, faced with perhaps months of boredom at Fern Place, was only too ready to divert herself with a new, if somewhat inept, admirer.

For the first time in her eighteen years, Cathie found herself bereft of her brother's companionship, no longer permitted to share his thoughts and pursuits. He had become almost a stranger, with time, it seemed, for no one but Rachel.

'A plague upon her!' Cathie thought uncharitably, and found Mary watching her with understanding. Mary did not like Rachel

any more than she did, but being older and wiser had learned to
guard her feelings.

'There's still something happening down there,' said Rachel.
'Oh, if only we knew what it was all about!'

'Mary has forbidden us to go out,' John murmured.

Rachel looked over her shoulder. 'She is concerned for your
welfare, no doubt.'

Her voice was silken-soft, but Mary flushed. 'In James's absence,
I *am* responsible for the household.'

'Of course.' Rachel sounded amused. She turned back to her
contemplation of the grey scene, over which the February sky
pressed down, heavy with rain-clouds.

Cathie glared at her behind her back, wishing, not for the first
time, that she had never come to Fern Place and disrupted their
lives. Yet, how could they have refused to take her in? She was their
cousin, after all, and moreover a widow, whose own home had been
seized by the Roundheads. She had nowhere else to go.

Annie came in, her rosy face drawn with anxiety. She had started
to work at Fern Place when she was a young girl, many years ago,
and now, middle-aged and matronly, held the position of cook.

'Did you hear it, my lady? Do you think it be they Roundheads
come at last?'

While Mary attempted to allay her fears, Cathie saw that John
slipped out of the room. Without a moment's hesitation she
followed him, guessing at once that he would go down to the bridge.

It took her but a moment to change into stouter shoes and throw a
warm cloak round her shoulders. Avoiding the avenue which led
from the front entrance to the main gates, she ran through the
garden and down the slope, almost losing her footing on the wet,
slippery grass and the patches of mud. She reached the gate in the
wall and went out into the lane. John was trudging towards the
bridge, his big dog, Shag, bounding ahead of him.

'John! Wait for me!'

He paused and looked back at her as she hastened after him.
'What are you doing here?' He did not sound very welcoming. 'Why
did you follow me?'

'I wanted to. What do you think we shall find?' She fell into step
beside him.

'I don't know. A few dead bodies, perhaps.' She shivered. 'You
should not have come. Go back to the house. Send Reuben, if you
like.'

Reuben was Annie's husband, and one of the few able-bodied men left at the house.

'No.' Her chin was set at a stubborn angle. 'I'm not frightened.'

They had reached the road that led towards the river. In a few minutes they would come to the group of trees and bushes that grew thickly a short distance from the little hump-backed bridge. Instinctively their steps slowed as they neared it. Shag had gone in among the trees and was lost to sight.

The stillness was profound, save for the stirring of the wind in the bare branches.

John was holding a long-barrelled pistol. He moved cautiously into the coppice with Cathie at his heels, eyes alert. Shag came up to them, whining in his throat, thrusting his muzzle into John's hand, troubled by the sense of death and desolation.

Something lay across their path, and Cathie clutched at John's arm.

'I told you—you shouldn't have come.' His voice trembled. He made himself go forward, peering down at the dead soldier lying spreadeagled on his back.

'There's another. Over there——' faltered Cathie. Her stomach churned. She turned blindly away and pushed through the bushes, to come out on the other side, near the bridge.

It was then that she saw the horse. He was standing, head drooping, his bridle hanging limply, nuzzling at something that lay inertly on the ground at his feet. She crept forward, heart in mouth. The horse raised his head, ears pricked, and looked at her.

'Hallo, boy.' Automatically she patted his neck.

She stared down at the soldier, lying on his face. In one hand he still held a pistol. Taking a deep, quivering breath, she forced herself to turn him over, and his head lolled back against her shoulder. His helmet had fallen off. Round his head was a soiled, hastily-tied bandage, stained with blood. His eyes were closed, his face ashen.

'He's dead!' she thought, and gulped.

Her gaze travelled from his face down to his chased body armour of back-and-breast, crossed diagonally by a blue scarf, over his buff coat. She saw then the dark wet patch on his side, high up, beneath his armpit. Her gaze returned to his face.

John was beside her, stooping to peer at the soldier. 'Leave him. He's dead.'

'No,' she said slowly, 'I don't think he is.' She bent her head

closer to the man's face. 'He's still breathing. We must get him to
the house.'

John frowned. 'He's a Roundhead!'

'I don't care!' Cathie flashed. 'We cannot leave him here to die! It
would be—it would be unchristian! Supposing it was James?'

'How are we going to carry him to the house? And in any event, he
will probably die before we can get him there.' .

'He will die if we leave him!' The man's head was heavy on her
shoulder. Her arm ached, holding him, but she would not, simply
would not, lay him down again. She glared up at John, her attitude
fiercely protective. 'No one else will bother to help him. The villagers certainly won't—you know that.'

The villagers, if they ventured out to the bridge at all, would
probably strip the unconscious man and his dead comrades of all
that was useful, and take his horse as a prize. Their sympathies were
with the Royalists, their loyalty given to the family at Fern Place. Sir
James Gifford had gone to fight for the King, taking many of the
men from the estate with him. No matter what happened they knew
he would remain true to the end, and so would they. They had never
seen a Roundhead soldier, but their hatred of them had been nur-
tured by the tales they had heard of rapine and plunder, of great
houses pillaged and burnt, of churches desecrated. No, they would
not help the wounded soldier.

Though this was the fourth year of the war, it had not as yet
directly touched this secluded valley hidden between the hills, in
which the village of Fernleigh stood. It was watered by the little
river Fern, which joined the more important Torridge that flowed
into the sea at Bideford, several miles to the north.

Now, however, the tide of war had turned towards them. The
Roundhead army—that New Model Army they had heard so much
about—was sweeping all before it. News spread like a leaping flame
through tinder-dry bracken. . . . Dartmouth had fallen, Exeter was
besieged, with little hope that it would hold out against a determined
onslaught. Fairfax was advancing. He was at Crediton. And then he
was at Chulmleigh.

And Chulmleigh was but a few miles away. . . .

Cathie looked up at her brother. 'We cannot leave him here.' Her
voice had a firm, determined note in it he recognised only too well.
Cathie in this mood was inflexible.

'Oh, very well!'

He straightened, and then gave an audible sigh of relief. Reuben, a sack over his shoulders to keep out the cold, was plodding towards them.

'Her ladyship sent me to find you, Master John.' His tone was reproachful. 'She were worried about you both.'

John and Cathie exchanged looks. Poor Mary had enough to bear already.

Reuben bent over the soldier.

'He's not dead,' Cathie said swiftly, 'just wounded. We must get him home.'

'If we could lift him over the horse——' John began.

He and Reuben managed it between them, staggering a little, for the man was heavy in his thick buff coat and armour. They fastened him securely, and then began the slow progress back to the house, with Cathie carrying his helmet.

Their advent was greeted with cries of shocked horror. A Roundhead! Better to have left him where he was! This from Annie. The maidservants, clustered behind her, also looked askance at him.

Mary, having recovered from her first surprise, gave swift orders. He had best be placed in the second guest chamber. A fire must be lit, hot bricks put into the bed, clean linen brought for bandages, water and medicaments. . . .

The daylight was fading. Cathie fetched a branch of candles and led the way upstairs, while John and Reuben carried the wounded man up between them into the cold bedchamber. Susan, who apart from her other duties, also acted as Cathie's tiring-maid, scuttled across to the fireplace and knelt before it with a tinder-box. Woodshavings placed beneath the dry logs soon caught alight, but it would be some time before the room was really warm.

'That's right, Master John. Lay him down,' grunted Reuben. 'We'd best take 'is boots off first. That's it. Now 'is sword-sash and belt.'

They began to unbuckle the leather straps that held his back-and-breast in place, exposing the buff coat with its ominous wet patch.

'Ar,' muttered Reuben. 'See, Master John. That be where the ball went in—here, at the side, between the fastenings. A lucky shot, that.'

Mary entered with Annie at her heels. Over her arm hung one of James's nightshirts, which she handed abstractedly to Cathie. She looked harassed.

'Have you undressed him?'

His shirt was of the finest linen. They untied his collar, edged with delicate lace, unfastened the shirt and eased him carefully out of it. Mary drew a quivering breath. Reuben gave her a quick look.

'Do 'ee leave this to me, my lady. You be in no fit state to remain 'ere.'

'But the bullet——'

'I can draw it out. Don't 'ee fret.'

Mary moved away from the bed. Her gaze fell upon Cathie, who was hovering anxiously nearby, having placed the nightshirt before the fire.

'What are you doing here, child? This is no place for you. Go downstairs at once.'

Cathie opened her mouth to protest, caught a swift look from John, and nodded.

'Very well, Mary.'

Rachel was sitting comfortably before the fire in the winter-parlour. 'How is he?' she asked idly as Cathie entered.

Cathie sighed. 'It is difficult to say; but at least we haven't left him to die of exposure.'

Rachel spread out her white hands before the leaping flames. 'All this fuss over a Roundhead!'

During the night the wind rose, rattling the windows, blowing eerily down chimneys and under doors. The day dawned wild and stormy.

Reuben had gone down to Fernleigh before darkness had fallen on the previous day, and the two dead men had been taken away to await burial. He had slept in the room with the wounded Round-head, on a straw pallet near the fire. Annie was vexed at this. She shared Rachel's opinion of Roundheads.

Cathie's first thought was of the soldier. She tiptoed in to see him before breakfast and found him lying on his back, covered up to the chin. It seemed to her that he was barely breathing. Her anxious gaze lifted to Reuben's face.

'He's in the Lord's hands,' he said cheerfully, and put some more logs on the fire, while he told her that when he had extracted the pistol-ball he had found it was not as deeply embedded as he had at first supposed, having been deflected by the side straps which fastened the man's back-and-breast. As for the head wound, it was apparently an old one, and nothing to worry about.

'I'll come back and sit with him after breakfast,' said Cathie, adding, as Reuben eyed her enquiringly, 'I feel responsible for him.

I *was* the one who found him.'

She said much the same to Mary and the others at the breakfast table. They ate off pewter, most of the plate having been sent two years before to the Mint at Exeter, to be melted down and stamped into coins to help swell the King's coffers.

'Reuben has his work to do,' she told them. 'One cannot expect him to remain upstairs all day.'

'Of course not,' Rachel murmured drily, helping herself to mustard and spreading it over her slices of cold beef.

'I don't know whether you ought to,' Mary said worriedly.

'Someone will have to sit with him.' Cathie glanced round the table.

'Don't expect *me* to!' Rachel flashed. 'I don't intend to go near the man. The sooner he is out of the house, the better.'

'*I* can't,' John said quickly. 'I've already made arrangements to go hunting in Holm woods this morning, with Joe.' Joe was head groom.

Mary frowned. 'The weather is none too good, and—and there may be more Roundheads about.'

John drained his tankard and wiped his mouth with his napkin. 'We'll take care.' He rose to his feet and strode out.

Mary sighed. When James had left to join the King's forces his steward, Miles Hendy, had still been alive and had taken much of the running of the house and estate upon his own capable shoulders. Since his death in the previous summer, however, the responsibility had devolved upon her. John helped, of course, but he was inclined to become impatient with her. She was so anxious to make a success of things that she often vacillated between one course and another.

James had managed to obtain a few days' leave when he had heard the news of Hendy's death. Mary had hoped he would remain for good, but he had told her he must go back. The war was not yet over. Until that happened, his place was with the Royalist army in the West. He had gone, and her heart had gone with him. He was dearer to her than anyone else in the world. She dared not contemplate life without him, should he never return.

As a result of those few precious days, she had become pregnant and, as the months passed, grew more and more harassed and troubled. She felt at times that she was near the end of her tether. John seemed unwilling to do anything to please her: he only wanted to be with Rachel, whose own restlessness transmitted itself to the boy, as did her continual complaints of the dreariness of life buried in this backwater.

Mary rose from the table and with a murmured word to the others, left the room. She should, she knew, go to the kitchen to have a word with Annie, but before she did so she went slowly up to her bedchamber, and sank down on the stool before the toilet table. The child within her moved, and she caught her breath. Only a few short weeks to her lying-in. If only James could be with her. . . .

She blinked away a sudden rush of tears and picked up her hand mirror, examining her reflection. How pale she was! James had always admired her pink-and-white complexion, her soft grey eyes and shining fair hair. What would he say if he could see her now? Pregnancy gave some women added radiance, but it had taken hers away.

She bit her lip and then, putting the mirror down, turned resolutely towards the door. It was no use giving way.

She went downstairs again, and met Cathie coming up.

The latter smiled at her. 'I'm going to sit with the Roundhead.'

'Oh.' Mary had forgotten him. She continued on her way to the kitchen, a frown between her brows. His presence in the house was yet another care to add to those already weighing on her.

As Cathie entered the guest-chamber, Susan rose with alacrity from the stool beside the bed, only too happy to be able to leave.

'He hasn't moved,' she reported, and scuttled out.

Cathie sat down and regarded him worriedly. Was he warm enough? He appeared to have plenty of blankets over him, and the fire was blazing cheerfully enough, but one could never tell. There was a clean bandage round his head. A lock of hair fell over it at one side of his forehead, a dark curl that looked somehow out of place. One did not imagine a Roundhead soldier with curling hair. One did not, come to think of it, imagine one with a fine linen shirt and a lace-edged collar. John and Reuben had concluded that he must be an officer, and they were probably right. No ordinary trooper would be dressed so elegantly.

His cheeks were sunken, his nose seemed all the more prominent. His mouth was drawn with pain, his breathing shallow. His face was pale, save for two bright patches of colour on his cheekbones.

As she watched him, his lips moved. Without warning, he opened his eyes, became aware of her presence and turned his head towards her on the pillow. He looked at her, but she felt he did not really see her: she was merely a vague shape to him.

Again his lips moved, and she bent over him. His voice was barely audible.

'Rom?'

Just the one word. For a moment she was at a loss to understand what he meant; then it occurred to her he was probably referring to his horse.

'He is quite safe,' she assured him.

His face cleared. 'Good.' He closed his eyes and then, after a minute or two, he re-opened then. 'Thirsty——'

She poured out some water, slipped a hand beneath his head and raised him slightly so that he might drink. He sipped a little of it and then shook his head.

'Enough, thank you.'

His eyes closed, and he appeared to drift into sleep. Cathie had brought some needlework with her—a dress she was making for Mary's baby—and while he slept, she busied herself with her sewing.

About the middle of the morning she heard horses approaching the house. At first she thought it must be John and Joe returning from their hunting, and then realising her mistake, rose and went quickly to the window, peering out through the rain-streaked panes.

Her eyes widened. It was James, at the head of a small column of troopers. He looked up and waved to her. She waved back, and stood there watching them as they dismounted, milling about the horses before leading them away in the direction of the stables. James turned and strode swiftly into the house.

One of the maidservants had already flung wide the great oaken door, and he stepped over the threshold, to find Mary waiting for him in the hall. His arm went round her. 'My love!' He kissed her, and then drew away with a laughing grimace.

'Help me take my armour off, then I can really kiss you!'

'Why have you come? Is something wrong?' Mary could not keep the anxious note out of her voice.

He led her across to the massive old fireplace. 'No, no. Nothing is wrong. How are you, my love?'

Her fingers were unfastening his shoulder buckles. 'Well enough,' she returned lightly; but she saw his keen glance search her face, and when he had laid aside his armour and buff coat, his arm went round her again.

'Sweetheart, are you sure? The baby—everything is well?'

'Yes, of course!'

Rachel came lightly down the shallow stairs. 'James—this is a delightful surprise!' She paused for a moment, her hand on the carved newel-post, before crossing the hall and lifting her cheek for his kiss.

'How are you, Rachel? In good health, I hope?' His expression was quizzical.

She shrugged, glancing up at him through her lashes, smiling. She liked him. She liked all personable men, especially those who could be of use to her.

'Indeed yes; and grateful to be here and not in Exeter, I assure you!'

It was the first time they had seen each other since she had become a guest in the house, though Mary had written to tell him of her coming. They went into the winter-parlour. From the kitchen came the sound of men's voices, laughter, the shuffle of heavy boots.

'I fear we are taxing your resources,' James said apologetically, 'arriving like this without prior warning. I hope Annie will be able to cope. A dozen hungry men will soon empty her larder.'

'How long are you here for?' Mary asked.

'Only for dinner. I wish it could be a longer stay, but——' He broke off and went over to the window, looking out at the desolate garden.

The door opened and Cathie came in, delighted to see her brother. He kissed her and then held her at arms' length.

'You've grown quite a young lady since I last saw you!'

She laughed, wrinkling her nose at him. Releasing her, he took his seat beside Mary on the settle near the fire, with Rachel taking the chair opposite them, and Cathie a stool nearby.

'John has gone hunting,' Mary explained. 'He's hoping to kill a stag in Holm woods. Oh, that reminds me!' She looked suddenly anxious. 'There was some trouble yesterday, at the bridge——'

'I know.' James took her hands in his and pressed it reassuringly. 'Some of my men were involved. Indeed, that is why I have come today—to explain the reason for yesterday's happening.'

He went on to tell them that Lord Hopton had brought his army over the Cornish border into Devon, as far as Great Torrington, where they were now quartered.

'Torrington!' Cathie exclaimed. It was their nearest town, and one she knew well.

James gave her a fleeting smile. 'We—that is to say, the Royalist horse—are stationed on the Common, when we are not busy elsewhere.' He turned to Mary. 'Hopton's intention was to try to get to

Exeter to attempt to raise the siege, but when we heard that Fairfax had advanced to Crediton, he had to abandon that plan.'

'Fairfax has left Crediton. He's at Chulmleigh,' Rachel put in swiftly and James nodded grimly.

'Yes, we know that, *now*. I sent out a scouting party yesterday afternoon to gather what information they could of Fairfax's army. They came this way, along by the Fern, and had crossed the bridge when they spotted some enemy troopers riding towards them, seemingly on another scouting mission. Bassett, my sergeant, is a resourceful fellow. He decided to ambush them.'

'And they rode into the trap,' Cathie said slowly.

'They did.' James's tone was one of triumph. 'It was all over in a few minutes, without loss to our men. Three of the enemy were killed, including their officer. The rest put up a half-hearted fight and fled back to their quarters. Bassett picked up a wounded man and brought him back. He told us they were foraging, but that Fairfax had no intention of bringing his army in this direction—too far out of his way.'

'Thank heaven for *that*!' Rachel murmured.

'It was from our prisoner we learned that Fairfax had reached Chulmleigh.' He pulled a face. 'Until then we'd had no idea the enemy were so close. They could have taken us completely by surprise had not luck favoured us yesterday. As it is, we are barricading all the approaches to Torrington, and have stationed men at Stevenstone House, in St Giles-in-the-Wood. Their task will be to hold up Fairfax's advance for as long as possible.'

For Rachel's benefit he explained that Stevenstone House was situated about a mile from the town, on the route that the New Model Army would have to take to reach Great Torrington.

'We are doing all we can to prepare for the battle,' he said; and feeling Mary's hand tremble in his, turned to her, his voice ringing with confidence. 'Don't fret, my love. We are all in good heart and ready to fight. We have the finest of leaders in Hopton and Webb and Capel. If yesterday's skirmish is any criterion, we shall soon vanquish the Roundheads.'

She managed to smile. 'I know you will! But tell me, what provisions have you? Are you short of meat? You could take some of our sheep——'

He shook his head. 'We have brought flocks of sheep and oxen with us, which were intended for the people of Exeter, had we been able to reach them. So you see, we are well provided for!'

Cathie's thoughts returned to the ambush. 'Did you say the Roundhead officer was killed yesterday?'

'Yes. One of Bassett's men fired point-blank at him and he fell from his horse. Why do you ask?'

Cathie eyed him warily. 'He—he isn't dead. John and I found him when we went down to the bridge to see what had happened. We brought him here, with Reuben's help. He's in bed upstairs. Reuben took the pistol ball out and dressed his wound.'

James stared at her in surprise. Then he rose swiftly to his feet. 'I must take a look at him!'

Upstairs, in the guest-chamber, he stood gazing down at the wounded man. It gave him an odd feeling. Here was an enemy, helpless, barely conscious; one who should, by rights, be dead. Would probably have died, had John and Cathie not gone down to the bridge.

He returned to the winter-parlour.

'You aren't angry with us?' Cathie asked.

He grinned at her. 'Of course not, silly goose!' He glanced at Mary. 'Have you found any means of identifying him? Letters, a pocket-book?'

She shook her head. 'No. Only a kerchief, with the initials "P.D." embroidered on it, and he was wearing a signet ring with the same initials. Would you like to see his armour and sword?'

It was while he was examining these that John arrived home, hastening in, his face alight, when he heard his brother's voice. The two spent some time in the book-room talking together before dinner, discussing estate matters and also, Mary suspected, the prospects of battle.

Not until the meal was over did she have James to herself for a while. Once again his eyes searched her face.

'It won't be much longer, dearest.' He was referring to her confinement, she knew, but her own thoughts had turned to the coming conflict. She went into his arms, resting her cheek against his comforting shoulder, safe in his embrace. Just for a moment; then she raised her face to his, smiling.

'Only a little while! Perhaps—the next time you come home—it will all be over.'

She watched him ride away, holding back the tears until he had gone from her sight. A gust of wind tugged at her cloak. Rain stung her cheek. She turned and went inside. The house seemed empty without him.

CHAPTER
TWO

JOHN had had a successful morning's hunting, returning with a fine stag. Everyone was pleased. Though there still remained a plentiful supply of the meat salted down in the previous autumn, it was always a pleasant change to taste fresh venison.

Mary thought it was time to change the wounded man's bandages, and went to the guest chamber with Cathie and her own tiring-maid, Betsy, in attendance. Cathie had insisted upon being present and Mary had given dubious permission. They were easing him out of his nightshirt—no simple task—when the man's eyes opened. He groaned.

'Adam?'

Mary's eyes met Cathie's, a look of helpless appeal in them.

Cathie said swiftly, 'Adam isn't here just now.'

He groaned again. 'What are you doing?'

'We have come to change your bandages. You were wounded—remember?'

He frowned, and then stiffened as Mary, having uncovered the wound, began to cleanse it.

'It's been bleeding again,' she murmured. 'I had intended to look at it this morning, but James's arrival put it out of my head. I'm sorry. I did not mean to hurt you.'

The ghost of a smile hovered at the corners of his mouth. 'I'm—sure—you did not.'

He compressed his lips, maintaining a stoic silence while they completed their task, and helped him into a clean nightshirt. Betsy left the room with the basin of blood-stained water and the soiled bandages, her attitude one of disapproval.

Cathie glanced at Mary. She looked drawn and pale.

'Do you go,' she said gently. 'I will sit with him for a while.'

'I don't think——' Mary began.

'Oh, nonsense! You are tired. Go and rest.'

Mary hesitated, but finally allowed herself to be persuaded. 'Just for a while,' she said, and went quietly out.

Cathie turned to the wounded man. 'Would you care for a drink of water?'

His lids lifted a little and then he looked up at her and nodded, thanking her when she had held the pewter mug to his lips and he had drunk from it.

'So—I was wounded. Can you tell me what happened?'

She seated herself beside the bed and gave him a brief account of the ambush and its sequel; how she and her brother had found him lying near the bridge, and with Reuben's help had brought him back to the house.

'I am much obliged to you all,' he murmured faintly.

'We do not yet know your name,' she said. 'Mine is Cathie—Catherine Gifford.'

'God save you, Mistress Cathie.' He held out his hand, and as she took it he added: 'Piers Denham, at your service. Or would be, if it were possible.'

She smiled, and released his hand. 'As to that, sir, I am not so sure.' Her tone was demure. In response to his look of surprise, she went on: 'You forget—you are in the enemy camp.'

Surprise turned to amusement. 'Was there ever so sweet an enemy?'

She flushed. 'I—I think you should rest. You will tire yourself, talking.'

His hand drifted up to his forehead, touching the bandage.

'Does it hurt you?' she asked.

'No. I had forgotten—'tis an old wound. I knocked my head—was it yesterday?—and it started bleeding again.'

He lapsed into silence for a moment, his head turned towards the windows. 'How stormy the sky looks.'

'We have had bad weather all day—strong winds and heavy showers.'

'The bridges will be down,' he muttered, brows drawn together. 'It will hold up our advance.'

She said nothing, remembering James and his brave body of men, riding away with cheerful faces, knowing that soon they would be facing the enemy in battle. If Fairfax was held up, even for a day or two, it would give them a little more time in which to prepare.

She found that her hands were tightly clasped together in her lap. She let her fingers relax and gave him a swift, wary look. His head came round on the pillow.

'Whatever the outcome, I shall not be there to see it.' His words were tinged with regret. Then he added, as though to himself, ''Twill be the first time since Winceby, in October, '43.'

He lapsed into silence once more, and in a little while his eyes closed. She remained beside him, watching him, as the room darkened about them and the storm clouds gathered overhead.

Afterwards she found herself recalling his words '. . . *I shall not be there to see it.*'

Strange that their effect upon her should be one of thankfulness. It did not occur to her that she had already identified herself with him when she had held him in her arms by the bridge, refusing to abandon him there.

After breakfast next morning Reuben reported that Mr Denham had had a restless night, but had since fallen into a more peaceful sleep.

'He were muttering about bridges and storms and someone called "Adam" and someone else called "Tom". 'E were in a rare ol' taking!' Reuben shook his head.

'Oh dear!' Mary looked worried, an expression which was almost habitual to her by now. She decided to wait until Mr Denham awoke before tending his wounds.

She and Cathie were in the still-room when they were suddenly interrupted by one of the maids, who burst in without ceremony, crying that a party of Roundhead troopers were coming up the avenue towards the house.

'What'll us do, m'lady?' she quavered fearfully.

Mary took a steadying breath and rose to her feet. 'Go back to the kitchen, Polly. There is nothing to be frightened about.'

For all her seeming calmness, however, Cathie could see that the news had alarmed her. 'Stay here, Mary,' she said swiftly. 'John and I will deal with this.'

'No, that would not be right. I must see what they want.' Mary went to the door.

'Then I will come with you.'

They found, when they entered the Great Hall, that Reuben had admitted the officer and some half-dozen of his men. The latter were standing in front of the carved wooden screen, a silent, watchful bodyguard.

'Sir, what can we do for you?' Mary's voice was admirably controlled.

He bowed correctly. 'Major Dowd, my lady, of the Captain-

General's army.' His speech was strange to their ears. He was from the North country.

Rachel glided across the hall towards them, with a rustle of silken skirts. The group of troopers stared at her, but she took not the least notice of them. Major Dowd glanced at her, gave a stiff nod, and addressed Mary once more.

'I have orders to take your sheep and cattle.'

Her hand went to her throat. 'Oh, no! I——' She turned as John strode in, Shag bristling at his heels. 'John, did you hear that? We cannot allow them to take them.'

His jaw set. 'How can we prevent them?'

He looked at Major Dowd, a glint of anger in his eyes. 'Must you do this?'

'Yes, sir, I must. You will be given a receipt for them, and will be able to claim compensation at fair market prices, later.'

Rachel laughed contemptuously. 'When did Fairfax bother to haggle over a flock of sheep?'

He eyed her coldly. 'The General does not take what he wants without paying for it. My lady, I have already given orders to the rest of my men to round up the beasts. I regret that we are forced to do this, but unfortunately it is necessary. The district round Chulmleigh is a poor one, with little to provide in the way of fresh meat.' His harsh voice deepened. ' 'Twould seem the Royalists stripped it the last time they went through. I wonder—did *they* pay for what they took?'

Rachel tossed her black ringlets. 'They did not have to!'

'Must you have *all* the cattle?' Mary asked desperately. 'Could you not leave us one or two milch cows?'

His gaze went swiftly over her thickening figure. 'I will see,' he conceded.

'You will not—slight the house?'

He looked surprised. Before he could answer her, Rachel said silkily: ' 'Twould be a pity to do so when one of your own officers lies helpless upstairs.'

For a moment he stared at her, completely taken aback. Then, recovering, he turned to John. 'Take me to him!'

Having led the way upstairs, John opened the door of the guest-chamber. Major Dowd stepped inside and came to a halt beside the bed. John, following him, saw his expression change to one of incredulous relief.

'Piers Denham!'

The wounded man opened his eyes, and blinked. ''Swounds!' he murmured. 'Jack Dowd! Did Tom send you?'

'Aye, but not to find *you*. Eh lad, we thought you were dead!' Dowd's speech lapsed into the vernacular for a moment. 'Tha's made a reet mess o' things, falling into t'trap like that!'

The other grinned ruefully. 'Happen I did!' he mocked. 'Could thisen ha' done better?'

Dowd grimaced. 'Tha'll ha' summat t'answer for when tha' sees Black Tom!'

'How is he?'

'Plagued with the rheumatism, thanks to this wet weather. Confound the rain! It's holding us up. The bridges have washed away, and we cannot get across the river.'

'I thought that would happen. What is he going to do?'

Dowd glanced pointedly at John, who took the hint and left the room, taking care however to leave the door fractionally open. Standing with his ear to the crack he tried to hear what was passing between them, but to his disappointment could catch little of their low-voiced conversation. He did manage to gather that 'Black Tom' was growing impatient, aware that there was little enough in the district on which to feed his army, and few villages in which to quarter them; aware too that the men themselves were impatient to advance and come to grips with the enemy.

He caught the words 'Torrington' and 'tomorrow, mayhap'.

He wondered whether it would be of any use riding to warn James—but Hopton would surely be prepared by now.

Downstairs again, Dowd was a little more expansive than before. Captain Denham, he informed them, was on the General's staff and was, moreover, a cousin to Lady Fairfax.

Rachel's eyes suddenly narrowed. 'He would be a personal friend of General Fairfax?'

'Aye, he would,' Dowd said laconically, and turned to Mary. 'I will see that his servant is sent here as soon as possible, to take care of him.'

When the Roundheads had left, Reuben came in from the kitchen premises, his expression thunderous.

'They rounded up every sheep they could find on the place, m'lady, and most of the beeves as well. What Sir James 'll say when 'e knows——' He shook his head.

The livelihood of the estate, including the village, depended upon the wool trade. With the loss of their sheep, things would be very black for them all.

'I know, Reuben, but what could we do?' Mary looked at him helplessly.

He passed a hand over his face, and heaved a sigh. 'Well, they didn't take the poultry. That's *one* blessing.'

'And if they have left us a few cows as well, I suppose that may be counted as another,' Rachel remarked idly.

'We probably have Captain Denham's presence to thank for that,' Cathie flashed. 'Had we not taken care of him, they might have removed the lot!'

'That being so, you had best go and thank him,' said John sardonically. 'He is awake. He and Captain Dowd had much to say to one another.'

'Oh! He may be hungry.' Cathie made for the stairs.

As she did so, she heard Rachel say in a mocking aside to John: 'Lud! What solicitude!' She glanced back at them over her shoulder. They were laughing together and it hurt, that laughter. Once John would have flown to her defence.

She swept into the guest chamber and up to the bed. 'John said you were awake. I wondered whether you might care for something to eat.' She broke off. He was regarding her with raised brows, a deep-rooted twinkle of amusement in his dark eyes.

'Good morrow, Mistress Cathie. I trust I am not the cause of your displeasure?'

'Oh.' She eyed him uncertainly. 'No, of course not.' His level gaze made her feel very young and slightly foolish. She gave him a wavering smile. 'Good morrow, Captain Denham. I beg your pardon—I should not have burst in upon you like that.'

'Not at all.' The twinkle had grown. 'I am only too delighted to see you.'

'Indeed?' She thought it best not to pursue the matter further. 'Major Dowd mentioned that he would be sending your servant, but he will scarcely arrive before evening, and probably not until tomorrow. It will take the Major and his men some time to reach their quarters, I should think.' She paused, and then added significantly: 'They came for our sheep and cattle. Some they slaughtered on the spot and took away in their wagon, the rest they are driving before them.'

'Yes, I know. Had I not failed in my mission the other day, *I* should have been the one to take them. If it is any consolation to you, they will be much appreciated by a host of hungry men.'

'No doubt.' Her tone was short.

'Incidentally, where do you pasture the sheep? I could see nothing but hills and woods when I rode through the valley.'

'You did not ride far enough. There is a broad stretch of common land, known as High Moor, behind the house. It stretches down to the village, and away into the distance in the opposite direction. Reuben said your men had taken all the sheep they could find, but there are many gullies hidden by the rocks in which they shelter from the weather, so it is quite likely they missed some. Oh!' She broke off, her expression one of consternation. 'You won't tell Major Dowd that, will you, if he should come back again? We rely on our sheep, for the wool. Every cottage in the valley has its spinning wheel.'

'I won't tell him,' he promised gently.

Her face cleared. 'Thank you. And now, shall I fetch you something to eat?'

She returned within a short while with some gruel, which he eyed with a noticeable lack of enthusiasm. He had been given the same fare for last night's supper. She saw his look.

'Yes, I know it is not very interesting, but until you regain your strength a little you will have to make the best of it.'

'I suppose so,' he muttered gloomily; and then gave her a rueful smile. 'That was ungracious of me. Who am I to complain, when I have such a charming nurse to tend me?'

She propped him up against the pillows, tucked a napkin beneath his chin, and seated herself beside the bed. Dipping the spoon in the gruel she began to feed him, her cheeks a trifle rosier than they had been. He forbore to point out that on the previous evening Susan had merely handed him the bowl and left him to feed himself. As he had said, Mistress Cathie was a charming nurse, and he was quite enjoying the situation. He fancied that *she* was, too.

She appeared to be in no hurry to leave him when he had finished his gruel, and had politely declined a second helping.

'Is General Fairfax annoyed with you for being ambushed?' she enquired tentatively.

He grinned wrily. 'I suspect his attitude is one of exasperation rather than annoyance,' he replied, adding whimsically: 'I am not a very good soldier, Mistress Cathie.'

She looked startled. 'But surely, if that were so you would not be in a position of command!'

His lips twitched. 'Perhaps I should put it in another way. I am inclined to forget the needs of the moment. I see a beautiful land-scape, and fail to note that there may be a whole cavalry regiment pounding across it towards me until someone jogs my elbow. Or I find myself riding into a pretty little village, and admiring the old church without noticing the sharp-shooter who is training his mus-ket at me from behind the tower of that self-same church. I suppose I should account myself fortunate to have escaped death so many times.'

'You nearly didn't, the other day,' she reminded him.

'Yes—and do you know why? Because I was lost in contemplation of the trees and thinking how beautiful they are in the early spring, and entirely forgot to send a couple of men on ahead to scout out the lie of the land. Had I done so it is probable they would have spotted the ambush before we all fell into it.' He sighed. 'That is one reason why Tom Fairfax is the Captain-General of the New Model Army, while *I* am merely a junior officer.'

'Do you mind?'

'No, not really.' He smiled at her. 'Soldiering is in Tom's blood. I have long since come to the conclusion that it is definitely not in mine.'

'Yet you became a soldier—why?'

Had she stopped to think, she might have phrased the question a little less bluntly. Mary would definitely not have approved of her open curiosity. But by this time Captain Denham had won her rapt attention and, what was perhaps more important, her sympathetic interest.

'My soldiering began in the Scottish campaign of 1639, and continued in that of the following year. I went with Tom when he joined the King. He had already seen action in the Low Counties under Lord Vere, before he married Nan.'

'Nan?'

'One of Vere's daughters.'

'Oh.' Enlightenment dawned. 'Your cousin!'

'Did Dowd tell you? Yes, that is so.'

'And you joined Lord Fairfax again when this present war started?'

'No—not until after Chalgrove Field.'

She eyed him questioningly.

'I should explain,' he said, 'that my home is in Buckinghamshire, and that my father is loyal to the King. It would never occur to him to be otherwise. But I—well, I had divided opinions; divided loyalties, if you like. I knew my father expected me to join the King's forces. He could not understand why I hesitated so long. To him the King's cause was right and just—as it may seem to you, Mistress Cathie—and Parliament's defiance of his absolutism, an act of treason.'

She nodded, her gaze fixed on his face.

'To me it was nothing of the sort. It was the action of men driven beyond endurance, striving to defend their rights, their freedom. To them the King's demands were those of a tyrant——'

'But he *is* the King!'

'True. It was that thought that restrained me from taking up arms against him ... until Chalgrove Field.' Once again he paused, staring into space, while she waited for him to continue. His head turned towards her on the pillow. 'Have you heard of John Hampden?'

She frowned. 'Ye-es. Was he not charged with refusing to pay his Ship-Money tax? I seem to recall my father mentioning it. The trial was made much of at the time, but that was years ago.' She paused for a moment, deep in thought, and then exclaimed, 'Of course! I remember now. He was killed, wasn't he, fighting against the King?'

He nodded. 'He was wounded in the shoulder at Chalgrove Field, and died a few days later. I went to his funeral. Our homes were not far apart, and I had come to know him well, and to respect his views. He was a man of great integrity, much loved, deeply lamented. It was his death that finally decided me upon the course I took. I rode north and found Tom in Hull, and with him was Hampden's cousin, Oliver Cromwell. He was a Colonel at that time. I saw my first fighting of the war at Winceby soon afterwards. Perhaps it was a happy omen that my first battle should prove to be a victory for the Parliamentarians, though I must disclaim any credit for that. It was Colonel Cromwell's masterly handling of the cavalry that won the day for us.'

'He now commands the cavalry in your New Model Army, does he not?'

'Yes. He is our General of Horse.'

'Were you at Marston Moor and Naseby?'

'Yes.' He looked into her eyes, wide and wondering, and smiled gently. 'And at the siege of Bristol, too.'

She sighed. 'Ah yes, when Prince Rupert was finally defeated. And now—you are here.'

'Lying in a comfortable bed, miles away from the war, talking to *you*.'

She acknowledged this with an absent smile. 'How did your father take your decision?'

'Not very well.' His quiet voice held regret. 'He found it hard to accept that I really intended to fight against the King. Even on my last evening at home, he still could not quite believe it. He felt bitter, I knew that. But we had said all there was to say, over and over, for and against. We parted with respect for each other. I wrote, often, to tell him my news. For a while he returned only the briefest of replies; and then, gradually, longer ones. I think he has forgiven me by now, but he will never understand.'

'Have you been home to see him simce you left to take up arms?'

'Yes, two or three times. The last occasion was after the fall of Bristol in September last year. He had not been well for some time—he suffers from the stone.'

'I am sorry.'

'I wonder what he would say, could he but know of my present situation?—Probably that it was more than I deserved.'

His glance lingered warmly on her face. She was still trying to think of a suitable rejoinder when Mary entered, looking none too pleased.

'So here you are, Cathie!—Good morning, Captain Denham. I trust you are feeling a little better this morning. Betsy has come to assist me in tending your wound.' She glanced quickly at the bowl in Cathie's hand. 'You had best take that down to the kitchen. . . .'

CHAPTER
THREE

THE storm blew over in the night and next morning dawned fair and bright. The thoughts of everyone in the house turned to Torrington. Would General Fairfax advance, now that the weather had turned in his favour?

They were soon to know. Not long after breakfast a solitary horseman rode up to the house, dismounted, and knocked on the outer door for admission. It was opened to him by Reuben, who looked him up and down and then in surly tones demanded to know his business.

The stranger smiled, seemingly not one whit disturbed by Reuben's uncompromisingly hostile manner.

'My name is Adam Potter. I am Captain Denham's body-servant.'

'Are you, indeed? Then you'd best come inside.'

Having admitted him, Reuben sent one of the maids to inform her ladyship of Adam Potter's arrival, and took stock of the newcomer. Stockily built, he was clad in the familiar buff coat crossed by the tawny-orange sash of the Parliamentarian troopers. Despite his prejudice against the Roundheads, however, Reuben was forced to admit that there was something about this man that was at once likeable and dependable, with his frank, open countenance, cheerful expression, and twinkling blue eyes.

He condescended to address a few remarks to him, ascertaining that he had been in the Captain's service for the past twelve years, accompanying him when he had joined General Fairfax's army.

Mary came into the hall. 'Adam Potter?'

He stepped forward and bowed respectfully, explaining that he had been sent to look after the Captain during the latter's enforced stay in the house. General Fairfax himself had requested him to thank her ladyship for her kindness in succouring the wounded man, expressing himself as greatly obliged to her.

Mary, a trifle flustered at hearing this, found herself thanking *him*. Her heart had lightened a little when she had learned of his arrival, for it meant that someone else would now be responsible for

Captain Denham's welfare. It lightened even more when she saw what manner of man Adam Potter was. She had not been looking forward to having him in the house—to have one of the enemy there was bad enough. But now she had met him, her fears dwindled away.

She told Reuben to take him up to the guest-chamber and returned to the linen-room, where she had been sorting sheets and pillow-beres with Betsy, setting aside those that required mending.

Cathie had just finished giving the Captain his breakfast gruel when Adam came in. She saw the Captain's face light up.

'Adam! It's good to see you!'

'Not nearly as good as it is to see *you*, sir!' The man's face split into a wide smile. 'When I heard the news of the ambush—well, I never thought to set eyes on you again, and that's the truth! You ought never to 'a done it, sir! Riding into it like that.' His tone was one of mild reproof.

Cathie, looking swiftly at the Captain, found him grinning ruefully. 'I know, Adam.' He caught Cathie's speculative look. 'Did I not tell you what a poor soldier I am?—Mistress Cathie, allow me to present Adam Potter to you. Without him I am lost, and he knows it. Adam, this is Mistress Cathie Gifford, to whom I owe my life, for she was the one who found me and insisted upon bringing me here—so Reuben told me.'

'Indeed, sir.' Adam's blue eyes beamed upon her. 'Then I'm more'n glad to meet you, mistress.'

Reuben coughed in the doorway, his bulky frame almost filling it.

'Be you wanting your gear brung up?' he enquired; and Adam said swiftly that he would come down and fetch it straight away, as soon as he had delivered General Fairfax's letter to the Captain. He produced the letter and Captain Denham took it and broke the seal, scanning the contents.

He glanced up at Adam. 'So he is on the move again.—The General writes that he has given the order to advance to Ring Ash, which he says lies within a few miles of Torrington.'

'That's right, sir. The cavalry, under General Cromwell, started to move out early this morning. General Fairfax decided to advance, whatever the weather. We were in poor quarters there. As it happens, the day has turned fine for us.'

'Yes.' Denham glanced at Cathie. She was sitting very still, staring down unseeingly at the bowl she held in her lap. 'Very well, Adam,' he said absently, 'bring up the baggage.' And when Adam had disappeared with Reuben, he turned to her again. 'You are thinking of your brother in Torrington, Mistress Cathie?'

She nodded, lifting her gaze to his face. There was a shadow of regret in his eyes.

'It is very hard for you, for all of you, to have to wait for news. I trust that whatever the outcome of this day's affair may be, he will be spared to return home.'

He saw her eyes mist over. They were lovely eyes, blue-grey, set beneath winged brows. Her hair was lovely, too; golden brown and softly curling over her shoulders.

'He is in God's hands,' she returned unsteadily.

It was an interminable day of waiting. That battle would be joined was certain. What the result would be was in the lap of the gods.

Mary, unable to rest, went from one room to another. She sat for a while by the fire in the winter-parlour, her needlework in her hands, but could not concentrate on it. The others shared her tension. Cathie went to stand on the small landing half-way up the staircase, gazing out of the window across the valley to the far hills, where Torrington stood high above the Torridge. It all looked so peaceful and tranquil. . . .

Adam, coming down the stairs on an errand for his master, halted.

'There is no word yet?'

'None,' said Cathie.

'Time passes slowly when you are waiting for news, mistress.'

'Yes.' She paused, and then added tentatively: 'Captain Denham says he is a poor soldier, but somehow I find that difficult to believe.'

Adam's eyes twinkled. ''Tis just his way of speaking, mistress. In battle there's none braver. You'll have seen his head wound, no doubt? He received that while defending Major Dowd during the storming of Bristol last autumn. The Major had been knocked from his horse and while he was lying there, on the ground, one of the enemy aimed a pistol at him and might well have killed him, had not Captain Denham seen what was happening. He hacked his way through the press and brought his sword down on the man's wrist, forcing him to drop his weapon.'

'So Major Dowd was saved.' Cathie was listening attentively.

'Aye, he was, mistress. But in rescuing him, Captain Denham was hit by a stray bullet striking across his forehead. It seems likely he'll bear the scar to his dying day.'

'Yes.' Cathie turned back to the view from the window, but she was no longer aware of it. Instead she could see in her mind's eye the scene of the battlefield, conjured up by Adam's words, with Captain Denham, a gallant, heroic figure, risking his own life in order to save his friend.

Adam, seeing the faraway look in her eyes, smiled to himself and went quietly away.

Evening came. There was still no news; and Torrington was too far away for sounds of fighting to reach them. Mary made but a poor pretence of eating at supper-time. Of them all, only Rachel seemed to be at ease, though Cathie noticed that her laughter sounded brittle, her conversation a trifle forced. Clearly she was also anxious for news.

'Do you know whether your—friend, Lord George Randolph, is at Torrington?' Cathie enquired innocently.

She saw John look up, his gaze going swiftly to Rachel. The latter avoided his glance.

'Yes, he is. I asked James the other day.'

'Are you not worried about him?' Cathie pursued.

'I shall be thankful to hear news of him.' Rachel's gaze swept over her. 'Why do you ask?'

'I was under the impression he was a very close friend of yours.'

'What do you mean by that, pray?' Rachel's tone was suddenly sharp.

Cathie shrugged. 'I was merely interested.'

'I do not care for your tone, or for your choice of words!'

'I did not mean——'

'I know exactly what you mean. You made it perfectly clear! And even if it should be true, you forget that I was alone, unprotected, my husband dead, my home taken from me.' Rachel's voice broke and she snatched a wisp of lace-edged lawn from the low-cut bodice of her shimmering red gown, and dabbed at her eyes. 'I had no one, no one at all. When George offered me his protection, what choice had I but to accept?'

She looked round the table at them, her eyes wide and tragic. Mary frowned, compressing her lips, but John rose swiftly and bent over Rachel, his hand on her shoulder.

'Rachel dear, don't distress yourself—*please*!'

She looked up at him, and put her hand over his, smiling wanly. 'You don't know how much it has meant to me, to be here——'

His eyes kindled. 'This is your home for as long as you wish. You know that, Rachel.'

She sighed. 'Thank you.'

He looked across the table at Cathie. 'I think you should apologise to Rachel.' His voice was curt.

Cathie met his look. For a moment she remained silent and then in a flat, expressionless voice said: 'I am sorry, Rachel.'

Some time later, on her way to bed, Cathie paused for a moment on the half-landing, peering out into the darkness, wishing they could know what was happening.

A soft murmur of voices reached her. She looked down into the hall, dim and shadowy. Two people stood close together before the wide stone fireplace. The dying fire glimmered on a full red skirt, on white arms and bosom, on a boy's eager face.

Cathie saw Rachel turn and look up at John, saw her draw his head down to hers.

She drew back and went blindly away, finding herself all at once outside Captain Denham's room. She hesitated and then, without really knowing why she did it, knocked softly on his door. It was opened to her by Adam, who looked out enquiringly and then, seeing her, smiled and stood aside.

She went in and came to a halt halfway to the bed. Denham's head had turned towards the door.

'This is a pleasant surprise. I did not think to see you until the morrow.'

'I didn't know—I thought you might be asleep. It is getting late. I hope I have not disturbed you.' Her voice was uneven.

His eyes beneath their level brows surveyed her keenly, and then softened. 'Not at all! Come and talk to me for a minute. I have seen nothing of you since breakfast. I was beginning to think Adam had driven you away.'

She smiled and advanced to the bed, standing there, her hands clasped loosely in front of her. 'No, but now you have him to look after you——'

'——I am to be denied the pleasure of *your* company? Mistress Cathie, I cannot believe you would be so hard-hearted.'

Despite herself, a small chuckle escaped her. 'I do have other things to do, you know.'

'Yes, of course; of far more importance than tending a mere wounded soldier!' He cast a mournful glance at her. 'Adam deserted me this afternoon to visit the stables, and here was I, all alone.'

'Now, sir!' Adam grinned broadly at him, glad to see him in this light-hearted mood. 'You did ask me to make sure your horse was comfortable and I was only gone for a short while.'

'Gossiping with the grooms, I have no doubt, and telling them blood-curdling tales of battle. Mistress Cathie, allow me to warn you. Don't believe all Adam tells you. He is an incorrigible liar!'

'Sir! How can you say that?'

'Because it's true, you rogue!'

Adam caught Cathie's eye. 'Not always, sir.' He gave her a significant look. 'I do tell the truth sometimes!'

Denham laughed; and then caught his breath with a gasp. He found them both watching him with some concern.

''Twas nothing. I shall have to remember to control my merriment until this wound of mine has healed.'

'Yes, sir, you will,' Adam agreed gravely.

Cathie's troubled gaze travelled over Denham's face, noting the lines that pain had carved on each side of his mouth. 'I should not have come in and disturbed you,' she said contritely. 'I only wanted to bid you goodnight.'

'I am glad you did,' he returned, his voice soft. His eyes held hers. 'Very glad.'

When she had left him, he lay frowning into space. Adam, making his preparations for bed, glanced at him from time to time, but did not speak. He knew when to keep silent. Finally, however, he went across to the bed. The Captain's gaze turned to him.

'Well, Adam?'

'Shall I close the bed-curtains, sir? There's quite a draught tonight.'

'There's always a draught.' The Captain's tone was gruff. He met Adam's worried look and shifted awkwardly against the pillows. 'I'm sorry. It is not your fault. I was just wishing something foolish.'

'Indeed, sir?' Adam deftly tucked the sheet in.

'I was wishing I wasn't—an enemy.'

Cathie had gone to the Great Chamber to say goodnight to Mary before making her own preparations for bed. 'Try to sleep, Mary dear,' she counselled. 'I'm sure we shall have good news in the morning.'

Mary sighed. 'Indeed, I hope so. John has offered to ride into Torrington, or at least in that direction, to try and find out what has been happening today.'

'Good.' Cathie took a quick breath. 'I'm sorry, Mary, for what happened at supper tonight. I should not have spoken to Rachel as I did.'

'No, it would have been better had you kept your tongue between your teeth.' Mary rose from her stool and went slowly, heavily, to the window. Drawing aside the thick curtain, she looked out. Cathie went to stand beside her. The night was dark and quiet. Only a few miles separated them from Great Torrington, but it might have been half a world away.

Mary let the curtain fall back into place. 'Go to bed, Cathie. It is late.'

They kissed each other affectionately as Betsy came quietly in. At her own insistence, she had recently taken to sleeping in a truckle-bed in a corner of the Great Chamber, to be near Mary should she require her urgently during the night.

Cathie went to her own bedchamber, but when she was ready for bed, a warm bed-gown over her night-smock, her curls tucked away beneath a dainty, frilled cap, felt strangely reluctant to blow out the candles and climb into the four-poster. Instead, having dismissed Susan, she chose to sit for a while before the small fire, chin cupped in her hand.

Her roving thoughts went from John and Rachel to poor Mary, trying so valiantly not to show her fear, and thence to James who might at this very minute be fighting for his life.

She wrenched her thoughts away from him with a brief prayer for his safety, and found herself thinking instead of Captain Denham, and of the way he had looked at her. Her expression softened, and she gave an involuntary little sigh.

Some time later she became aware that she was cold. The fire was nearly out. She rose with a shiver: the candles were guttering. Crossing to the toilet table she snuffed them, wrinkling her nose at the acrid smell of the smoke.

She was drawn to the window. Through the gap in the curtains she could see, far above, the pricking of stars in the darkness. She was about to turn away when, without warning, the whole sky to the west was suddenly and violently rent by a vivid flash that threw the tree-crowned hills into stark relief against it. She started back with a cry of alarm. What could it be?

She heard hurrying footsteps, raised voices.

'——An explosion!'

Rushing to the door, she pulled it open. John was in Mary's room, talking excitedly, sweeping aside the curtain, pointing to the bright glow in the sky. Mary and Betsy joined him at the window, and Cathie followed them. They peered out at the frightening spectacle.

'What—what could it have been?' Mary's voice trembled so much that her words were scarcely coherent.

'They must have blown up the powder store, or something.'

'Oh, no——' Mary swayed, and with a little moan collapsed into John's arms.

Rachel appeared in the open doorway. 'What has happened?' She was attired in a lace-trimmed, beribboned undress-gown, her black hair loose and flowing over her shoulders.

Cathie's glance swept over. 'Mary has fainted,' she answered curtly, as John placed the inert figure carefully down upon the bed.

'Oh dear!' said Rachel. 'Can I do anything to help?'

Cathie, chafing Mary's cold hands, did not look up. 'She's coming round.—John, fetch some cordial, will you?'

He rushed away, and in the doorway cannoned into Adam, his shirt hanging out of his hastily-donned breeches. The latter explained that the Captain had sent him to enquire if he could be of assistance. He understood there had been some sort of explosion, and perhaps the ladies were alarmed.

Cathie glanced at him. John had disappeared upon his errand. Betsy was clucking anxiously over her mistress, while Rachel was still standing at the foot of the bed, for once finding herself ignored. From the expression on her face the experience was not to her liking.

'It was very thoughtful of the Captain,' Cathie said. 'Tell him that—that Lady Gifford was upset by the explosion, but she will be better in a short while.'

'Very well, mistress.' Adam quietly withdrew.

John returned with the cordial, and Cathie helped Mary to sit up, so that she might drink it.

'As you appear to have the situation under control, I may as well return to my bed,' Rachel announced coldly. 'I see no point in us *all* standing about here.'

'No, of course not,' John agreed hastily. He sprang to open the door for her, and touched her hand. 'You are frozen! I will come and put some wood on your fire for you.'

They left the room together. Cathie compressed her lips, and then for Mary's sake forced a smile. 'Are you feeling better now, Mary dear?'

'Yes, thank you,' Mary murmured. 'I'm sorry I was so silly, fainting away like that.'

'Nonsense! You could not help it. Are you warm enough?—Betsy, perhaps——'

Betsy was already coaxing the dying fire into flame. 'Master John did ought to 'a tended this one first,' she muttered, rising painfully from her knees. She was beginning to feel her years, for she had been Mary's own nurse when the latter had been a baby, remaining with her ever since.

'Do 'ee go back to bed, Mistress Cathie,' she said; and as Cathie hesitated, drew her aside, adding in low tones: ''Twas Master John, frightening her with his talk of explosions. The boy should have more sense, knowing her condition! And then, to fuss round that drazel in such a manner—making himself a proper looby over her!' She sniffed.

'You will call me if—if you need me?' Cathie asked anxiously.

Betsy patted her arm. 'Aye. To be sure I will.'

Cathie returned wearily to her room and divesting herself of bed-gown and slippers, climbed quickly up into the bed, pulling the bed-curtains close.

It was a long time before she fell asleep.

Before John rode away on his mission early the following morning, he took Cathie aside into the winter-parlour.

'Why were you so rude to Rachel last night?'

'Rude? Do you mean at the supper table? If you remember, I did apologise to her.'

'I was not referring to that, and you know it! When she came to Mary's room to offer her help, you treated her with the utmost discourtesy. She was most hurt by your attitude.'

Cathie took a deep breath. 'And what of your attitude towards Mary? Had you not burst in upon her, shouting about explosions, she would never have fainted.'

'I didn't shout!'

'You did! I could hear you quite plainly from my own room. Frightening her out of her wits like that! She is worried enough already, with James away fighting, and the baby coming.'

The shaft went home, and John looked suddenly crestfallen. 'I didn't intend to alarm her. I suppose I didn't think.'

Cathie eyed him steadily. 'No, you didn't, did you?' She should have left it at that, but before she could prevent herself, added: 'You are so infatuated with Rachel, you can think of no one else.'

'Infatuated! What are you talking about?'

'Oh, John! I'm not blind. Ever since she came here, you have fallen over yourself to please her. It's—it's *sickening*! Don't you see, she is only amusing herself? She doesn't really care for you. Why, if Lord George Randolph were here, she would have no use for you. It is only because there is no one else——'

His hands shot out and gripped her arms, giving her a furious shake.

'Be quiet! You don't know what you are talking about!' His eyes blazed down into hers. 'What do *you* know of such matters?'

'More than you think! Do you suppose I haven't seen the way she looks at you, and smiles up at you, so——' she fluttered her lashes at him. 'You cannot resist her, can you? You're just like wax in her hands.'

'You little bitch!' He slapped her hard across the face.

As Cathie staggered back, someone gave a horrified gasp from the doorway.

'John! What are you doing?'

Mary stood there, with Rachel by her side. There was sudden, shocked silence.

John looked at Cathie. She was staring at him, wide-eyed, a hand over her bruised cheek. 'Cathie, I—I'm sorry!' His expression was stricken. 'I didn't mean it—truly I didn't!'

Rachel gave a soft laugh. 'Dear me! Whatever has Cathie done to deserve *that*, I wonder?' Her tone was mocking.

Mary went forward to Cathie's side and put her arm round the girl's shoulders. 'John, how could you?'

'I've said I'm sorry!' He turned away, unwilling to face the reproach in her eyes. 'I'd better go.'

He settled his plumed beaver hat on his brown curls, fastened his riding-cloak securely at his throat. Rachel handed him his gloves. 'John, dear, would you do something for me when you are in Torrington?'

'Of course.' He did not look at Cathie.

'Would you enquire after Lord George Randolph? I have had no word from him, as you know. I cannot help wondering—' She broke off, and then continued huskily, 'He has been good to me. I dread to think that something may have happened to him.'

'I will make enquiries for you,' he said gruffly.

'Thank you.' She touched his hand for a moment. 'I should be most grateful if you would.'

He took his leave of them, and strode out. Joe was walking the horses up and down, and they mounted and rode away. Rachel watched them from the window, and then turned back into the room. Her glance went to Cathie's cheek. She said nothing, but there was an unmistakable air of satisfaction about her.

'I'll put some ointment on that for you,' Mary said, and took the girl to her still-room.

'He won't listen to reason!' Cathie burst out. 'He cannot see that she is only diverting herself.'

Mary took the jar of ointment from the cupboard and smoothed some gently over the bruise. She herself was looking pale and drawn this morning, but had refused to stay in bed. 'Give him time,' she murmured.

Cathie went slowly up the stairs, pausing as she always did, on the half-landing. The sky was overcast. Clouds hung low over the hills. As she stood there Rachel came down the stairs towards her, with a rustle of tawny skirts.

'I wonder how long it will take John to reach Torrington.'

Cathie turned away, unwilling to stand in conversation with her. 'I have no idea.'

'Are you going to see your Roundhead?'

'He's not *my* Roundhead.'

'Oh?' Rachel's tone was cool. 'I thought he was.'

Cathie glanced back at her. There was a derisive glint in Rachel's long green eyes. 'I cannot think why you should.'

Rachel laughed. 'Can't you?'

Cathie's hand tightened on the baluster rail. She continued to the head of the stairs and went swiftly away, leaving Rachel to her contemplation of the landscape.

When Cathie entered the Captain's room she found him propped up against his pillows, reading a small, battered leather-bound book.

'Shakespeare's sonnets,' he explained, having returned her greeting. 'Adam brought it with my gear yesterday.' He looked at her with a half-smile. '*Shall I compare thee to a summer's day? Thou art more lovely and more temperate.* Come and sit down and talk to me.'

'Perhaps you would rather read.' His choice of quotation had disconcerted her.

He closed the book with a snap. 'I was reading to pass the time. I would far rather talk to you.—What *have* you done to your cheek?'

Her hand went instinctively to the bruise. 'I—I bumped into something.' His eyes held concern and she had the feeling that he did not believe her. She said swiftly, 'John has ridden into Torring-ton.'

'Yes, so Adam told me. I wish he had come to see me first. I would have given him a letter to take with him. It might have helped him.' He saw her enquiring look. 'It is likely he will be stopped and asked his business.'

Her cheeks whitened. 'You think that Fairfax has taken the town?'

'I do, Mistress Cathie,' he said gently.

She sat there for a moment, staring at him. 'Poor Mary.' Her voice shook. 'What will she do, if James——' She broke off, looking down at her hands, twisting her kerchief round and round. 'What will—*he* do now?'

'Fairfax? He will advance into Cornwall.'

Her head came up. He read despair in her eyes.

'There will be—nothing left—for us,' she whispered. 'He will push our army back and back. They will have to—to surrender.'

He said nothing.

She rose and walked to the window, standing there with her back to him, shoulders drooping. Tears stung her eyes. She wiped them swiftly away.

'What will happen to the King?'

'He will have to come to terms with Parliament,' he said quietly. 'There is nothing else he *can* do, now.'

'The Prince of Wales is in Cornwall.' She was thinking aloud. 'If Fairfax advances, he will have to be sent to safety.'

'He will probably be taken to France, to join the Queen.'

'It was all so different four years ago.' She turned and faced him. 'Everybody thought the King would win.—*Everybody*!'

'Yes,' he agreed wrily. 'He had such fine armies and experienced leaders, it did not seem possible that he would ever be defeated. After all, what had Parliament to throw into the field against him?—Raw, half-trained men. What cavalry had we to stand up to Prince Rupert's?' He paused, and then added quietly, 'Our victories would never have come about had we not had men with vision; or perhaps I should say, one man who had the wisdom to see that we must have a properly trained, properly disciplined force if we wished to meet the Royalist armies on equal terms, and beat them—General Cromwell. He was the guiding spirit behind our New Model Army, and has inspired the men with a new belief in themselves and in their cause. . . . He is himself deeply religious.'

'Oh yes,' she said swiftly, 'I have heard that your chaplains exhort the men with great fervour before the battle.'

He smiled slightly at the disdain in her voice. 'True. They fight all the better for it, knowing that God is with them.'

She made a gesture of repudiation.

'It is not easy,' he pointed out, 'to have to go into battle on a bitterly cold morning, with perhaps only the heel of a stale loaf in your stomach; and the enemy cavalry charging down upon you. It needs more than ordinary courage to face that.'

Her glance wavered and fell. 'I suppose it does.'

'I *know* it does!' he said with conviction.

She returned to his bedside, and sat down. 'You think then that without General Cromwell you would not have been so victorious?'

'Yes, I do.' Again his lips curved in that ghost of a smile. 'I must confess, though, that he does not return my admiration. He has little time for my kind—gentlemen officers who have no real military skill. He considers us to be worse than useless, and would sooner have the army officered by butchers and bakers and candlestick-makers, should they happen to possess the necessary ability.'

She stared at him in amazement. 'How extraordinary!'

His smile broadened. 'He is an extraordinary man!—Not, of course, that all our officers were tradesmen before the war. There are a few of my kind left, though I have the feeling that, if General Cromwell could have his way, they would be swept out of the army and back into civilian life, where they would be of less trouble to him. As for myself——' he made a wry grimace '——were it not for Tom Fairfax, Cromwell would have sent me packing long before this! We have never seen eye to eye.'

'Yet you admire him?'

'Yes—for what he has achieved; even though I do not really care for him as a man.'

'What is he like?'

He screwed up his eyes in thought. 'In looks, plain to the point of ugliness, not always as careful of his personal appearance as he might be—he has too much on his mind to bother with such mundane things.' He was speaking slowly, measuring his words. 'He is forceful and often blunt in his manner, but he can also be a persuasive and powerful speaker. I have heard him in Council. He has a wonderful understanding and command of men; what one might call, I suppose, the gift of leadership. He is also a born soldier with the ability to plan a battle, and to overcome disadvantages.'

'A better soldier than your General Fairfax?' she asked quizzically.

'In some ways, perhaps he is. But he has no, shall I say, *compassion*. One feels that though he might spend hours wrestling with his conscience—I told you he was an extremely religious man—he would still be incapable of feeling deeply for those who might suffer as a result of his actions.'

'And General Fairfax is not like that?'

'No.' He was gazing into space. 'I've seen Tom heartsick after a battle; unable to share Cromwell's exultation over victory, remembering the suffering and the slaughter.'

'Yet he fights on.'

'He fights for the things he believes in—liberty, justice, honour. For him, there is no turning back. There never was, once he had taken the first step. He will go on until the end, until our cause prevails.'

She was watching him closely. 'You feel the same way, don't you? There will be no turning back for *you*, even if—you might sometimes hate what you have to do.'

His eyes met hers. 'I shall go on for as long as Tom needs me,' he replied quietly.

She looked suddenly wistful. 'I wish we could have met under different circumstances.'

The words were spoken before she realised it. She sat there, scarlet with confusion. What must he think of her? Mary was always saying that she let her tongue run away with her.

She said hastily, 'It will soon be dinner time. I will go and see if Annie has remembered to set out your tray. I believe you are to have chicken broth and a spiced custard today. Are you not pleased to hear it? It will make a pleasant change from gruel.'

She had already risen, and was speeding towards the door.

'Mistress Cathie!'

Something in his tone made her pause, and turn a trifle uncertainly towards him, her cheeks still warm.

'Must you rush away? Adam will bring up my dinner.'

'I—I think I must. Mary will wonder——'

He let her go and fell back against the pillows, his eyes shadowed.

Rachel, meeting her downstairs, did not miss Cathie's glowing colour. Her gaze sharpened. 'He must be quite a man, this Captain Denham! Whatever has he been saying to you, to make you look like that? I think I had better make his acquaintance.'

'Why?' Cathie was immediately on the defensive. 'I thought you said you wanted nothing to do with him!'

'That was before I realised he might be of interest to me.'

She moved away, leaving Cathie staring after her, aware of a prickling of unease.

CHAPTER
FOUR

LONG before they reached Great Torrington, John and Joe came across evidence of the previous day's advance of the New Model Army when they emerged on to the main highway. The surface of this, never very good at the best of times, was in an even worse condition after the passage of cavalry and heavy baggage wagons. The foot soldiers—pikemen and musketeers—must also have come this way, trudging through the mud, stumbling in and out of the ruts and potholes.

'I've 'eard tell they bain't allowed to swear,' Joe remarked. 'They be fined, else.' He chuckled. 'I'll wager many a man called down curses on this road under his breath!'

'More than likely.' John spoke absently, his thoughts troubled.

They received their first check when they reached the village of St Giles-in-the-Wood, where they were challenged by Roundhead sentries who demanded to know their business.

'We are on our way to Torrington,' John answered brusquely.

A sergeant appeared, a middle-aged veteran, with a scarred face. So they were going to Torrington, were they? His keen gaze swept over them. For what purpose?

John, smarting inwardly beneath the man's authoritative manner, explained briefly. The sergeant gave a sour smile. Maybe they had not heard that General Fairfax had taken the town? They would do better to ride home again and wait *there* for news of Sir James Gifford.

'I cannot do that,' John protested. 'I promised Lady Gifford I would find out what had happened to her husband.'

The sergeant stroked his greying moustache, and then nodded resignedly. 'Very well. Ride on. But you're likely to be turned back.'

As they went on their way, Joe said: 'What'll you do, sir, if they won't let us into the town?'

'They will.' John spoke confidently. 'I shall ask to see Major Dowd. They can scarcely refuse such a request.'

He was right. At the mention of the Major's name, the guards stationed at the outskirts of the town allowed them to enter, with instructions to proceed to the Market Place where Dowd was most likely to be found.

As they picked their way up the hill, they could not fail to see the devastation left by the battle—tumbled barricades, houses with their doors and shutters smashed, shattered glass and tiles strewn everywhere, together with pieces of armour, broken pikes and muskets abandoned by the fleeing Royalists. Over all hung the acrid smell of smoke from the still smouldering buildings which had been set alight by the flames from the explosion.

They saw several working parties of soldiers helping the weary citizens to clear away rubble and restore some order to the narrow streets.

John, catching sight of a familiar face, reined in. 'Mr Woodnutt! What happened last night? The explosion——'

Woodnutt, a woollen merchant with whom the Giffords had done much business in the past, paused and looked up at John with red-rimmed eyes.

''Twas St Michael's church. Hopton had stored some fifty or more barrels of gunpowder in it. The Roundheads had fought their way into the town, and the Royalists were trying to make a stand, and I suppose in the confusion the stuff became ignited.'

'Were many killed?'

Woodnutt nodded. 'Royalist prisoners were being held in the church under guard. They say some two hundred of them were killed. I heard that Fairfax had a narrow escape when a sheet of lead fell from the roof and killed a man standing in the street beside him.'

'You have no news of my brother, have you?'

'Sir James?' Woodnutt shook his head. 'I've heard nothing of him.' He made as if to move away. 'Pray excuse me, Mr Gifford, I must get back to my wife. She is in a sad way after the terrible happenings of last night.'

Upon entering the Market Place, John was astonished to find a crowd of people assembled there, citizens and soldiers alike, listening to the preaching of a Puritan divine. John reined in, with Joe beside him.

'He has a powerful flow of words,' the latter commented.

'Yes.' John leaned towards a young soldier standing nearby. 'Who *is* that fellow?'

The soldier eyed him stonily. 'That, sir, is Hugh Peters, chaplain to the New Model Army.'

'Peters!' John's eyes kindled. 'I've heard of him!'

'Doubtless you have, sir. His name is known the length and breadth of England——'

'For preaching sedition against the King, and no quarter for the Royalists!'

The soldier's face flamed. 'And are *they* any different?'

'At least they do not wage war against innocent and defenceless women!'

'What do you mean by that?'

Their dispute was becoming heated. Heads were being turned in their direction; voices commanded silence.

Joe moved his horse nearer to John's. 'Sir—hadn't us best be going?'

John did not heed him. Glaring into the soldier's face, he said fiercely: 'What happened when Basing House was stormed in October last year? Is it not true that Peters boasted to Parliament, when he made his report to them, that he witnessed its destruction and the slaying of many unarmed men *and women*! And did he not say that several ladies of rank, when attempting to escape, were captured by the common soldiers and vilely misused by them? From all accounts, he appeared to find it amusing. And he has the effrontery to call himself a man of God! What have you to say to that?'

''Tis lies! They were whores—painted and bedizened daughters of Baal!'

His voice had risen to a shout. Fists clenched, he looked ready to spring at John and drag him forcibly from his saddle. Next moment, however, came an interruption. Another horseman had come into the Market Place, an officer of the New Model Army. Having become aware of the altercation, he had threaded his way through the crowd towards the two antagonists. Within seconds the young soldier was despatched summarily about his business; and John found himself confronted by the very person he had come to see—Major Dowd.

The latter recognised him in the same instant. 'Mr Gifford! So it's you, is it?' His tone was anything but friendly. 'Might I suggest that the next time you wish to pick a quarrel with one of my men, you do so in a less public place?'

Without waiting for an answer, he swung his horse about, and rode away, leaving John sitting there, seething.

Joe coughed. 'Hadn't you best go after him, sir?'

With a face like a thundercloud, John did so, coming up with Dowd as the latter halted outside the Black Horse inn and dismounted.

He looked up at John in some surprise. 'Yes? Did you wish to speak to me?' He handed his bridle to a soldier, who immediately led the horse away.

'Yes, I did.' John got swiftly down, and tossed his own bridle to Joe. 'I have come to Torrington to try and find some news of my brother. I was hoping you might be able to help me.' In the face of the other's unwelcoming attitude, his own was truculent.

Dowd eyed him keenly beneath drawn brows. 'You'd better come inside. Your groom can take the horses round to the stables. You—what is your name?'

Joe stiffened. 'Joe Seaton, sir.'

'Well then, Seaton. Tell them I gave you permission to stable your horses and bait them. Come along, Mr Gifford. We'll see what news we can find of Sir James.'

Once inside the inn, he ushered John into a room in which several other officers were congregated, some busily writing letters or reports, others talking briskly together. The hum of conversation died down as the two newcomers entered, and John was momentarily disconcerted at finding himself the cynosure of all eyes.

His own gaze passed over them, and came to rest upon a number of Royalist standards, many with their poles broken, propped forlornly in a corner. The fruits of victory, he thought bitterly; and all at once his brother's face seemed to swim before his eyes, not as he had last seen it, cheerful and smiling, but haggard and drawn. What if he had been one of those two hundred men killed in the church? Or had been cut down in the carnage in the streets?

Hitherto he had been so wrapped up in his own affairs that he had failed to understand the true extent of James's involvement in the King's cause. He had taken it for granted that he would come riding home at the head of the column of fifty or so men who had volunteered to go with him to the war. Now it occurred to him, with a sudden stab of pain, that he might never see James again, and he remembered that out of those fifty men, eight had already been killed or had died of their wounds, and four others had been so badly crippled that they would never be able to do a day's work again.

He heard Dowd introducing him and explaining the purport of his visit to the town, and he looked from one man to another, scarcely daring to hope they would have some news of James. But they all shook their heads.

In despair he turned to Dowd. The latter gave him a quick, intuitive look. 'One of the prisoners should be able to supply the information you need,' he said.

It was one of James's own men who was brought to him: Hal Pridham, a year or two older than John, whose family owned a small manor-house on the other side of Fernleigh.

'James?' he said. 'Oh, he got away.'

'Thank God!' John felt limp with relief.

They were in a small store-room at the back of the inn. Here Dowd had tactfully left them alone together, with a guard posted outside the door.

'He was one of the lucky ones,' Hal commented. 'He escaped without a scratch, as far as I know.' His own arm was heavily bandaged and held in a sling. He explained that when the church had been blown up he had been struck by a piece of falling masonry, and knocked from his horse. '——And when I came to, I found myself lying in the street with the poor animal dead beside me.'

John sympathised. 'Is there anything I can do for you?'

'I'd be obliged if you could tell my parents I am still alive. After last night, they'll be worrying. Incidentally, I have heard that the wounded are to be released soon, as long as we promise not to fight against the Roundheads again.'

'That is good news! Tell me, Hal, what happened yesterday?'

Nothing loth, Hal launched into his tale. 'You have probably been told that Hopton sent a party of men to Stevenstone House, with orders to delay the enemy advance. Well, they held out as long as they could, but in the end they had to retreat into Torrington. Meanwhile, General Webb was making a series of skirmishes against the enemy, which he kept up all day, and that also helped to delay them.' He grinned reminiscently. 'There is nothing more annoying than being fired at from behind a hedge when you least expect it!'

John smiled. 'No, I suppose not. When did the Roundheads reach the town?'

'After dark. They had advanced as far as the barricades on the outskirts about late afternoon. We had some infantry there and they held them off for a while, but after darkness fell Hopton ordered everyone back into the town. By that time, the light was so poor you couldn't tell friend from foe! There was only one way to distinguish them—the Royalists had handkerchiefs tied round their right arms, and the Roundheads had sprigs of furze in their helmets.'

'And I suppose you had a password?'

'Oh yes! "We are with you!" And I am told that the Roundheads' password was "Emmanuel, God with us".' He shifted a little on the bench they were occupying. 'It seems He was, last night.'

He described how the enemy had forced the barricades and fought their way in, beating the Royalists back and back; how the latter, with no time to reload their muskets, had had to use them as clubs in order to defend themselves. By that time the fighting had become general all through the town.

'Pretty desperate, it was,' said Hal gruffly. 'Hopton himself was wounded in the face by a pike. He had already had one horse killed under him.'

'What did he do?' John was hanging on his every word.

'He and Lord Capel talked things over with some of the officers, wondering whether it would be possible for the cavalry to break through the enemy and try to reach the King at Oxford, but they decided against it. The odds were too great. So Hopton had no choice but to retreat into Cornwall. Before he could give the order, however, the barrels of gunpowder we had stored in the church blew up——'

'We saw the flash from Fernleigh! Mary was terribly upset.'

'Yes, she would have been.' Hal looked grave. ''Tis as well you can tell her that James escaped. When I came to, after I was hit, he was rounding up the men and ordering them to retreat. He saw me and asked if I was badly hurt, and said he was sorry he'd have to leave me behind.' He looked anxiously at John. 'You'll surely be hearing from him soon?'

'I hope so.'

They conversed together for a while longer, discussing the battle and its aftermath. Hal was of the opinion that the war was as good as over. 'What can Hopton do now,' he said, 'with so many men killed or taken prisoner, and others deserting by the score?' His brows drew together. 'Some four hundred of our men were captured during the battle, and they say half of them have already gone over to Fairfax!'

'What!' John stared at him in disbelief.

''Tis true! Miserable fellows, the lot of 'em, with no real loyalty to the King. The Roundheads have offered them good terms, so——' He gave an expressive shrug.

They sat in silence for a moment or two, then John said, 'I heard Hugh Peters preaching in the Market Place. He seemed to be creating a good impression on the crowd. He was telling them that they and all the other people living in Devon had suffered enough at the hands of the marauding Royalist Army in the West. According to him, they took their livestock and their food, their forage and wagons—and all without so much as a "by-your-leave" or a penny offered in payment. What fools they are to swallow such nonsense!'

Hal shook his head. 'Can you in all honesty blame them? This was a prosperous little town once. After four years of war it is far from that! And with last night's violence fresh in their minds, is it not natural that they should turn to someone offering them fresh hope?' Hal gave a wry smile. 'I fear they have little to thank the Royalists for, with their houses shattered and their streets strewn with debris, *and* the casualties caused by the explosion.'

It was a point of view which had not occurred to John before, but as he turned it over in his mind he was forced to the reluctant conclusion that Hal was right.

When Hal had gone, escorted by his guard, John found Dowd at his side.

'I trust you had good news of your brother, Mr Gifford?'

'Yes, I did. He escaped with Lord Hopton.'

Dowd allowed himself a fleeting smile. 'Then he will be across the Tamar by this time. There was so much confusion after the explosion that we had to give up all thoughts of pursuing the Royalist cavalry.' He turned towards the inn's dining-parlour. 'It is approaching midday. You are doubtless hungry.'

John hastily demurred, saying he would prefer to return home in order to set Mary's mind at rest.

Dowd nodded understandingly. 'Yes, of course, she will be worried. Nevertheless, I must ask you to postpone your return for a while. The General wishes to see you before you go, but being much occupied at present with urgent matters, he suggests that you partake of some refreshment in the meantime.'

'The General?' John was startled. 'Lord Fairfax? Why should he want to see *me*?'

Dowd shot him an amused look. 'To enquire after Captain Denham's health. He is naturally concerned about his wife's kinsman, and I should also like to know how he fares. Is his wound healing cleanly?'

After a dinner of mutton stew and apple pudding, washed down with excellent ale, Dowd conducted John upstairs to the main guest-chamber, a big, low-ceilinged room overlooking the street. Here guards armed with pikes stood at the door, whilst within Lord Fairfax paced slowly to and fro, dictating a despatch to his secretary, who was seated at a table littered with maps and documents, some of the latter bearing the Parliamentary seal.

While he waited with Dowd inside the doorway, John looked curiously about him at the large curtained bed and the other items with which the room was furnished—the oak chest, the carved press, the stools and toilet table.

The Black Horse inn, built in Tudor times, was the largest and most important hostelry in the town. It had received many guests in its time, but surely never one as illustrious as the man who now occupied its best chamber.

Overriding the smells of beeswax and lavender-scented sheets, were the more masculine ones of tobacco smoke and leather. On the oak chest the General's black armour was set out, dented ominously here and there, dimly reflecting the flames that licked round the logs in the wide fireplace. A leather-bound Bible lay on the stool by the bed. Silver-backed brushes, a hand-mirror, and other personal possessions of the General's were strewn across the top of the toilet table. A miniature portrait of a woman caught John's eye. Lady Fairfax, perhaps?

His gaze turned to the General himself. Thin and haggard from lack of sleep, the left side of his face still bore the scar of the wound he had received nearly two years before at Marston Moor. He was dressed in black, with a wide collar of fine lace tied at the throat. With his black hair and sallow skin, it was easy enough to see how he had come by his nickname. He was 'Black Tom' indeed!

Fairfax finished his dictation and turned to John and Major Dowd, his serious, sensitive face lightening as he smiled and bade them come forward to the fire.

'Ah, Dowd! So this is Mr Gifford?' He stuttered slightly, John noticed, and the thought crossed his mind that such an impediment might present certain difficulties when, for instance, he had to address his troops or make his report personally to Parliament.

'I apologise, sir,' the General said to him, 'for keeping you waiting; but as you see——' he waved a hand towards the littered table '——my time is not my own. I trust you have had good news of your brother?'

'Oh—yes.' John was taken aback, not only by the unexpectedness of the question but by the genuine concern in the General's tone. 'He escaped unharmed; or so I am informed.'

'I am glad to hear it.' Fairfax kicked a smoking log back into the fire. 'When Major Dowd informed me you were here, I asked him to bring you to me in the hope that you could give me news of Piers Denham which I can pass on to my wife when I write to her.'

'He is progressing well enough.' John made an effort to recall what Mary and Cathie had had to say regarding the Captain's recovery, and wished he had paid more heed to their words. Like Rachel, he had little interest in the matter. 'His head wound does not trouble him, but the other is—is more serious.'

Fairfax nodded, his thoughtful gaze never leaving John's face. 'He had some fever, I believe?' Evidently Dowd had told him.

'Yes, but that has passed. He is still weak, though his appetite is improving.' Had not Mary mentioned that he was now able to take more solid food? 'My sister-in-law, Lady Gifford, has been dressing the wound herself. He could not be in better hands, she has a wide knowledge of medicaments.'

'Pray thank her on my behalf. I am indeed grateful to her—to *all* your family—for your good care of him.' His lips lifted in a wry smile. 'I am aware that the situation is not an easy one for any of you.'

John murmured a disclaimer; adding, 'He now has his body-servant to look after him.'

'Ah, yes—Potter.' Fairfax picked up a sealed letter from the table. 'Would you be kind enough to take this to the Captain, and convey my respects to him?'

'Of course.' John tucked the letter inside his doublet, and prepared to withdraw. Before he could do so, however, the door was flung open and without ceremony a heavily-built man in stained buff coat and muddied boots strode in, the guards standing stiffly to attention as he passed them.

To John, the very air in the room trembled with his coming, as though he brought with him an echo of battles past, a wild clamour of thundering hooves and crashing cannon-fire, borne on a cold, rushing wind. There was a fervour about him, a robust strength, before which the slender, weary figure of Fairfax seemed to shrink a little.

John, stepping hastily aside to allow the newcomer to pass, was left with an impression of a plain, weather-beaten face dominated by a nose both broad and long and red in colour, of untidy brown hair streaked with grey beneath a large, broad-brimmed hat, and a pair of piercing, heavy-lidded eyes that flashed him a look of acknowledgment as he stood back.

He found Dowd at his elbow. 'I will see you out, Mr Gifford.'

John went, with a backward glance at the two commanders; the quiet, courteous aristocrat and the bluff, forceful man of the people. He had already guessed the latter's identity.

'That was General Cromwell, wasn't it?' he asked, as he followed Dowd down the stairs.

'Aye,' Dowd said gruffly, 'it was.'

John grinned. 'He is well named "Ruby Nose".'

Dowd's answering smile was reluctant. 'Aye, well I'll grant you he is no Adonis, neither does he aspire to be the gentleman in manner or dress, but all the same, he is our inspiration and strength. Without him we would not have prospered nearly so well.'

Back home once more, John gave the others a detailed account of the day's happenings, passing on the General's message to Mary, and repeating Hal's assurance that James had managed to escape, unhurt.

'And what of Lord George Randolph?' Cathie asked, with a glance at Rachel.

'Hal said he escaped with the others.' John could not help noticing Rachel's look of relief. He turned away. 'I have a letter from Lord Fairfax for Captain Denham. I will take it up to him.'

It was the first time he had entered the Captain's room since the day of Dowd's arrival at the house, and he was at once struck by the improvement in Denham's appearance. It seemed almost a miracle that the man he had dismissed as dying, but a few days ago, was now propped up against his pillows, able to converse with him.

Denham was eager to hear his news, and John found himself sitting by the bedside and recounting his tale for the second time.

'So Tom—General Fairfax—looked ill and tired,' Denham commented. 'He is not a strong man. He forces himself to overcome physical weakness, but the strain tells on him.'

John remained with him for a while, his initial constraint evaporating under the warmth of the man's personality. Indeed, he had to admit to himself that his preconceived ideas of the Parliamentarians, and his antagonism against them, had been considerably shaken during his day in Torrington. He was aware of a feeling of guilt. James, after all, was fighting for the King; Denham for Parliament. Was it right to like an enemy?

Some of his uncertainty conveyed itself to Denham. He had deliberately set out to overcome John's distrust: he found the boy likeable. He had the same direct, open manner and youthful appeal as his sister. Both were a mixture of adolescent and adult. Studying John, however, he was inclined to the opinion that of the two, Mistress Cathie had the stronger character.

He read his letter as soon as the boy had left him, and acquainted Adam with the contents.

'The General writes to assure me he is well and that victory was theirs after a hard struggle. Hopton has withdrawn his troops—such as are left to him—into Cornwall. The General proposes to advance as soon as possible.'

Adam grinned cheerfully. 'There'll be no stopping him now, sir!'

Denham relaxed against his pillows, eyes half-closed, deep in thought. Adam left him alone. After carrying the supper things down to the kitchen, he remained there, talking over events with the servants, his bright blue eyes following Susan as she went to and fro at Annie's bidding, with the other maidservants.

Susan was a buxom little thing, very much to his taste. It was a pity she appeared to harbour no feelings of liking for him, or for any Roundhead in fact. She had made that quite clear to him when he had attempted to draw her into conversation upon his first excursion to the kitchen. Yes, it was a pity. She was the prettiest little wench he had seen for many a day, with those big brown eyes and rosy cheeks, and a waist small enough for a man's two hands to span. Ah well, he was not one to be put off by a rebuff. The barricades might be up, but perseverance would breach them, in time.

Rachel retired early to her bedchamber that night. She wished to be alone, for she had much on her mind.

Sitting before the inadequate fire she thought, 'Surely John would have heard if George *had* been killed? Major Dowd would have mentioned it. He *must* have escaped with the rest. . . .'

She sat there, frowning at the slow-burning logs, crouched on the stool, hugging herself, her eyes narrowed, her brain working feverishly. Finally she got up, smoothed her skirts, and went over to the toilet table. In the light of the branch of candles standing there, she examined her reflection carefully in the hand-mirror, patted a curl into place, and then, satisfied that she was looking her best, put the mirror down and left the room.

A few moments later she stood outside Denham's door. Hearing no response to her knock, she knocked again, and then opened the door and went in. The room was shadowed, lit only by a couple of candles, and Adam was not there. Her gaze went to the bed. The Captain appeared to be asleep.

Closing the door quietly behind her she advanced towards the bed and stood there, gazing curiously down at him. His face was in shadow. The bandage had been removed from round his head. She bent over him, peering at the scar that went diagonally across his forehead.

As she did so, he stirred, and opened his eyes, gazing blankly up at her. She realised he was not fully awake, was but half aware of her presence. She drew back a little.

'Forgive me; I did not intend to disturb you. I came to see if there was anything I could do for you, but I will leave you to sleep. Until tomorrow, Captain Denham.'

She went away and he lay there, still only half awake; wondering indeed whether he had dreamt it—a soft, seductive voice in his ear, a cloud of perfume, a whisper of silk. In the dim light it had been difficult to distinguish her features clearly, but he had gained the impression that she had been more than usually attractive, with night-dark hair and white skin.

By the time Adam returned, he was wide awake. 'Who,' he demanded, 'was in my room just now? A dark woman, young, beautiful——'

Adam looked wise. 'That would have been Mistress Devereux.'

He recounted all he knew of her, culled from servants' gossip. Those at Fern Place had little time for her or for her tiring-woman. Mistress Devereux made no attempt to conceal her boredom, and was for ever complaining of the dull life they led here. As for Grace, she was a high and mighty piece, deeming herself to be far above the others.

'They haven't a good word to say for her,'Adam said, adding: 'There's nothing wrong with her that a tumble in the hay wouldn't put right—not that *I'd* suggest it to her!'

Denham chuckled. 'If she is anything like her mistress, I wonder you haven't!'

'Too thin for my taste. Mistress Devereux, now—she's something different!'

'So I believe.'

'I'd like to know why she came in here. She's never set foot inside the door before.' Adam gave Denham a significant look. 'I'd be wary of her if I was you, sir. That kind are for ever causing trouble.'

Denham's eyes gleamed. 'True. Nevertheless, I am considerably intrigued by her sudden interest in me. Perhaps I shall discover the reason for it tomorrow.'

CHAPTER
FIVE

REUBEN had reported to Mary that some of the cottages on the estate had had their thatch badly damaged by the storm that had swept the countryside a few days before.

When, on the following morning, John announced that he was going to call upon Hal's parents to give them his news of him, Mary asked him to go and inspect the damage on his way back. It seemed she would have to give her consent for it to be made good. She hoped the re-thatching would not prove to be extensive, for she felt uncomfortably certain that the halcyon days of Fern Place were over, and they would be forced to keep expenses to a minimum.

The loss of their sheep was a blow from which it would be hard to recover; and apart from that the future was extremely uncertain. No one knew what would happen when the war was over, but the reckoning would have to be paid.

She went heavily upstairs to the linen-room, a frown between her brows. From the Captain's room she heard a sudden rippling laugh, and paused in surprise. Rachel—in *there*? She was the last person she would have expected to find with the Roundhead officer. Her frown deepened.

Rachel had waited until John had ridden away and Cathie was occupied in the stillroom, before going upstairs and tapping on Denham's door. In her hand was a book. 'I thought this might help to pass the time for you,' she said, having exchanged polite greetings with him.

He glanced at it and then up at her. 'Thank you. I have not read John Milton's *Comus* before. I shall look forward to doing so. Pray, sit down, Mistress Devereux.'

She did so, aware that she looked her best in red, the bodice cut low to reveal white shoulders and bosom. She saw his eyes quicken with interest while she conversed lightly with him concerning his wound, explaining that she had not wished to bother him before he was well enough to receive visitors.

He acknowledged this with a smile, saying it was most thoughtful of her. His eyes met hers with a slightly quizzical look in their depths that sent a sudden pricking of awareness through her. She had the uncomfortable feeling that this man would not be easy to deceive. And he was certainly no dedicated Puritan—not with those eyes!

Her first glance had told her he was not handsome: his face was too angular, his nose too prominent. Yet despite that, he was one of the most attractive men she had ever met. There was something about him that was at once exciting and challenging. She set herself out to charm him, while making no secret of his own effect upon her.

It did not take her long to discover his background; that he came from a wealthy family with a large estate in Buckinghamshire, and a house in Covent Garden. Their conversation turned to pre-war days. Casual enquiry rewarded her with the information that he had been no stranger to Court circles at one time.

Rachel's interest deepened. Originally she had intended to pay him but a fleeting visit in order to take his measure. She would then depart, with a promise of another visit on the morrow. But that had been before she had met him. . . .

She was still there some time later when Cathie tapped upon the door and in answer to the Captain's bidding entered the room, coming to a sudden halt when she saw Rachel.

Her eyes widened. 'Oh—I did not realise——'

Rachel looked at her, managing to convey the impression that she was interrupting a private conversation which would be resumed immediately upon her departure.

The look was not lost upon Denham, and he smiled at Cathie. 'Good morning to you. I trust you are well?'

'Well enough, thank you.'

His eyebrows rose a fraction at the curtness of her tone. He saw her gaze go to his forehead, and touched the scar.

'As you see, it is healing. Adam removed the bandage last night. I must remember not to knock it again.'

'Indeed you must not.'

Rachel, aware that the chance of an intimate discussion with him had gone, rose languidly and smoothed her skirts.

'I will bid you adieu, Captain Denham, for the time being.'

She smiled at him, her eyes shadowed by their long lashes. Cathie saw, resentfully, the way the Captain smiled back.

She turned swiftly away and attacked the fire, replenishing it with a great clatter of logs. When she had finished she found that Rachel had gone, and the Captain was surveying her with a certain amount of amusement.

'For one moment I thought you were going to bombard me with them!'

She pushed back a fallen lock of hair, her face hot from bending over the fire. 'Why should you think that?' Her expression was defensive.

He beckoned her over to the bed. 'Come here.' And when she had obeyed him, slowly, unwillingly, he added: 'Never let your enemy see your weakness. Give me your kerchief, you have smudged your cheek. Come along—I cannot possibly reach you if you don't lean towards me.'

She did so, feeling a trifle foolish. He wiped away the smudge of dirt, and regarded her critically. 'That is better.' His hand was on her shoulder, holding her there. 'Your bruise is fading,' he observed, and let her go, returning the kerchief. She stood beside the bed, eyeing him uncertainly. 'Sit down,' he said gently.

'Are you sure you want me to? I thought perhaps you might have had enough of—conversation.'

He gave her an enigmatic look. 'That would depend upon the person conversing with me.'

She seated herself and then could think of nothing to say, frowning down at the kerchief twisted between her fingers. She became aware that he was watching her.

'John has ridden into the village,' she said hastily. 'Several of the cottages were damaged in the storm. He has gone to see what can be done.' Her voice trailed away, and she looked at him. 'What did you mean—about not letting the enemy see your weakness?'

His eyes began to twinkle. 'Do you really need me to tell you? You positively looked daggers at Mistress Devereux when you found her sitting here; which fact I am sure did not escape her. You play card games, I am sure. Have you not learned to guard your expression? Not to give yourself away to your opponent?'

'Ye-es.' Her face cleared. 'I understand!'

'I thought you would.'

When Adam came in, they were deep in a discussion of music and Court masques. After Cathie had gone, he said, 'So Mistress Cathie brought you a book to read, sir.' He himself could read and write and was very proud of that fact, in an age when it was not considered necessary to educate the humbler classes of society.

Denham picked up the copy of *Comus*, lying on the coverlet. 'No, Adam. Mistress Devereux did.'

Adam looked startled. 'She's a deep one, sir.' There was a warning note in his voice.

Denham smiled at him. 'She is indeed.'

He fell silent, lost in thought. The antagonism that existed between her and Mistress Cathie had struck him at once. He wondered what had caused it. It was not merely the jarring of two completely opposite personalities, but something far stronger than that.

He thought of each of them in turn: of the beautiful woman, painted, perfumed, exquisitely gowned; of the young girl, artlessly charming, with her simple toilette. The one assured, calculating to a nicety the effect she was making, dangerously inviting. The other inexperienced, unversed in the ways of the world, with many lessons yet to learn—among them the art of hiding her feelings. He smiled to himself, remembering the look of furious resentment on her face when she had seen Mistress Devereux sitting beside his bed.

He would not be honest with himself if he did not admit that Rachel Devereux attracted him; she was the kind of woman who would attract any man with red blood in his veins. The kind with whom he might have had an affair, once; whom he would have been proud to own as his mistress, to deck in fine clothes and jewels, to show off to his friends.

Once—but not any more. Looking back over the past few years, he acknowledged the fact that he had changed. His values had changed, too. What he would have accepted without question in the old days now seemed meaningless. It had taken the war to show him that; the war, and his decision to fight for Parliament against the King.

He thought of the Court and its frivolities. It seemed incredible to him now, that he could have borne that butterfly existence; yet at the time, he had not wanted anything more. He knew he could never return to that way of life when the war was over and it was time to pick up the pieces and start again. Though he was not quite sure yet what exactly he did want, he had the strangest feeling that the answer was there somewhere, waiting for him to find it. . . .

Adam was beside him with his dinner.

Denham's appetite was improving, and he ate his meal with enjoyment. Adam observed this with a beam of satisfaction, thankful to see his master so much better.

Afterwards, as he lay back against his pillows, Denham's thoughts returned to Cathie. She had warmth and tenderness; she would make a good wife and mother, one day. Perhaps in a year or two she would marry. Maybe she was already betrothed. . . .

He blinked. Strange, that that had not occurred to him before. She had not mentioned it—but why should she? For all he knew she might be betrothed to someone serving with her brother; waiting for news of him, living only for the day of his return.

'Sir?' said Adam; and Denham realised he must have uttered some word—an oath probably, judging from Adam's startled expression.

'I was—thinking,' he said lamely.

He opened *Comus*, but found he could not concentrate. He threw the book down.

'I shall be very glad,' he said vehemently to the puzzled Adam, 'when I am no longer tied to this bed! The sooner I am out of it, the better.'

It was several days before they received news of the Royalist army.

One evening before supper a messenger arrived, weary and spent. He had come, he said, from Stratton, over the border in North Cornwall, at the request of Sir James Gifford, who was now quartered there under Major-General Webb; taking care to avoid any place where he might be challenged by Roundheads.

Lord Hopton had received orders from the Council of the Prince of Wales in Pendennis, to hold the enemy at Stratton should they attack. Word had been received from Lord Jermyn, at present with the Queen in France, that French troops would soon be on their way to the West Country.

'——Though whether that is true or not, I would not care to say,' added the messenger, who had introduced himself to them as Cornet Edmund Hill. He divested himself of his rain-sodden hat and cloak, having ridden for hours in a steady downpour, and then produced a letter from his doublet which he handed to Mary. It, too, was damp, but she took it over to the fire, broke the seal and smoothed it out with trembling haste, her lips moving silently as she read the hurriedly-scrawled words.

Mulled sack was brought for Cornet Hill, and he drank it gratefully while his wet things were taken away to be dried in the kitchen. Mary, having read her letter, called him over to the fire, and questioned him concerning the welfare of her husband and his companions. He answered her cheerfully enough; but to the others he had already spoken of hardship and bad quarters, poor food and, what was perhaps the worst blow of all, the loss of their baggage and guns, which had had to be abandoned in the retreat from Torrington. Men were deserting daily. In his opinion the Royalists would never be able to withstand a determined attack. . . .

'You must be famished,' Mary said to him. 'Supper will be ready soon. Cathie, will you see that a bedchamber is prepared for Mr Hill? He will stay here overnight.'

'Thank you.' The young officer smiled gratefully from her to Cathie. He was a fresh-faced boy from Bideford, the son of one of the town dignitaries, as he presently told them, having taken the edge off his appetite. He spoke highly of James—it was evident that he greatly admired his skill as a soldier and considered him to be the best of officers.

'Will you be going on to Bideford in the morning?' John asked him.

He shook his head regretfully. 'No, I must return with all speed to Stratton. Fairfax may cross the Tamar at any moment, and I want to be with Sir James when he does.'

He was gone after an early breakfast the next day, riding away with their good wishes ringing in his ears, and Mary's reply to James safely tucked away inside his doublet. John rode with him for a mile or so, taking a roundabout route in order to avoid Torrington, and then parted from him, having offered to go to Bideford to let his parents know of his visit to them, and to give them the letter Edmund had written on the previous evening.

They parted on the best of terms, Edmund promising to call upon them again one day if all went well with him.

'Pray remember me to your sister,' he added as they shook hands.

John grinned. 'To be sure!' He had been somewhat amused to observe the effect Cathie had had upon Edmund. Rachel had noticed it too, murmuring in an aside to him that she appeared to have made a conquest.

His grin faded as he rode along. Thoughts of Rachel had brought to mind her growing interest in Captain Denham. Ever since her first visit to the Captain's room she had visited him every day, much to John's displeasure.

When he had remonstrated with her, saying that she had gone back on her first avowed intention regarding the Roundhead officer, she had raised her fine eyebrows, replying coolly that she had decided it might be more politic to be on favourable terms with him, as it seemed certain the Parliamentarians were on the verge of a complete victory in the West, and would doubtless go on to conquer the few places still remaining to the King.

With that John had to be content, but he did not like it. He made it his business to go to the Captain's room when he knew Rachel to be sitting with him, finding them deep in conversation concerning matters about which he knew little or nothing—Court balls and masques, river pageants, great houses, all the pomp and glitter of Whitehall. His resentment grew. He felt himself to be gauche and awkward, with none of the polish, none of the easy assurance, that distinguished the Captain. His feeling of accord with him evaporated. He even resented the fact that Denham did his best to include him in the conversation, changing the subject to something of more general interest—as though he were some country clodhopper who had to be humoured!

It seemed to his jealous fancy that Rachel had completely changed towards him. Where before she had been content to be in his company and had encouraged him to believe that she really cared for him, her manner had become almost indifferent. He was miserably convinced that Captain Denham had supplanted him in her affections.

She would be there at this moment, he thought, sitting beside Denham's bed, turning her smile upon him. Rain stung his cheek. He tugged at his hat brim, and urged his horse into a faster pace.

It was evening when he arrived back at Fern Place. Edmund Hill's family, consisting of his parents and younger sister and brother, had made him very welcome, giving him an excellent dinner, over which they had lingered for some time. He was thankful to reach home, for it had been raining for most of the return journey, and he was as wet as Edmund had been on the previous day. He hoped the young Cornet had managed to reach Stratton in safety.

Adam had heard the news brought by the messenger, and reported it to Denham. The latter looked thoughtful.

'It's seven days since the battle at Torrington—time the General made a move. Come to think of it, it is time *I* made one too!'

'Sir?'

'Oh, I have no intention of galloping off to Cornwall! But I think I have stayed long enough in this bed. Tomorrow, Adam, I propose to dress and try my legs.'

Adam regarded him dubiously. 'If you think you're strong

enough, sir.'

'I do, so you may get out my clothes in readiness.'

Adam did so, murmuring that he didn't know what Mistress Cathie would have to say about it when she found out.

'Not that we've seen so much of her recently,' he added pointedly, with a swift glance at Denham, who told him he was well aware of it and said he supposed she was busy elsewhere.

Adam had formed his own opinion regarding Cathie's less frequent visits to the Captain's room, but he kept it to himself. The following morning, however, found her tapping on Denham's door. Upon entering the room she instinctively turned her gaze towards the bed, then she came to an abrupt halt. It was empty.

'Good morrow, Mistress Cathie,' said a voice from the other side of the room; and to her surprise she saw that Denham was seated in a high-backed chair by the fire.

'Why, you are dressed!' she exclaimed, and went over to him. 'Do you think it is wise?'

'You are as bad as Adam,' he returned. 'Allow me to assure you I should not have attempted to get up if I had not felt equal to it.'

His doublet and breeches were dark red, of fine quality cloth, the doublet fastened with silver buttons and elaborately trimmed with silver braid. His linen collar and wrist-bands were edged with heavy lace, his breeches tied at the knee with loops of red ribbon over black stockings. His shoes were black leather, with ribboned rosettes and red heels. The whole effect was one of quiet elegance.

'I did not feel capable of stamping into my boots,' he remarked.

'I should think not!' Cathie exclaimed. She sat down on the stool beside his chair and told him about Edmund Hill's brief visit, and of the news he had brought to them. 'Oh, how I wish this war would end!' she said, in despairing tones.

He looked at her downbent head. Her hair had fallen forward on each side of her face, leaving the nape of her neck uncovered. He had a sudden desire to kiss it, but before he could do so Rachel tapped upon the door. Biting back an oath, he bade her enter.

'Why, Captain Denham!' she cried. 'I am delighted to see that you are now well enough to leave your bed.'

In her emerald green gown with the wide lace collar, she looked graceful and elegant, her black hair drawn back from her face into a heavy coil, the side pieces dressed in fashionable little ringlets. It seemed to Cathie that the Captain's gaze dwelt upon her with appreciation. All at once she felt her own gown to be plain and ordinary, the blue ribbon threaded through her curls too childish.

Rachel looked at her. 'Mary sent me to find you. She is in the still-room.'

'Oh!' Cathie got to her feet. 'I had better go. Pray excuse me, Captain Denham.'

She found Mary measuring out a dose of physic for Polly, who was troubled by a cough.

'So there you are!' Mary exclaimed, giving Cathie a sharp glance. 'I suppose you have been sitting with Captain Denham. Why you must be for ever going in to see him, I don't know! Belittling yourself in such a forward manner!' Ordinarily she would never have spoken so openly before a servant, but for once she allowed her feelings to get the better of her.

Polly accepted the physic, swallowed it down and bobbed a curtsey. 'Thank you, m'lady.'

She thereupon returned to the kitchen, all agog to recount what she had heard. Annie and the others shook their heads, and agreed that her ladyship had been quite right to speak so firmly to Mistress Cathie. Sir James would never have countenanced such unseemly behaviour. She was only demeaning herself—and with a Round-head, too!

Later, recalling Mary's words of condemnation, Cathie was forced to acknowledge to herself that, much as she might resent them, they were nonetheless justified. In her heart of hearts she knew she had been wrong to spend so much time with Captain Denham unchaperoned. Mary had said she was belittling herself. Could *he* be of the same opinion? Somehow it hurt to think that.

Mary had apparently mentioned the matter to John, who told Cathie in blunt, brotherly fashion, to stop making a fool of herself—the Captain was no concern of hers. In future she had best keep out of his room. The servants were already talking.

Bristling at this no less than at his manner, she retorted that it was a pity he did not say the same to Rachel, who appeared to spend far more time in the Captain's bedchamber than she did in any other room in the house.

His face darkened ominously. 'Leave Rachel out of it! You never have a good word to say for her! If she wishes to sit with the fellow, let her!'

He flung himself off, leaving her staring after him, struck by the savage note in his voice. Could it be that he was at last losing his infatuation for Rachel, and if so, was it due to the fact that the latter was finding Captain Denham's company more attractive than his?

With a sudden rush of compassion, she went after him. 'John, don't let us quarrel. *Please!*'

He looked at her, then shrugged. 'Very well.' He hesitated and then in offhand tones, added, 'I am going up on to the moor. You can come, if you like.'

It was a long time since he had invited her to accompany him anywhere, and her face lit up. 'I'd love to!'

'Don't be long, then, I will wait for you in the stables.'

Cathie changed swiftly into her warm riding-dress and thick shoes. Her hat was of black felt, its wide brim adorned with a sweeping plume. She put it on, and snatched up her riding cloak. Downstairs she paused only long enough to tell Mary where they were going, before running out of the house to join John.

On the moor the horses picked their way along the track between the furze bushes and clumps of heather, the scattered, stunted trees and outcrops of rock. 'It seems strange to see so few sheep,' Cathie commented.

John scowled. 'We have the Roundheads to thank for that!'

They rode on in silence. The wind was keen up here on the open moor, where there was little shelter. The sheep kept to the gullies, their backs to the wind, moving slowly from one patch of grass to another. It was the lambing season. Down in the valley pens had been erected to shelter the ewes, many of whom had already dropped their lambs; but there were pathetically few of them compared with other years. Cathie tried not to think about it, but it was difficult not to do so.

A glance at John showed that his expression was forbidding. 'Damned Roundheads!' he exclaimed forcefully. 'I'd like to see every one of them thrown into that bottomless Pit they are always preaching about!'

'John! They are not all cast in the same mould! You said yourself how thoughtful General Fairfax was; and Captain Denham——'

It was the wrong thing to say, as she realised at once. He turned a furious face upon her.

'Captain Denham is as bad as the rest of them! Lying upstairs, pampered like an honoured guest, while he knows perfectly well his precious General Fairfax has taken our livelihood away! I tell you, Cathie, he is laughing up his sleeve at us. And I'll tell you something else—if he knows what is good for him, he'll leave here as soon as he is able to straddle a horse—or take the consequences!'

'What do you mean?'

'Never you mind! Let's go back.'

Before she could question him again, he spurred his horse away from her, thudding over the ground.

She sat there for a moment as though turned to stone. Then, with a sudden little shiver of foreboding, she turned her horse and followed him.

CHAPTER
SIX

MARY had learned from Adam that Captain Denham had left his bed. While John and Cathie were riding on the moor, she went upstairs to see him, conscious of a feeling of guilt which stemmed from the fact that since Adam's arrival she had barely bothered to go into his room.

Everything was a strain for her now, and she felt both mentally and physically tired. If her calculations were correct, her baby was due at the beginning of April, in about five weeks' time. Betsy had spoken of getting out the wooden cradle and preparing it in readiness with the little blankets and other things, but Mary had put the matter aside. James was of more importance to her than her unborn child. She carried his letter inside the bodice of her gown, a talisman against evil; just as she had once carried his love-letters in the days before their marriage.

Denham stood up when she entered, moving stiffly and with obvious effort.

'Sir, you must take care!' she protested.

'I do not think I shall come to any harm,' he replied, smiling; and taking her hand, led her over to the chair he had just vacated, seating himself on the padded stool Adam brought over to the fire.

Mary sat down thankfully, albeit with a feeling that he had more need of a back-rest than she. When she attempted to tell him so, however, he waved her words aside.

'I shall be quite comfortable here. Would you care for a buffet for your feet? Adam will fetch you one from downstairs.'

At a nod from him Adam departed, returning shortly with a footstool for her. She placed her feet upon it and slowly relaxed, feeling, for the first time for weeks, comforted and protected.

She had never conversed with Denham for more than a few minutes at a time before; now she discovered how easy he was to talk to. He had a warm, receptive manner. While conscious of his charm, she was nevertheless aware of an underlying candour and strength of purpose in him. Before she knew quite how it had come about, she found herself confiding some of her troubles to him regarding the estate, finding him to be a sympathetic listener.

It was hard, he said gently, for a woman to be left as she had been to cope with everything single-handed.

'I do have John to help me,' she said. 'He does his best, but——' She left the rest of the sentence unspoken, with a rueful smile.

'He is young yet,' he said quietly.

They both fell silent, looking into the fire. The logs hissed, and there was a scent of apple-wood.

'Lady Gifford,' he said hesitantly, 'would you consider it amiss of me to offer *my* help to you while I am here? I know something of the running of an estate.' He told her of his home, explaining that he had taken much of the responsibility of it upon his own shoulders as his father was not physically strong. 'Fortunately we have a capable steward, so he is able to cope while I am away. If you would let me advise you, I should be only too glad. I know very well I owe my life to you, and to—all who have looked after me with such care. This will in some measure repay that debt.'

'I—I don't know——' she said uncertainly.

'Think it over. I could at least take some of the burden from your shoulders.' He paused, then added: 'I shall be coming downstairs tomorrow. I have been too long a slug-abed. It is time I found my feet again. We will talk about this another time.' He left the subject and went on to something else.

Mary remained with him a little longer and when she went away it was with a feeling of warmth and well-being such as she had not experienced for many a day. With almost a sense of shock did she remember that this man was an enemy; that he and James were on opposing sides.

True to his word, Denham came downstairs next day, with Adam at his elbow. Having seen him safely into the winter-parlour and to a chair by the fire, the latter left him and took himself into the kitchen to find Susan.

Shortly afterwards Cathie entered. It seemed to Denham that she was ill-at-ease; as indeed she was, being mindful of Mary's admonition. He gave her a quizzical look. 'You are not going to run away, I hope? I have seen so little of you recently.'

'You saw me yesterday,' she pointed out.

'For five minutes! Come and sit down and talk to me.'

'I'm not one of your troopers, to be ordered about!'

'Oh! I beg your pardon.' He got to his feet and made her a bow.

'Pray forgive my discourtesy, Mistress Cathie. Believe me, I have never regarded you as anything but a most charming and delightful young lady. I should be blind indeed to think of you as—um—a trooper.' He took her hand, smiling down into her startled face. 'I should be greatly honoured if you would be so kind as to sit with me awhile.' With a flourish he deposited her on the settle, bowed again, and returned to his chair on the opposite side of the fireplace, sinking down into it with an unmistakable sigh of relief. 'I am stiffer than I thought,' he commented wryly.

'Would you care for a cushion?' She took one across to him from the settle, and placed it behind his back, bending over him for a moment with a look of concern. 'Is that better?'

'Yes, thank you.' There was about her the scent of lavender, very different from the heavy perfume used by Mistress Devereux. It reminded him of his home, of his mother's herb garden, beech-woods and chalk hills.

He began to talk to her, describing the Chiltern country he knew so well: the bare, grassy slopes, the dense woods and thickets, the little villages tucked away in secluded hollows, safe from the ravages of the weather.

She sat enthralled as he painted his word-pictures for her, pictures which showed how deeply he loved his home, how much he missed it. Every now and then she would put in a word, but for the most part sat silent, content to listen. They were completely in harmony with each other.

And then abruptly the spell was broken. Rachel entered, exclaiming with pleasure at seeing Denham. He rose to greet her, and the conversation became, with her coming, brittle and lively. Cathie excused herself, saying she had promised to help Mary patch some torn sheets. Denham's gaze followed her as she went out.

In the hall she met John, who had ridden down to the village again to oversee the repairs to the cottage roofs and was now on his way to report progress to Mary. 'Who is in the winter-parlour?' he asked, hearing the hum of voices.

'Rachel and Captain Denham.'

He came to a sudden halt. '*Denham*? I didn't know he was well enough to come downstairs yet.'

'I don't think he is, really. John——' she hesitated, searching his dark face. 'You—you won't do anything to cause trouble, will you?'

He guessed she was referring to his threat. 'Don't be silly!' He strode away to find Mary.

Cathie went upstairs to the linen-room, her happy mood dispelled by John's manner; aware once again of a sick feeling of foreboding.

She found herself watching John as he, in his turn, watched Rachel and Denham. There was an undercurrent of tension that Rachel did nothing to dispel. Where once she had turned her charm upon John, she treated Denham to the same flattering attention, giving the impression that she greatly preferred his more mature personality.

Cathie wondered what he made of it all. He appeared to be impervious both to Rachel's blandishments and to John's ill-humour, steering a course between the two with an air of amused indifference. All the same, thought Cathie miserably, no man could possibly be expected to resist Rachel for long. It would only be a question of time before the Captain capitulated; and when that happened, she dreaded to think what her brother might do.

John took himself off with Joe for a morning's hunting in Holm woods, returning in an even worse humour than before. He had found a group of Roundheads there, from the garrison at Torrington. When he had remonstrated with them, informing them they were trespassing on Fern Place property, the sergeant in charge had answered that if he wished to press the matter he had best get in touch with his commanding officer, adding insolently that even if he did, he would probably only be wasting his time.

'I wish you could have heard him!' John's eyes were blazing as he recounted the incident to the others. He was so incensed that he could not keep still and was pacing swiftly back and forth, flinging out his arms to emphasise his words. 'He addressed me as though I were some ignorant dolt! Of all the insufferable——' He drew a deep breath. 'I could have rammed his musket down his throat! I would have done, had he not had half a dozen skulking clods with him!'

Mary's glance went nervously to Denham. 'John,' she murmured, with a warning shake of her head.

He ignored her. Swinging round upon Denham he glared down at him. 'Is this the way your fine army behaves? I thought you were supposed to pay for everything you took? That, at least, was the impression your friend Dowd was so careful to make . . . not that we have received one groat in payment for our sheep and cattle. Nor does it seem likely we ever shall! What restitution can we hope to obtain for our game?' His voice had risen. He was furiously angry. 'Things have come to a pretty pass when your confounded soldiers

are sent to plunder our estate and to take whatever they have a mind
to, without so much as a "by-your-leave"! I suppose the next thing
we may expect is for them to come here and sack the house!'

'You need have no fear of that!' Denham's voice was crisp. He
turned to Mary. 'Lady Gifford, I can only apologise for this regret-
table incident. I will write to the garrison commander and request an
explanation. Adam will take the letter for me.'

'That is most kind of you,' Mary said, while John glowered at
him.

The letter was duly written and sent, an apology received from
Torrington, and the incident was closed so far as everyone except
John was concerned. He did not forget it, nor did he forget the
treatment he had received from the sergeant. It became one more
grievance to add to those he already had against the Roundheads in
general and Captain Denham in particular.

Adam had arrived back from Torrington at supper-time. He went
straight to the dining-parlour with the letter, which he handed to
Denham. The latter read it and passed it to Mary, then he glanced
up at Adam.

'Any news, Adam?'

'Yes, sir. The General crossed the Tamar two days ago.'

At his words all eyes were turned upon him.

'Crossed the Tamar!' John's voice cracked. 'Has he advanced to
Stratton?'

'Yes, sir.' Adam hesitated and then, in an apologetic tone, said:
'They heard in Torrington this morning that he had reached Launceston.'

Mary uttered a stifled exclamation, and her hand closed tightly
round the sheet of paper she was holding. With a quick glance at
her, Cathie asked the question Mary could not bring herself to voice.

'What happened to the Royalists at Stratton?'

'They were beaten back, mistress, and forced to retreat.' Adam's
gaze returned to Denham. 'I heard that General Fairfax entered
Launceston with little resistance. They say the Royalist army is
falling apart, that men are deserting by the score and only the
diehards refuse to accept defeat.'

Cathie rose swiftly and went to Mary's side, placing an arm round
her shoulders. She looked beseechingly at Adam.

'You did not hear any news of Sir James?'

'No, Mistress Cathie. I'm sorry.'

Rachel was staring at Denham. 'The Royalists are trapped, then?'

Her voice was thin. 'None of them will be able to break through and return across the Tamar?'

'To join the King? Is that what you mean?'

For a moment she appeared to hesitate, then nodded. 'Yes, that is what I meant.'

He regarded her thoughtfully. 'I should imagine that Fairfax will block all the roads between Cornwall and Devon to prevent such an eventuality, though in any event I imagine the Royalist horse will by now be too weary to contemplate making the attempt.' He turned to Mary, his expression one of sympathy. 'Believe me, I understand how you must be feeling. I trust you will soon receive good news of your husband. If there is anything I can do——'

John jerked to his feet, his stool crashing to the floor. 'You and your kind have done enough! We do not want your help!'

'*John*!' Mary pushed herself up from her chair at the head of the table. 'I will not allow you to behave in this manner towards a guest in our house.'

'A guest!' He uttered a bark of derisive laughter.

'If you cannot be civil, I suggest you leave us.'

There was a sudden hush. John, completely taken aback, stared at her for a moment. Then, recovering himself, he glanced at Denham, muttered something that might have been an apology and flung himself from the room.

Mary looked at the others. 'If you will excuse me—I think I will go upstairs.'

'Of course.' Denham came to her side. With a hand beneath her elbow he helped her across the room to the door, Adam opening it for them.

As Cathie followed them out she glanced back at Rachel. The latter was still sitting at the table, staring into space, apparently oblivious to the fact that everyone else had gone. . . .

All next day they waited for news. Denham despatched Adam to Torrington again, but when he returned in the late afternoon he had little to add to the information he had brought on the previous evening, save that General Fairfax had freed all the prisoners he had taken at Launceston and given each of them a shilling and a pass to return home.

'Very magnanimous of him!' John sneered.

For Mary's sake the others tried to keep the conversation away from the war during supper. They had nearly finished the meal when Shag, lying at John's feet, suddenly raised his head and growled. He then got up and went over to the door, ears pricked.

A moment later they all heard the sound that had disturbed him—approaching hoofbeats. Mary's hand went to her throat, and John rose. 'I will go and see who it is.'

He left the room, Shag bounding out before him. The others waited tensely. They heard the murmur of voices, and then John returned. With him was a man, travel-stained, moving stiffly after his hours in the saddle, his face set in lines of weariness. He removed his beplumed hat and bowed.

'Pray forgive me for disturbing you.'

'Have you come from my husband?' Mary's tone was sharp with anxiety.

Before he could answer her, John said, 'No, Mary. He has not come from James, though doubtless he can give us news of him—Rachel, allow me to present this gentleman to you. His name is Francis Wilmot, and he has brought you a message from Lord George Randolph.'

For a moment she stared at him; then her expression changed to one of eagerness. 'A message? Give it to me, please.'

Wilmot smiled and bowed. 'Certainly, Mistress Devereux.' He produced a sealed letter which she almost snatched from him in her haste, hurriedly breaking the seal, and scanning the contents.

Wilmot, in response to Mary's enquiry, was telling her something of the events of the past few days, and of the difficulties he himself had encountered since he had set out on his journey at cockcrow that morning. He had had to make many detours in order to escape detection by Parliamentarian troops. She had a place laid for him at the table, and food brought to him. He was very hungry.

Cathie looked at Rachel. 'Is it good news?'

Rachel raised her eyes from the letter. She was frowning abstractedly. 'He is well. He says very little.' She turned to Wilmot. 'Did you have an easy journey today?'

'No, Mistress Devereux.' He repeated what he had already told Mary. Rachel listened intently, still with that little frown between her brows. His gaze travelled over her, admiration in his eyes, but she appeared indifferent to it.

'Have you any news of my brother, Mr Wilmot?' John asked abruptly.

Wilmot pursed his lips. Yes, he had heard that Sir James had taken part in the battle at Stratton and had been one of those who had got away to safety. To the best of his knowledge, he was now in Bodmin with Lord Hopton. Mary gave a small sigh of relief. Her lips moved silently. Cathie gave her an encouraging smile.

'Is Lord George Randolph in Bodmin too?' she enquired.

'No.' Wilmot glanced quickly at Rachel, who had made a sudden movement. Denham's gaze sharpened. The look had held a warning.

Wilmot picked up his glass and drained it. John leaned across and refilled it for him, and he smiled his thanks.

'No,' he repeated, 'Lord George is with Sir Thomas Bassett. I believe he is at Lostwithiel.'

'You do not seem very certain,' John observed.

'I left him when we received orders to move out of Launceston,' Wilmot replied. 'He asked me to come here with the message for Mistress Devereux.'

'Will you be returning tomorrow?'

Wilmot looked down into his wine glass. 'Probably.'

To Denham the man seemed ill at ease, though when the conversation turned to other matters he relaxed his guard and grew more expansive. Nevertheless, though he drank deeply, it was apparent that the wine did not loosen his tongue to any great extent. Denham could not help wondering what Lord George had said in his letter. Mistress Devereux had been remarkably vague about it.

When the meal was over and the company repaired to the winter-parlour, he excused himself, sensing that they would probably feel freer to talk if he were not present. As he crossed the dim, shadowy hall, someone came after him: light footsteps, the rustle of silk. He knew, before he paused and turned, that it was Rachel Devereux.

She looked up into his face. 'Captain Denham, may I ask you something?'

He thought he could guess what it was, and said firmly, 'You may rest assured I shall not despatch Adam to Torrington in the dead of night to summon the garrison out here to capture Mr Wilmot. Nor do I intend to do anything to hinder him when he leaves here—whatever his purpose may be.'

Her hand touched his sleeve. 'Thank you!'

For a moment she swayed towards him, and her perfume enveloped him. He was deeply aware of her. Taking her hand, he raised it to his lips. She smiled.

Out of the corner of his eye he caught a sudden movement and turned his head sharply, but there was no one there. All the same, he could have sworn someone had been watching them, and felt pretty certain it had been John.

Rachel drew back, with a swift glance into the shadows. 'Good night, Captain Denham.' She wandered off in the direction of the winter-parlour, while he continued on his way upstairs.

Something made him pause on the darkened half-landing. As he had expected, he heard the sudden swift murmur of voices. He looked down into the hall. It was difficult to distinguish anything clearly in the dim light, but he could discern the shapes of two people, a man and a woman, standing in the shadows: Rachel and, he supposed, John.

At that moment Rachel turned and crossed over to the fireplace. He saw her hand go up to the bodice of her gown, pull out something white, tear it across and throw the pieces on to the fire. His eyes narrowed. She was burning Lord George Randolph's letter.

The man followed her. The glow from the fire lit his face, and Denham caught his breath. It was not John—it was Wilmot.

Unobserved, he waited. Wilmot was talking urgently, in low tones; Rachel answering in the same way. By now their conspiratorial manner had thoroughly roused his curiosity.

A door opened and closed, and someone came into the hall. The two stepped apart, began a casual conversation.

'Oh, there you are, Wilmot.' It was John. 'Did you find your pocket-book?'

'Yes. Mistress Devereux was helping me.'

'Good. Shall we return to the winter-parlour?'

They moved away and disappeared out of sight. Denham waited for a moment and then went cautiously down the stairs and into the hall. He crossed to the fireplace, bent down and peered into the fire. The logs were nearly burnt through.

He saw what he had been looking for—one or two scraps of paper, charred at the edges. Not many, but enough perhaps to give him some clue. He snatched them away before the little flickering flame from the logs consumed them.

Upstairs in his bedchamber he spread the pieces out on the toilet table, and while he enlightened Adam as to what had occurred, examined them carefully, moving them about until they appeared to be in the right order.

He straightened. 'What do you make of *that*, Adam?'

The man bent over then, rubbing his chin ruminatively. 'It says something about being prepared to leave at a moment's notice . . . and to tell no one.' He looked at Denham. 'What's it mean, sir?'

'It seems that Mistress Devereux will shortly be leaving us. It would appear that the Royalist army in Cornwall is being deserted not only by its men but by its officers as well; one of those officers being Lord George Randolph.'

''Slud!' exclaimed Adam. 'But—but sir! You could warn the garrison at Torrington to keep a check on the roads.'

'No, Adam. That is something I cannot do, not now.'

Adam eyed him enquiringly, waiting for him to continue; and when he did not do so, said doubtfully, 'Very well, sir. But all the same——'

Denham roused himself from the fit of abstraction into which he had fallen. 'All the same, we had best be prepared for trouble.'

He crossed to the press and opened it, taking from it a long-barrelled wheel-lock pistol.

'It is time I loaded this again,' he observed.

Mr Wilmot left early on the following morning. Annie had given him his breakfast of bacon rashers and bread and ale. Reuben had told her to forget him. The Roundheads might be after him, he said darkly. If they should call at the house and start asking questions, it would be best to pretend ignorance.

Annie spoke to Cathie about it.

'Do you s'pose Reuben be right, Mistress Cathie?' She was twisting the corner of her apron as she spoke, her expression taut with anxiety. 'If they Roundheads come 'ere, what ought us to say to 'em? I be proper frightened of the likes o' they.'

'I don't think you have any cause to worry,' Cathie assured her. 'Mr Wilmot told us he took good care to avoid being seen by any Roundheads.'

Annie regarded her doubtfully. 'We-ell, that's as may be. But *someone* might 'a seen 'im.'

'If they *should* come here you will have to do as Reuben suggests—pretend to know nothing.'

'Ar, that be all very well, but you bain't reckoned with Captain Denham. He'll tell 'em, sure enough! And where'll us be then?'

—And where *would* they be? Cathie thought, when Annie had returned to her kitchen. If the Roundheads did come to Fern Place searching for Mr Wilmot, what would the Captain do? Would he tell them all he knew, or keep silent?

She gnawed her lip, uncertain and troubled. She realised she had completely overlooked the fact that he was a Parliamentarian officer on the previous evening—they all had. They had discussed the latest developments in Cornwall and their probable effect on Royalist policy quite openly in front of him. Supposing Mr Wilmot had been in possession of some important information and had confided it to them at the supper table? It would have been too much to expect the Captain to refrain from doing something about it. He would have felt himself obliged to pass on that information as soon as possible.

She sat staring down unseeingly at the sheet she was patching. Should she speak to Mary about it? She did not really want to trouble her—she was far too worried already. It would be no use approaching John, for he would probably use it as an excuse to pick a quarrel with the Captain. He might even insist upon his leaving the house at once. There was only one person she *could* talk to: the Captain himself.

She rose, set the sheet aside, and went resolutely in search of him, finally running him to earth in the book-room.

He glanced over the top of his book at her, and then rose to his feet with a welcoming smile.

'Mistress Cathie! They told me you were busy patching sheets.'

'Did they?' She spoke abstractedly.

'What is troubling you?' he asked.

She turned away and wandered across to the window. 'It is a little difficult to put into words.'

'Is it?' He was beside her. 'Suppose I hazard a guess and say that it is something to do with Wilmot's visit—would I be right?'

She looked swiftly up into his face, her expression startled.

'Yes, but how did you know?'

'Intuition. Shall we sit down? It is pleasant here, in the sunshine.'

They sat a little distance apart, on the window-seat. The spring sunshine poured in through the small panes, touching Cathie's hair with soft highlights. Denham's gaze lingered upon it, and travelled down to her face. He was conscious of her youth; of the years that lay between them, and felt suddenly weary.

'I will hazard another guess—you have come to ask me not to betray him. You need not worry. I have already given my word to Mistress Devereux. She was of the same mind as yourself.'

'Oh, I see.' Her tone was flat. 'There is no more to be said, then, is there? I will leave you to your book.'

She made as if to rise and then found, to her surprise, that he was holding fast to her skirts.

'Captain Denham!'

'You are always running away from me. Am I such an ogre?'

'No, of course you are not—only——' She paused, uncertain how to continue.

'Only—I am an enemy, is that it?'

'No!'

She stared up at him, struck by the harsh note in his voice, his changed manner, the way he was looking at her, as though she had in some way displeased him.

'I never think of you as an enemy,' she faltered. 'You have become a—friend.'

'A friend? Someone to be trusted? *Do* you trust me?'

'Yes,' she whispered.

His eyes searched hers. He read bewilderment, hurt, in them, and his own softened. 'I am sorry. I *was* behaving like an ogre, wasn't I?'

Her hands were clasped tightly together in her lap. He put his own hand over them.

'Mistress Cathie, will you always trust me, whatever happens?'

There was an underlying seriousness in his tone. She sensed that her answer was of great importance to him.

'Yes, always,' she said.

She saw his face change, his eyes light up. His hand tightened over hers. 'Thank you,' he murmured; and then, without warning, bent his head and kissed her swiftly on the mouth.

While she was still sitting there, utterly taken aback, he rose, drew her to her feet and smiled quizzically down into her confused face.

'I am not going to apologise for that! It is something I have wanted to do for a long time.' He paused, and then added lightly, 'I trust I am not poaching on another's preserves?'

'Poaching? Oh—no.' Her heart was still hammering. She looked up at him, and then down again. Her hands were held fast in his. 'I think I ought to go. I haven't finished my sewing.'

She pulled her hands away, turned, and sped towards the door.

He made no attempt to stop her; content, for the moment, to have learned the answer to a question that had been troubling him, even though he still refused to acknowledge to himself its true significance.

As for Cathie—she sat staring into space, with the sheet across her lap, without adding one stitch to the patch. He had kissed her! No one had ever done such a thing before. He had said: 'It is something I have wanted to do for a long time. . . .'

She was unable to look directly at him at dinner-time, feeling that if she did she would betray herself. No one seemed to notice. They all appeared to be occupied with their own thoughts.

After the meal she returned to her patching and sat dutifully over it until her fingers and toes were numbed with cold and the afternoon was nearly over. She rose, folded the sheet, placed it with the others and went to her room to tidy herself for supper.

She found, when she went downstairs, that Rachel and the Captain were absorbed in a game of piquet, apparently oblivious of all else. John was sitting nearby, watching them sullenly. Mary, on the settle, was occupied with her needlework.

Cathie went to the fire and warmed her chilled hands. She stole a glance at Denham: he looked up at the same moment. Their eyes met, and she was unable to prevent the colour rising in her cheeks.

Mary had observed the incident. 'Oh heavens!' she thought wildly. 'The child is in love with him. *Now* what am I to do?'

She realised she had been half-expecting it, ever since Cathie had shown such an interest in the Captain and had insisted upon sitting with him in his room. It was a natural development. Cathie was young, ready for love; the Captain was that much older, an experienced, attractive man. She did not want Cathie to come to any harm. She did not want her hurt. She would have to speak to her, warn her. It was a task she did not relish.

If only James were here! she thought. If only he had not gone away to fight. She looked into the fire, her heart aching for him, longing for news.

That night she went to Cathie's room, and found her brushing out her long curls. She looked surprised to see Mary.

'You are looking very serious! Is something wrong?'

'No, I just wanted to talk to you.'

Cathie's expression became guarded. 'What about?'

Mary sighed. It was not going to be easy. 'Has it ever occurred to you that if this war had not come to us, you would probably have been married by now? When James comes home I expect he will arrange a suitable match for you.'

Cathie's throat felt dry, and she swallowed. 'I don't care for arranged marriages.'

'They are often the best. Mine was arranged for me.'

'You and James were already in love with each other.'

'Yes, I know. But you will not be forced into a loveless marriage, Cathie. You know James would never do that! What I am trying to say is—don't do anything foolish meantime. It is so easy to make mistakes at your age, to believe one is in love, when all the time it is mere infatuation; especially when the man happens to be older. It often happens that way. Don't let yourself be hurt, Cathie.'

She put her hand on the girl's arm, her expression anxious, pleading. Cathie's mouth trembled. She said huskily, 'I won't, Mary.'

She smiled, a ghost of a smile that touched Mary's heart. She gave her a swift hug.

'Captain Denham will be leaving as soon as his wound is healed and he is able to ride any distance. We shall probably never see or hear from him again. He will go back to the war, and afterwards return to his own home. Regard him as a friend; nothing more. It is better that way, believe me. You will forget him in time.'

When she had gone Cathie sank down on the stool before the fire.

You will forget him in time.

'No,' she thought, 'I shall never do that. Never.'

CHAPTER
SEVEN

IN the morning it was raining, a filmy curtain that blotted out the landscape. It dripped monotonously from the roof and coursed in little streams down the window-panes, keeping everyone indoors.

Annie had a cold and was inclined to be short-tempered. Susan had the rough edge of her tongue. Adam found her weeping into her apron in the buttery.

'What's all this?' he asked, putting an arm round her shoulders.

'Nothing to do with you!' she replied in muffled accents.

'Ah, now! I don't like to see you cry.'

'Go away, then.'

'I have a better idea.' He took out a kerchief and dabbed gently at her face with it. 'Don't spoil those pretty eyes.'

'Think you're somebody, don't you, you gurt gomeril!'

He grinned. 'Somebody who's got a soft spot for *you*, my little maid.'

Her coif was askew, her dark hair curled in soft tendrils round her face. He touched it. She jerked away from him.

'Leave me be!' Despite her words, her voice had lost its sting.

'Maybe I would,' he said, 'if you were old and fat and ugly. Seeing you're none of these things, well—it's more'n a man can bear. Susan, love—give me a kiss.'

Her mouth opened, her cheeks reddened. She looked as though she would sooner give him a determined piece of her mind, but something in his manner checked her. He was standing there with a look of wistful entreaty on his face. She hesitated and then, standing on tiptoe, placed her hands on his shoulders and pressed her soft lips to his. Before he had time to recover his breath she had gone.

Mary rested in her room after dinner, with Betsy sitting nearby, mending a torn smock and talking quietly. Her words ran on, in the nature of a soothing monologue, expecting no answer. When she at last looked up she found that Mary had fallen asleep, and gave a satisfied nod. It was not the first time she had talked someone to sleep. Her ladyship had needed it, poor soul.

Cathie had once again taken refuge with her patching, her thoughts troubled and confused. John had gone to the stables. His horse had pulled a muscle and Joe was doctoring it with some embrocation of his own.

In the winter-parlour Rachel threw down her piquet cards.

'I'm sorry—I cannot concentrate.'

She rose to her feet and went to the window, standing there drumming her finger-tips on the glass, staring out at the dreary view.

Denham regarded her speculatively. All day her restlessness had been growing. She was unable to sit still for long at a time. This was the third occasion on which she had gone to stand at the window, looking out through the rain across the valley. One could see, in the distance, the road to Torrington on the other side of the little river. Her gaze was searching that road now, but it remained empty. She turned away from the window.

'Do you wish to continue the game, or have you had enough?' Denham enquired.

She came slowly towards him. 'I have had enough.' Her tone was resolute. She was regarding him with an oddly intent look; as though, he thought, she was measuring her chances.

'Captain—I would like to ask your help.'

She came to stand beside him and then with a swift, graceful movement sank down at his feet, her red skirts spread, tulip-fashion, about her, her face upturned to his, revealing the smooth, rounded column of her throat. Beneath her fine lawn collar her swelling breasts rose and fell. She placed her hand on his knee; he could feel the warm pressure of her fingers.

The whole gesture was wildly theatrical, yet some part of his mind could not but help register its effectiveness. At the same time his senses were fully alert: she was a dangerous woman, in every way.

'Ask away, Mistress Devereux,' he said.

'You are, I believe, a personal friend of General Fairfax, are you not?'

'That is so.'

'He would be willing to grant you some small favour?'

His face remained impassive. 'It is probable. What particular favour had you in mind?'

Her hand tightened its pressure on his knee. She began to speak swiftly, urgently.

'I want a pass for myself and a friend, to go to France. You could send Adam to Fairfax's headquarters. If he left at first light in the morning he could be back by nightfall, or soon after.' Her expression was one of supplication. 'If you would only do this for me, I should be extremely grateful to you, Captain Denham.'

Her eyes were brilliant, holding his. He was left in no doubt what form her gratitude would take.

'For yourself and a friend,' he repeated thoughtfully. 'Might I ask the identity of the friend?'

She blinked, and realised he had taken her off-guard. 'Grace, of course!' she said quickly. 'Who else would it be?'

'Why—to France?' He was not going to make it easy for her.

'I have no home in England now; no close family ties. Many of my friends have already left the country.' She gave a slight shrug. 'They considered it expedient to do so. Oh, if only you would do this for me'—her voice throbbed—'we could then go to France together in perfect safety, with no one to stop us.'

She broke off, with a sudden start. Unnoticed by either of them, John had entered the room. He was by their side in an instant, his expression dark with anger and suspicion.

'Rachel, what——?' He stood over her.

For a moment she remained where she was, too taken aback by his unexpected appearance to move. Then her eyes flashed. She rose to her feet, shaking out her skirts. Her manner was all at once cold, forbidding.

'Well, John? What was it you were about to say?'

'I—I was wondering what you were doing. It seemed odd that you should be—on the floor.'

'Indeed?'

'Rachel——' he put a hand on her arm. 'You were saying something about going to France. What did it mean?'

Her brows rose. She looked him up and down. 'I did not think you stooped to eavesdropping.'

Head high, she went swiftly towards the door. He hurried after her, all the anger gone from him, suddenly abject.

'Rachel, no—I didn't mean——'

The door closed behind them. Denham sat there, expression remote, deep in thought.

For the rest of the day he was conscious of John's watchful manner. At supper the boy was drinking heavily, but the wine, far from raising his spirits, only appeared to intensify his ill-humour.

He returned short answers to remarks addressed to him, his words becoming increasingly slurred as the meal progressed.

'Don't you think you have drunk enough, John?' Mary said quietly.

He scowled, and shrugged irritably. 'I'm not a child!' He poured himself some more wine with a belligerent air, and Mary sat back with a sigh of helplessness.

Rachel smiled sweetly at Denham. 'We didn't finish our game of piquet. Perhaps we could do so, after supper.'

'By all means,' he agreed gravely.

He guessed she was bent upon returning to the subject she had brought up before. He was quite ready for her: he had no intention of acceding to her request.

As it happened, she had no chance to talk to him alone. Though Mary and Cathie might be judged to be out of earshot by the fire, John had brought his stool close to the table at which they sat at their card table. He was strumming idly on a lute, breaking into snatches of recognisable tunes and then wandering off into odd harmonies and discordant notes. Every now and again he would throw out a remark, sometimes addressing Cathie, sometimes Rachel. The latter scarcely deigned to reply.

Altogether it was an uncomfortable evening, not enlivened by the sound of the rain pattering against the windows. Draughts swept through the room, making the candles flicker and the fire smoke. Shag lay at full length close to the fire, head on paws, warm and comfortable.

It was Rachel who made the first move to retire for the night, with the remark that she hoped it would be a better day on the morrow. This was said with a swift look at Denham, which was not lost on John. Cathie and Mary were not long in following her. Denham, left alone with John, wondered whether to try and talk him into a more reasonable mood, but decided against it. It would be better to let him sleep it off.

He bade him a good night, to which John responded with a surly grunt.

On his way to his room Denham had to pass Rachel's door. It was partly open. As he reached it, her voice called to him. He halted uncertainly.

'What is it, Mistress Devereux?'

She was sitting at her toilet table, half-turned towards the door, hairbrush in hand. Her black hair fell over her shoulders like a heavy curtain. 'Can you spare me a moment?'

She put down the brush and rose, her filmy undress-gown billowing about her as she came towards him. He glanced round the room. There was no sign of Grace.

'How did you know it was me?'

Rachel smiled. 'I know your step by now.' She laid a hand on his arm, drawing him farther into the room, pushing the door to behind him.

'Have you considered what I asked you?'

'Yes, I have.'

She was standing close to him, her face raised to his. Her arms went up, sliding over his shoulders; her hands began to caress the nape of his neck. She pressed herself against him.

'You will do it for me?' she breathed.

A nerve twitched in his cheek. 'Mistress Devereux——' he began.

Before he had time to finish the sentence, the door crashed open. John stood there, swaying slightly.

'Get away from her!' In his hand was a pistol.

Rachel gave a little choked cry, and Denham put her quickly from him and turned to face John. One glance was enough to tell him it was no use trying to reason with him. Jealous resentment had turned into blind, murderous fury.

'You took me for a fool, didn't you?' John's voice rang out wildly. 'I heard what you said—you're planning to go to France together. You're not going anywhere, Denham! I intend to kill you!'

Denham instinctively took a step towards him. 'Don't be a dolt!'

Immediately the pistol raised. 'Keep away!' John shouted.

There came a sudden rush of footsteps, a cry of horror. 'John—no! *Don't*!'

Without warning, Cathie flung herself at her brother, her hand closing round the pistol. For a moment they grappled for possession of the weapon. Denham, heart in mouth, plunged forward, pulling her away. As he did so there was a violent explosion, followed by a scream from Rachel, and another rush of footsteps. This time it was Adam. He gaped at them through the smoke.

'Sir! What happened?'

'An accident,' Denham said curtly. The bullet had sped past him, burying itself in the wall. Cathie was trembling in his arms, and he looked down at her. 'You are not hurt?'

She shook her head, her face white with shock. He released her and turned to John, who was staring at him, wild-eyed. The pistol dropped from his nerveless fingers.

'Oh, God!' He put his hands over his ashen face.

'Adam, go and tell Lady Gifford there is nothing to worry about,' Denham commanded, and the man hastened away.

John stooped and picked up the pistol. Denham held out his hand for it. 'I think you had better give that to me.'

For a moment John appeared to be about to refuse; then he allowed him to take it.

'I—I don't know what to say. I think I—I must have lost my senses.' He looked at Rachel, his face distorted. 'Forgive me.'

She said nothing. He turned away, head bowed, and stumbled out.

'Perhaps I ought to go to him,' Cathie said uncertainly.

Denham gripped her arm. 'Leave him. He will be better on his own.' He glanced at Rachel. 'I will bid you good night, Mistress Devereux.'

Before she could answer, he ushered Cathie outside and took her back to her own room.

She had left the door wide open in her haste. A branch of candles on the toilet table showed him that she had been making preparations for bed when she had been disturbed by John's shouting. Garments lay across a heavy oak chest standing at the foot of the four-poster, a stocking had fallen to the floor. He picked it up and handed it to her.

She took it from him, her expression still dazed. His gaze went over her. She was enveloped in a bed-gown adorned with bows of ribbon, her feet in little slippers. She looked very young. Some colour had returned to her cheeks, but she was still obviously shaken.

'Would you like me to fetch Betsy?' he asked in concern.

She shook her head. 'Is it true? *Are* you going to France with Rachel?'

''Od's death, no!'

'But John said——'

'John was under a misapprehension. If Mistress Devereux wishes to travel to France, she will have to look for an escort elsewhere.'

'I see,' she said slowly; and then, in a voice that shook, 'You might have been killed! John——' Her voice broke.

'Oh no,' he countered swiftly. 'You must not think that!'

'He meant to kill you!' The horror of that moment had returned to her. 'I heard him say so!'

He forced himself to speak lightly. 'I doubt whether he really meant it. Even if he did, your timely intervention prevented him from carrying out his threat. That reminds me, I have not yet thanked you for coming to my rescue.'

She smiled wanly. 'What are you going to do with that?' She indicated the pistol.

'I shall probably return it to him in the morning. I hope by that time he will have come to his senses.'

'So do I!' she said, feelingly. He was thankful to see that she was calmer.

Footsteps approached and Mary came in, her expression anxious, her manner distraught. Denham did his best to allay her fears: it was nothing—just a pistol exploding accidentally; no one was hurt, the bullet had gone harmlessly into the wall.

'Thank God!' she exclaimed.

He went wearily to his bedchamber and found Adam there, on tenterhooks to know what had happened. Denham told him, and Adam whistled.

'*Are* you going to send to the General for a pass for Mistress Devereux?' he enquired.

'I am not!' Denham's reply was emphatic. 'I never had the least intention of doing so, and this night's events have only strengthened my resolve. It's no thanks to that lady that I am not at this moment bleeding to death on the floor of her bedchamber. I shall have a few words to say to her in the morning.'

The few words were said immediately after breakfast, in the seclusion of the book-room. For a moment she stared at him, uncomprehendingly.

'You mean—you *won't*!' Her tone was incredulous.

He regarded her coldly. 'Mistress Devereux, has it never occurred to you that there are some men who are not to be bought?'

'I should never have said you were a prude!' she flashed.

'I am not, but I do happen to have certain principles.'

'How very convenient! Would it have hurt you to have done as I asked? All I wanted was a pass——'

'For yourself and a *friend*. At the risk of calling you a liar, may I say I do not believe for one moment that you intended taking Grace with you? In fact I would express the opinion that the friend in question was not a woman at all, but a member of the opposite sex.'

'Indeed!' Her eyes snapped. She was breathing quickly.

He had not finished with her. 'Even had I considered helping you, what happened last night would have changed my mind for me.'

'Are you referring to John's extraordinary behaviour?'

'You have treated him abominably. It is no wonder the boy was ready to commit murder. Had he succeeded, *you* would have been responsible. He is at a susceptible age, ready to believe anything. I can guess to what extent you have encouraged him—he must have proved an easy conquest for you. And then, when you considered *I* might be of use to you, you turned your charms on me and left John to kick his heels in jealous frustration.'

'He will get over it!'

'It is to be hoped so—but that is not the point, is it? *I* am no susceptible boy, Mistress Devereux, whom you can twist round your little finger, ready to believe that your flattering interest is genuine. In other words, I dislike being gulled by an unscrupulous woman whose only object is to use me for her own ends.'

He had perhaps spoken a trifle more strongly than he had intended. He saw her face change, her pupils dilate with fury.

'How dare you speak to me like that!' She flung herself upon him, clawing at his face.

Just in time he jerked his head away; caught her wrists and held them in an iron grip, feeling a sudden sharp stab of pain in his wounded side with the effort of holding her at bay. She spat out a stream of invective, twisting and struggling to free herself. Her heavy coil of hair became unfastened, slowly unwound and fell over her shoulders. He stood there, implacable, until she came to a gasping, sobbing halt. Then he freed her.

'You had best go and tidy yourself, madam!'

For a moment she faced him, bosom heaving, expression ugly. Then she drew herself up.

'I will make you pay for that, if it is the last thing I do!'

She turned, rushed to the door and went out, slamming it violently behind her. The ensuing silence seemed all the more profound.

The rain had ceased in the night, and as the morning advanced the sky cleared and the sun came out from behind the clouds.

Cathie went out into the garden, thankful to be in the fresh air, away from the house and Rachel's disruptive influence. As she paced the gravelled paths, Shag accompanied her, bounding off every now and then after some scent. John had eaten a solitary breakfast before the others had come down, and then disappeared. He was probably up on the moor. Cathie wondered whether she should go after him. Once she would have done so without question, but now they were so far estranged from each other she felt he would only resent her concern for him.

Denham was watching her from the book-room, where he was joined by Mary.

'I don't know what I should have done without Cathie,' she observed, 'especially now.' It was the first time she had referred, however indirectly, to her pregnancy. 'I shall miss her when she leaves here.'

He looked at her. 'When she leaves?' he repeated sharply.

She seated herself on the window-seat and returned his look. 'When she is married.'

'I understood she was not yet betrothed,' he said carefully.

'Not yet.' She studied his face. He was gazing once more out of the window, with an air of brooding abstraction. She decided to change the subject.

'I wanted to speak to you about last night,' she said.

'Last night?' He looked at her blankly; and then with an effort marshalled his thoughts. 'Of course——'

'I should like to know exactly what happened. You told me at the time it was an accident, but I am perfectly certain it was more than that. Please tell me, Captain Denham.' As he hesitated, she added, 'I was in the hall this morning when Rachel stormed out of this room. I had already heard your raised voices. It needed little deduction on my part to guess that you were quarrelling. Was it because of John?'

He seated himself. 'Yes—or at least, partly.' He decided to be frank with her, telling her everything that had happened.

When he had finished, she said: 'So you believe that Rachel is going to France with Lord Randolph?'

'Yes, I do.'

'Yet you have done nothing about it? You have sent no word to—to anyone?'

'No. I thought it better to let things take their course.'

'His capture would be of great value to the Parliamentary cause. You know, of course, that his father, the Duke of Wentworth, is one of the King's advisers?'

'Yes, I do.' He gave a faint smile. 'I was slightly acquainted with the Duke in the days before the war. I met him at Court.'

'Then I cannot understand——'

'If I had advised the commander at Torrington, he would by now not only have set a watch on all the roads, but would also have sent a troop here to this house, to lie in wait for Randolph should he succeed in slipping through the net.' He paused, and then added, 'I doubt if he will come alone. He will have others with him, ready to sell their lives dearly. Do you suppose they would submit without a fight? I do not want that to happen here.'

Mary was staring at him, wide-eyed. 'It had not occurred to me.' She thought about it for a moment. 'If they *should* come here and then manage to escape to France, will you not be blamed for it?'

'That is a chance I must take.'

'And you are willing to do that? For an enemy?'

He smiled faintly. 'Let me make it clear, Lady Gifford, that if you and your family were not involved, I should have no hesitation whatever in doing everything in my power to capture Randolph. As it is—I would rather let him go than have you all drawn into what might prove to be a fierce and violent conflict. I have seen enough of war to know what could happen here. I would not willingly bring that upon you.'

For a moment Mary was silent; then she placed a hand on his arm. 'Thank you, Captain Denham!'

She rose, and glanced out of the window. 'It is a pleasant morning. The sun is quite warm.' She smiled at him as he got to his feet. 'The garden is sheltered. Why not take the air for a while? I am sure you will come to no harm.'

'To tell the truth,' he said, with an answering smile, 'I had already considered it.'

A little later she saw him join Cathie, saw them stand for a moment in conversation before moving slowly away in the direction of the sundial in the centre of the garden.

Rachel saw them too, from the window of her bedchamber. Denham was gazing down at Cathie. It was impossible to see his face, for his hat brim hid it from her; but Cathie, her hood fallen back from her head, was smiling up at him. Watching narrowly, Rachel saw him put out a hand to touch the girl's cheek, saw the way Cathie bent her head in sudden confusion. She drew in her breath with a little hiss. So that was the way of it, was it?

Grace, sitting nearby, mending a tear in a petticoat with small, neat stitches, glanced up at her mistress, and caught the venomous expression on her face. She was thankful not to be the cause of it:

Mistress Devereux might be honey-sweet to those she wished to charm, but Grace knew the other side of her nature only too well.

At dinner, John was quiet and withdrawn. He looked heavy-eyed and slightly untidy, as though he had not bothered overmuch about his appearance.

After the meal Cathie faced him in the book-room. 'Have you apologised to Captain Denham for your behaviour towards him last night?'

'Apologised?' His face darkened ominously. 'Has your precious Captain told you I found him in Rachel's room with his arms round her? Ah, I thought not!'

'I don't believe you!'

He grasped her wrist. 'Why do you not ask him, then? See if he can deny it! Why should he be in her room, if not to make love to her? They are planning to go to France together. I overheard them yesterday afternoon.'

'No, John. You are wrong. Captain Denham told me himself you were under a misapprehension.'

He gave her a pitying look. 'And you believed him?'

'Why should she not, when it happens to be the truth?' a voice demanded from the doorway. In two strides Denham was beside them. His hand fastened over John's, forcing him to release Cathie's wrist. His eyes were burning. 'I thought last night's little episode had taught you a lesson. It seems I was wrong. Let me make it clear to you, once and for all—Mistress Devereux may be going to France, but she is certainly not going with me!'

For a moment John glared at him from beneath his brows; then, without a word, turned and left the room. Cathie, rubbing her wrist, glanced up at Denham. 'John said that you——' She came to a faltering halt.

His brows rose. 'John said what? Come, out with it!'

'He said he found you in Rachel's room——' Again her voice died away.

'I see. He doubtless painted the blackest possible picture of my misdemeanour.' He eyed her sardonically. 'And do you believe his tale?'

Her eyes met his. He read uncertainty, and his expression hardened. 'Judged and condemned—unheard!' he said harshly. 'I did not expect it from *you*!'

'I am *not* condemning you,' she denied in a choked little voice.

How could she explain her feelings to him without giving herself away? Rachel had taken John from her; she was quite capable of winning the Captain too. Compared with her, Cathie felt immature, desperately unsure of herself. She turned, and before he could stop her, rushed out.

Rachel was standing on the half-landing, scanning the valley. Cathie, head bowed, did not see her until she was nearly at the top of the first flight of stairs. It was too late then to turn back from the cool, measuring gaze that flicked over her. Rachel was the last person she wished to see. She made as if to brush past, but Rachel detained her.

'You'll never win him by running away, you know! Maidenly modesty is all very well, but a man likes a little encouragement.'

'So I have observed,' Cathie said shortly.

Rachel laughed softly. 'In that event, why not try it for yourself? —Unless, of course, you fear the consequences. You might find yourself out of your depth with him—or have you already done so?'

'Certainly not!'

'No—you would be a trifle too *gauche* for him, I should imagine. He would prefer someone more experienced.'

'Someone like yourself, for instance?' Cathie flashed. 'Yet it would appear even *you* have had little success with him!'

Rachel's smile faded. 'What do you mean by that?'

Cathie threw caution to the winds. 'I was referring to your proposed journey to France. I understand he has refused to assist you.'

Rachel's eyes snapped. 'How did you come to know that?'

'He told me so himself.'

Rachel caught hold of her arm. 'What did he say? Come, you have said so much, you may as well reveal the rest of it. I want to hear. Tell me!'

'I will not!' Cathie attempted to pull herself free, but Rachel's grip tightened, her nails digging into Cathie's flesh.

'*Tell* me! You *will* tell me!' she cried vehemently.

Mary heard their raised voices as she came out of her bed-chamber. She hastened towards them.

'Rachel—Cathie! Whatever are you doing?'

Startled, they looked up at her. Rachel released Cathie so abruptly that she almost lost her balance. Mary gave a cry of alarm as the girl swayed backwards, and grabbed at the baluster rail to save herself from falling.

'Cathie—careful!' Mary's face went white, and she pressed a hand over her heart.

'I will go and finish patching the sheet,' Cathie said shakily. She hurried away.

Mary sank down upon the window-seat, looking up at Rachel. 'Ever since you came to this house you have caused nought but trouble. You are a spoilt, selfish creature, with no thought for anyone but yourself. You care nothing for the harm you do to others. I can only say I shall be extremely thankful when you are gone from here for good!'

Rachel drew herself up, her mouth a thin red line.

'Don't think *I* shan't be glad to quit this place! It must be the dreariest hole in Christendom! You may rest assured that when I *do* leave, it will indeed be for good!'

Turning on her heel, she swept upstairs and disappeared.

Left alone, Mary closed her eyes for a moment. The events of the past few weeks had taken their toll of her: she felt she could not stand much more.

There was a rush of heavy footsteps, then Betsy was beside her, anxious and alarmed. 'My lady! Are you not well? Is it——?'

'No, no!' Mary forced a smile. 'I am merely tired, that is all.'

Betsy pursed her lips, eyeing her keenly. 'Let me help you upstairs. You should be resting. Come, now.'

She fussed over her and made her comfortable on the great four-poster. Then, with a determined air, she said, 'I think I will get out the cradle, my lady. 'Tis as well to be prepared.'

'As you wish,' Mary sighed indifferently. 'The baby is not due until the beginning of April.'

Betsy looked at her shrewdly. 'Babes come when they've a mind to, 'Tis already March. Yesterday was the first of the month.'

'So it was. I had forgotten. The days fly past . . . and so much has happened of late.'

'Ar. Too much,' Betsy said darkly.

Mary slept for a while, and when she woke, found that Betsy and Jane had brought out the cradle and cleaned it. It had held generations of Gifford babies, for it had been in the family since Tudor times. Betsy was on her knees beside the big carved chest at the foot of the bed, taking out the small blankets and the other things that would be needed, a tender smile on her face. She looked up and caught Mary's gaze upon her.

'It'll be good to have a babe in the house,' she said.

Denham returned John's pistol before supper when they were alone in the winter-parlour for a few minutes. The latter accepted the weapon with muttered thanks, his face reddening.

'I will put it away,' he said in low tones.

Cathie entered the room as he was leaving it. He went out without speaking, closing the door behind him. She looked warily at Denham, not at all sure what reception she would receive after their slight *contretemps*.

Seeing her hesitation, he said: 'Will you not join me? It is warmer by the fire.'

Polly had brought in the branches of candles a short while ago, and had drawn the heavy curtains across the windows. The large room was full of dancing shadows; the candle flames flickered in the draughts.

As Cathie moved towards him. Denham's gaze went over her appreciatively. She was wearing a gown he had not seen before, of rose-pink taffeta; he wondered whether it was her best one. Tightly laced, the high-waisted bodice, with its deep neckline, moulded her firm young figure to perfection. The fine lawn collar covering her shoulders was caught together at her throat with a small pearl brooch, from which it fell open in a wide vee to reveal a glimpse of the delectable hollow between her breasts. The full sleeves were slashed and lined with pale green, gathered into lace-edged cuffs just above the wrists. A pink ribbon was threaded through her curls.

He went forward, took her hand and raised it to his lips. 'You look enchanting!'

She said, in a breathless rush, 'Have you forgiven me for doubting you?'

His eyes crinkled. 'I would be an ungracious boor not to have done so! Is that why you were favouring me with such a wary look just now?'

She nodded, flushing.

He was still holding her hand. Looking down at it, lying in his, he said quietly, 'I fear I spoke in anger this afternoon. Had I stopped to think I should have realised I was being hasty. I jumped to conclusions.' He lifted his gaze to her face. 'As *you* did, I think?'

'Yes, I did.'

For a moment his gaze held hers; a questioning, searching look. Then he said, 'Shall we sit down, and change the subject?'

He led her to the settle, and when she had seated herself, sat down beside her. Cathie glanced at him and then away again, conscious of his gaze upon her.

Feeling suddenly light-hearted, she said: 'What would you care to discuss?—The weather? Mr Shakespeare's sonnets? Annie's cooking?'

'Spare me the rest of the list,' he retorted. 'I can think of far more interesting topics. When a man happens to be alone with a bewitching young woman, his thoughts do not generally dwell upon such mundane matters.'

'Oh? What *do* they dwell upon?' No one could have bettered her air of innocence.

Denham's eyes gleamed. 'If you don't know the answer to that, you must be singularly unimaginative!' He took possession of her hand once more. 'Has anyone told you that your eyes are like twin stars? Or that your complexion outvies the rose in loveliness?'

'Indeed they have not! And if they did, I would probably laugh at them!' She accompanied this declaration with an airy gesture, notwithstanding the fact that her heart was fluttering at his softly spoken words.

He shook his head at her in mock despair. 'You really are the most vexatious little creature! Here am I doing my best to flirt with you, and you refuse to respond! Any other woman——'

'But I am not "any other woman".' She turned her head and looked at him, her eyes indeed as bright as stars.

He regarded her in silence for a moment, then his expression changed.

'No, you're not, are you?' He sounded startled, as though he had just made an astonishing discovery. His hand tightened round hers. There was something in his eyes that caused her to feel suddenly breathless. 'Strange—I think I have always known it, and yet did not realise——'

What would have happened next, Cathie never knew, for at that moment Polly came to say that supper would be on the table directly, and the moment was shattered. With a rueful smile, Denham rose and drew Cathie to her feet.

'Allow me to escort you in to supper,' he said; and then broke off, turning his head away in a listening attitude.

'What is it?' she asked.

'Horses—coming towards the house.'

Polly, who had gone to make up the fire, gave a cry of alarm. 'Body o' me! 'Tis they Roundheads come to burn the place over our 'eads!'

'Nonsense, Polly!' Cathie admonished, with a glance at Denham.

'It is more likely to be a—a messenger from Sir James.'

He shook his head. 'I think not, Mistress Cathie; not this time.'

As the horses clattered up to the house, he led her swiftly from the room. They found the others already gathered before the fire in the hall, their eyes turned towards the screens. Shag barked once and then stood, quiveringly alert, at John's side.

Cathie looked across at Mary and to her surprise intercepted a warning glance between her and Denham. She had barely time in which to wonder at this exchange when there came a sudden loud knocking for admittance upon the outer door.

At a sign from Mary, Reuben went to answer it, returning after a brief parley to announce: 'My lady—'tes some gentlemen come ariding out of Cornwall——'

They came in on his heels, a travel-stained but nonetheless resplendent group. Wide-brimmed beaver hats on which the curled plumes danced; swirling cloaks over silver-laced riding dress; heavy lace-topped boots adorned with jingling spurs; decorated leather gauntlets; rich sword-sashes.

Rachel gave a shrill cry. 'George!' She ran forward.

Immediately, one of the newcomers went to meet her, an answering smile on his face.

'Rachel, my sweet!' He spoke with an affected drawl. 'It was worth all the long, dreary miles just to see *you* again! By my troth, it was!'

He swept her into his arms and kissed her. She gave a soft, gurgling laugh. 'Poor darling—have you had a terrible journey?'

'Terrible! Ankle-deep in mud. The roads are practically impassable after the rain. We had to ford the Tamar—couldn't get near a bridge. They are too well guarded. We were lucky to have a good guide. However——' he shrugged, '——the tale can wait.'

He turned towards the little group by the fire, sweeping off his hat, to reveal long fair curls. His eyes were blue and heavy-lidded, his face a trifle florid. On his upper lip he wore a moustache, the ends brushed upward in the fashion of His Majesty's, though his chin was clean-shaven.

Rachel led him forward; there was about her an unmistakable air of triumph. Her gaze passed swiftly over Denham and then fastened on Mary.

'Mary, allow me to present to you—Lord George Randolph!'

CHAPTER
EIGHT

THERE were six of them, all cast in the same mould—hard-living, hard-drinking, reckless, arrogant. They had seen the King's cause flourish and now saw it withering away. All were agreed that it was only a matter of days before that cause would be extinguished altogether, at least as far as the Royalist army in the West was concerned.

'The Ironsides have us beaten!' declared one of them, a hard-featured man whom Lord George had introduced as Sir Bevil Tarrant. 'I tell you,' he swept a look round the supper-table, 'this man Cromwell has surpassed Rupert at his own game; and 'tis said he has achieved that by disciplining his troops. One cannot but admire 'em in the field, however much one might despise 'em for the psalm-singing, mealy-mouthed sons of whores they are. Ecod! You should hear them before the battle!'

The young red-haired gentleman sitting beside him, Denzil Porteous by name, jumped to his feet. Rolling his eyes to the ceiling and pulling down the corners of his mouth, he folded his hands together and began to intone in high-pitched, nasal accents, 'Take fresh heart, my brothers, in this hour of peril. The Lord of Hosts is with thee. He that succoured Daniel in the lions' den; that led forth Moses out of Egypt; yea, He that smote the Amalekites and cast the worshippers of Baal into the bottomless Pit; He shall guard thee this day and shall give thee strength to strike and overcome thine enemies. For our God is not as their God. . . .'

At this point his voice was drowned by a great gust of laughter from his fellows. He subsided, grinning broadly.

Under cover of the laughter and the loud and somewhat ribald remarks that followed it, Cathie shot a quick glance at Denham, seated beside her. He had so far taken little part in the conversation. She wondered what he must be thinking after listening to that malicious piece of mimicry, but his expression gave nothing away.

From the moment she had intercepted the warning glance between him and Mary, she had become increasingly aware of a feeling of tension, of threatening danger.

Mary had introduced him to Lord Randolph and his party as plain 'Mr' Denham, and they had accepted him without question. Why should they not? There was nothing about him to indicate he was other than a Royalist guest in a Royalist household. Unless something untoward happened, they would never suspect his true identity.

There was only one she feared—a big-built man with a coarse, swaggering manner, who had seated himself on the other side of Rachel. Lord George had introduced him airily as 'My friend, Lord Somers'. He had stared hard at Denham, and once or twice Cathie had seen him frowning across the table at him, as though trying to place him; but fortunately his attention for the most part was fixed either upon his meal or upon Rachel, whose voluptuous charms were evidently much to his liking.

Lord George had made it clear they would be on their way again as soon as they had supped. There was about them a wild sense of urgency, even while they laughed and joked in a manner that reminded Cathie of a group of boys in holiday mood. They ate ravenously. Their horses had been led away to the stables by the servants they had brought with them. The latter were now partaking of their own supper in the kitchen, doubtless regaling Annie and the others with tales of their exploits, culminating in the escape they had made through the Roundhead lines.

Having taken the edge off their appetites, Lord Randolph and his friends were only too ready to embark upon their own account of the adventure. They told a tale of a hazardous journey, begun the previous day. Having informed Lord Hopton of their intentions, they had left their quarters in Bodmin, and successfully eluded the approaching Parliamentarian army. With the aid of a local man, who had guided them by little-frequented paths over Bodmin moor, they had reached Callington. From here they had pressed on to the Tamar, but had found it too swollen by the spring rains to attempt to ford it at this point.

'Having no desire to drown ourselves,' drawled Randolph, 'we turned northward to seek a better spot to cross over into Devon. Those God-damned Roundheads were everywhere. I swear 'twas nothing short of a miracle we escaped detection.'

'Their "Lord of Hosts" must have turned a blind eye to us,' Porteous asserted loudly, amid laughter. He tossed back his wine and poured himself some more.

Rachel said swiftly, 'What happened then? Where did you spend the night?'

It was not the first time she had prompted them. It seemed to Cathie that she was deliberately encouraging Randolph and the others to speak openly. Was it because she wished to impress those at Fern Place with the extent of Randolph's devotion to her, having risked his life to come here? Or had she some other, deeper, reason for doing so?

Cathie glanced at John, sitting at the foot of the table. He had said very little so far, but his eyes, guarded and watchful, missed nothing that passed between Rachel and Lord George. Mary, at the other end of the table, seemed ill at ease, and Cathie noticed that she had barely touched the food on her trencher. Her face was pale, and she was leaning back in her chair.

Again Cathie was aware of that feeling of tension. She found she had lost the thread of his lordship's discourse and had to force herself to concentrate. What was he saying? Something about pistolling their way through some village. . . .

'We arrived on the outskirts before we realised it. It was too late then to turn back.'

Now they were all talking at once.

'Rode straight into a troop of Ironsides. Fortunately for us they had dismounted outside an ale-house. Took them by surprise—should have seen their faces—that Sergeant—before he could order them to take cover—shot him through the head!' A gale of laughter.

Cathie shuddered, and looked down at her trencher. It swam before her eyes. A firm hand covered hers for a moment, then Denham leaned over and poured her some wine. 'Drink this,' he murmured. She did so, and managed to give him a wan smile. 'Good girl,' he said quietly.

Rachel was watching them, her eyes hard and glittering.

'Did they not follow you?' John asked.

'Yes, but by the time they had recovered from their surprise we were clear of the village. We managed to give them the slip.'

It was the elegant young gentleman sitting on Cathie's other side who answered him. His name was Sir Harry Wyndham, and throughout the meal he had done his best to engage Cathie in conversation, paying her fulsome compliments and ogling her in a manner she disliked intensely. His bold brown eyes raking her, he said, 'You do not care for talk of bloodshed, Mistress Cathie? To be sure, 'tis not a fit subject for such delicate ears. I would we could stay longer, that I might further my acquaintance with you, but alas it cannot be.'

She murmured words of regret, while feeling devoutly thankful he would soon be gone. It was enough to have him there beside her, breathing down her neck and nudging her at intervals with his knee.

John was following up his own train of thought. 'Those Round-heads will doubtless have reported to their headquarters in Torrington by now. The commander will send his men scouring the countryside for you. If they should come here——'

'If they should, we shall be ready for them!' Tarrant clapped his hand upon his sword-hilt, and there was a fierce shout of assent from the others.

Randolph drained his glass, and wiped his fair moustache. 'Nevertheless, it might be as well if we were on our way. Rachel, my sweet, you look delightful, but scarcely garbed for riding. Will it take you long to prepare yourself for the journey?'

'The journey?' John's expression was thunderstruck.

Randolph eyed him coolly. 'Rachel is coming with me. Surely you had guessed that by now?'

'Where are you going?'

'Ultimately, to France. 'Tis the only place left us. You seem astounded, Mr Gifford. May I point out that we have no alternative? The King's army in the West is well-nigh finished. Hopton will have to sign peace terms, and my companions and I have no intention of surrendering ourselves to any crop-eared, sour-faced Puritans. We value our lives and liberty too highly for that.'

'So you are escaping while there is still time? Might I ask where you propose to find a ship at such short notice?'

Randolph smiled. 'My good friend Wilmot will have arranged passages for us by this time. He should have reached Bideford on the day he left here.'

'If you set sail from Bideford, you will have to travel all round the Cornish coast before you can cross over to France, running the risk of being stopped and boarded. Remember, Parliament controls the Navy.' John looked at Rachel. 'Do you really intend to do this foolhardy thing? I beg you to consider the danger. If you should be hurt—'

She shrugged nonchalantly. 'I shall not be!'

'You will be safer here,' he pursued desperately. 'Rachel—' He leaned forward, his expression imploring.

'I have no intention of remaining here. Nothing would induce me to.'

'You can always regard this as your home—have I not already told you that?'

She gave a scornful laugh. 'You *have*—more than once! Perhaps I should have made it clearer to you that I never had any intention of staying here any longer than I had to.' She glanced at Randolph, lounging beside her, listening with slight impatience to the exchange. 'When George arranged for me to be brought here from Exeter, he promised he would return for me as soon as he could. As you see, he has kept that promise.'

John's hand clenched on the table. 'So it was true—you *were* planning to go to France!'

'Yes, but *not* with "*Mr*" Denham.' Rachel paused. Cathie, watching her, saw her look across the table at Denham. Something in her manner struck cold fear into her. She knew then, without any doubt at all, that Rachel was about to betray him. Instinctively she leaned forward, gripping the table.

'*No, Rachel*!'

The green eyes flashed, and Rachel smiled. 'No—*what*, Cathie?' She turned to Randolph. 'George, my dear, you have spoken very freely this evening, as well you might, believing yourself to be among friends; but I fear you have been acting under a misapprehension. The gentleman sitting opposite to you happens to be an officer of the Parliamentarian army. His presence in this house is entirely due to the fact that he was wounded in an ambush at the bridge a few short weeks ago. He was brought here so that his wound could be tended.'

She glanced from Randolph's astounded face to Mary's distraught one. 'What a pity Mary omitted to inform you of this,' she continued silkily. 'However, I am sure you will take the necessary steps to prevent him from passing on the information he has learned this evening.'

For a moment there was a stunned silence. Cathie looked quickly at Denham. He was sitting motionless beside her, his gaze unflinching as he faced his lordship across the table. Only the slight twitching of the nerve at the side of his mouth betrayed his inner tension.

Lord Somers suddenly sprang to his feet with an oath, thumping his fist upon the table with such force that he upset his wine-glass. A stream of wine shot across the white cloth and began to soak into it.

'I knew I had seen your face somewhere before!—Bristol—last

year! 'Swounds, I *should* remember it well enough.' He pulled up his sleeve, exposing an ugly scar across the wrist. ''Twas you gave me this—damn' near sliced off my hand! Remember?'

'I remember,' Denham said quietly.

'So it is true,' said Randolph heavily. 'You *are* a Roundhead officer?'

'Captain Denham, of the New Model Army,' Rachel interposed, with a sneer. 'A fine table companion for you, gentlemen!' She looked round challengingly. 'What do you propose to do about it?'

'*Do*!' Somers' face was ugly. There was a swish as he drew his sword. 'There is a quick answer to that!'

'*No*!' cried Cathie. She heard Mary also cry out in horror.

Randolph struck down Somers' arm. 'No, Nat.'

Somers turned on him. 'What! Would you let him go! Or would you prefer me to pistol him sooner than spit him on my sword? 'Tis all one to me.'

'Yes!' cried Wyndham. 'Take him outside and shoot him. Even that would be too good for him.'

'Hang him from the nearest tree,' Tarrant suggested.

There was a swift chorus of assent from the others. Cathie looked wildly round the table. 'You cannot do it! John—' she turned to her brother. 'Can you not stop them?'

Even as she spoke, she realised the futility of her appeal. He cared nothing for the Captain, or what might happen to him. Suddenly Mary spoke from the head of the table. She was grasping the arms of her chair so tightly that her knuckles gleamed white.

'My lord——' she addressed Randolph '——had Captain Denham wished to do so, he could already have warned the commander at Torrington of your coming, for he suspected it days ago. He remained silent because he had no wish to involve the members of this household in any conflict. He told me himself he would do nothing to prevent you leaving the country.'

'The word of a Roundhead!' Rachel cried contemptuously. 'How do we know he has not sent his servant into Torrington to warn them——'

'Yes!' Wyndham exclaimed. 'Don't believe him!'

Tarrant produced a pistol. 'Settle it with this,' he said deliberately. 'Let's have no more shilly-shallying.'

Cathie gave a gasp of horror. 'If you kill him, it will be murder! Captain Denham is a man of honour. If he pledges his word to you to remain silent, he will keep that word.'

'One might have expected *you* to defend him!' Rachel flashed. 'You've been hanging round his neck ever since you set eyes on him, making a fool of yourself!—George, the others are right. You cannot possibly trust him. Let them settle it *their* way!'

Randolph's gaze met Denham's level one. He was frowning in thought.

'I have a better idea. He will be of more use to us alive than dead.'

'What do you mean?' demanded Somers.

'We will take him with us. He will be our surety in the event of any trouble.'

The sixth member of the group, who had hitherto sat silent, now spoke. 'You mean—a hostage?'

'Exactly, Hollis. I presume he is known to the troops in the district?'

'He should be,' said Rachel swiftly. 'He is Lady Fairfax's cousin.'

'Indeed?' Randolph's eyes quickened with interest. 'Then he will certainly be of value to us. Porteous, order the horses to be made ready at once, and see that Captain Denham's horse is also brought round with the others. You have a servant, Captain?'

'I have,' Denham acknowledged.

'I want him here. Hollis, find him, will you?'

The two men went out.

Cathie looked at Randolph. 'My lord, Captain Denham has not yet fully recovered from his wound. He is in no fit state to ride far.'

'That is a chance we must take, is it not?' replied his lordship smoothly. 'Rachel, 'tis time you made yourself ready. As soon as the horses are saddled, we must be away from here. Time is passing.'

She went without a word, her lips pressed together. Things had not gone as she had wished.

Wyndham opened the door for her, bowing gracefully. He then returned to his place at the table, poured himself some more wine and, with an insolent nod at Cathie, said: 'Here's to you, Mistress Turncoat! May you profit by your conversion. What is it St Matthew tells us—"Love your enemies"?'

There was a sudden crash as Denham, eyes blazing, leapt to his feet, sending his chair toppling to the floor. 'Retract those words, or I will give you cause to regret them!'

'No!' gasped Cathie.

Somers, bearing down upon Denham, gripped him by the arms, forcibly restraining him. Wyndham was already on his feet.

'Let him be, Nat! If he is so anxious to spill blood I shall be only too happy to oblige him—though 'twill be his own that will be shed.'

'Don't be a fool. You're half-foxed,' Somers snapped.

'Half-foxed or not, I'll take *him* on. What! Do you think me but a pot-valiant dizzard? Let me at him!'

'Enough, Harry! We haven't time.' Randolph turned to Mary. 'Pray accept my apologies for this unpleasantness. We shall shortly be on our way, and will trouble you no more. Ah, here is Hollis.'

The latter entered with Adam, whose gaze went swiftly round the table until it alighted on his master's face. A look passed between them.

'You—fellow——' drawled Randolph.

'My name, sir, is Adam Potter.'

'Very well, Potter. Captain Denham is to ride with us. He will tell you what he needs. Fetch it here. Mr Hollis will accompany you to see that you play no tricks.'

Denham looked at Adam. 'You know what I need.'

'Yes, sir. Am I to come with you?'

Denham glanced enquiringly at Randolph, who answered for him, 'I think not. You understand of course that should you attempt to get in touch with your comrades at Torrington, Captain Denham's safety will be in jeopardy?'

'I understand, sir.' Adam bowed and went out, with Hollis at his heels.

Porteous entered. 'The horses will soon be ready. I've told the grooms to saddle one for Mistress Devereux.' He glanced at Cathie. 'They are taking yours, mistress. I trust that will be in order?'

She nodded with a slight movement of the lips, her eyes big and apprehensive in her pale face.

'I will see it is returned to you,' Randolph assured her.

'What of the tiring wench?' Tarrant asked; and was informed that she could ride pillion behind one of the servants.

'It will be a rough ride,' John observed. He had sat silent for so long that they had almost forgotten his presence. As they all looked at him, he added, 'You said yourself the roads were practically impassable. In the dark you are likely to lose yourselves.'

'I think not,' Randolph returned coolly. 'There will be a moon to light our way. In any event, we have a Bideford man with us. He should be capable of guiding us there.' He rose to his feet. ''Tis time we made a move. Nat, be so good as to keep an eye on Denham, will you?'

He went up to Mary. 'We are all most grateful to you for your hospitality. I wish I could have given you good news of your husband, but——' he shrugged, and brushed back a long curl that had fallen over his face '—— our paths have not crossed recently. I can only say that, to the best of my knowledge, Sir James is well and still remains with Hopton.'

Mary barely glanced at him. 'My husband will remain with him to the end,' she said with quiet dignity.

He acknowledged this with a slight inclination of the head, his face impassive. 'I trust you will soon have news of him. And now we must bid you adieu.'

He bowed to her, and the others followed suit before they left the room. Somers, pistol in hand, indicated to Denham that he was to precede him. Cathie watched them go and then, with a glance at Mary and another at John, who was sitting there frowning heavily at the table, she went swiftly out into the hall.

Rachel was already there, wrapped in her heavy, fur-lined cloak, with Grace, also suitably attired against the cold night air. Down the stairs came Reuben with a bulging cloakbag. Rachel indicated this to Randolph with an expressive gesture.

'As you requested in your letter, I am travelling light.' She turned to Cathie. 'I trust Mary will be good enough to keep the rest of my things for me, for the time being.'

'I am sure she will,' Cathie replied stiffly.

'Sir!' Adam crossed to Denham's side, and handed him his heavy boots. Denham, sitting down upon a joint-stool near the fire, pulled them on with a grimace. It was the first time he had worn them since he had been wounded. Having donned his hat, he held his hand out for the cloak Adam was carrying, neatly folded, across his arm.

'Right, sir,' Adam said quietly.

He was about to pass it to him, when there came an unexpected interruption. Randolph's servant burst into the hall, his expression one of alarm.

'My lord—Roundheads! We saw them in the moonlight—they are almost at the gates!'

Tarrant was the first to speak. 'Roundheads! 'Sblood, Randolph! What do we now?'

'Leave it to me!' Randolph brushed him aside and addressed his servant. 'Blake, get the horses out of sight at once. Be prepared for trouble!'

'Yes, my lord!' The man ran out.

Randolph turned swiftly to the others. 'Porteous—take that cloakbag. Rachel, you and your maid had best return upstairs and remain there.'

'What about——?' Somers jerked his head in the direction of Denham and Adam, standing near the fire.

'Captain—your hat! Give it to your servant. You will not be needing it—yet. Hollis, take charge of Potter. Wyndham, you have your pistol?'

'Yes, here it is.'

'Good.' Randolph turned to Denham. 'When they arrive, you will tell them we have already left and are making for Exeter. Do you understand?'

'Supposing I refuse?'

'I don't think you will; not while we have Mistress Cathie. We are desperate men, Captain. You would not wish her to come to any harm, would you? Wyndham—the girl.'

'With pleasure!'

Wyndham stepped forward. Cathie shrank back and made as if to turn and run, but he was too quick for her. His arm snaked round her waist, and she gave a little cry.

'Let her go!' Denham shouted furiously; and found his way blocked by Randolph, pistol in hand.

He had to stand, helpless and raging, while Wyndham half-dragged, half-carried the struggling girl away, and out of sight. The others, meanwhile, had melted away, some to the winter-parlour, the rest to the gallery above the hall, where they crouched, weapons at the ready.

'Remember, Captain!' Randolph warned. 'We have already left for Exeter. You had best make the story sound convincing. We shall be within earshot.' He paused, listening intently. 'Here they come! It is up to you to get rid of them.' He disappeared.

He had scarcely done so when there came a furious hammering upon the outer door. Reuben, who had been watching all that had occurred with growing alarm, looked enquiringly at Denham.

'Sir, I'd best open it afore they break it down. And—sir—you'll do as 'is lordship says, won't 'ee? For Mistress Cathie's sake?'

'You need have no fear of that, Reuben.'

'Aye.' The man went to open the door, his brows drawn. He had the uncomfortable feeling that the ground had been swept from under him. To think such fine gentlemen—and Royalists, as well—would behave so ungallantly! Why, they were no better than those whoreson Roundheads!

He opened the heavy oak door and stood aside as the Roundhead troopers burst in with a clatter and scrape of boots, candlelight gleaming on pot helmets and body armour.

He heard their Captain address Denham. 'Sir—Captain Denham, is it not? We have come in search of a party of malignants believed to have headed in this direction. Can you help us?'

A slight pause, and then Denham replied in a quiet, controlled voice, 'I am sorry, Captain, you are too late. They have already left.'

'Can you give us any idea of the direction they took?'

Reuben, peering round the troopers, saw Denham turn away towards the fire.

'They said they were making for Exeter.'

'Exeter! How long ago was this, sir?'

'Not long. If you hurry you may catch up with them.'

'Thank you. Come, lads, look lively. We don't want to have to ride all the way to Exeter!'

They hastened out; and Reuben, standing in the open doorway, watched them mount and ride away, disappearing swiftly in the direction of the gates. He closed the door and went back into the hall. 'They've gone, sir!'

Randolph had already stepped out of his hiding-place. 'Congratulations, Captain!' His tone was derisive. 'A most convincing performance. I could not have done better myself.' He raised his voice. 'Come! 'Tis time we were on our way! Wyndham—you may release Mistress Cathie.'

Wyndham appeared, still holding her by the arm. 'I never had so delightful a charge,' he said, lifting her hand to his lips and kissing it fervently. 'Farewell, my dove.'

She snatched her hand away and turned from him, straightening her collar, which had become sadly disarrayed and crumpled. Her eyes sought for Denham. It was as much as she could do to prevent herself running to him. His gaze met hers, giving her strength and courage, as she went to his side. She had lost the ribbon from her hair, and her curls fell over her shoulders. Her gown was disarranged. She looked young and defenceless.

'Captain!' Adam handed him his cloak, with a significant look.

Denham glanced about him. With the exception of Cathie, no-one appeared to be taking much notice of him. They were preparing for departure, drawing on riding gloves and hats. Again there was that sense of urgency.

Blake entered once more. 'The horses are ready, my lord.'

'Good. Did you hear that, gentlemen? Let us start on the last lap of our journey before those confounded Roundheads discover they have been sent on a wild goose chase!'

Amid laughter, there was a sudden surge towards the door. Blake, carrying the cloakbag, went out with Grace. Randolph offered his arm to Rachel, and turned to Denham.

'Come, say your farewells to Mistress Cathie. Time is getting short.'

Denham was holding his cloak. His gaze flashed round the hall. Apart from Rachel and Lord Randolph, only Somers remained.

'For you—yes,' he said, 'but not for me.'

'What do you mean by that?'

'I am not coming with you.'

'What! Why, you——' Somers strode forward; and then checked with a startled oath.

Denham had dropped the cloak. In his hand was a pistol. His eyes gleamed with sardonic amusement at the expression of shocked disbelief on their faces.

'Allow me to repeat what I said just now—I am *not* coming with you. Oh, I have no intention of killing you, unless I must; neither do I intend to prevent you from leaving. You have my word I will not send the troopers after you—whether you care to accept it or not.'

For a moment they stood staring at him. Rachel was the first to speak. 'George, you cannot allow this to happen!' Her voice was shrill, her face a mask of fury. 'Don't believe him! He will betray you—he will send his servant to fetch those troopers back!'

Randolph did not take his gaze from Denham's face. 'It would seem we have but little choice, Rachel. He has the advantage of us. We must bow out gracefully.' She opened her mouth to protest, but he silenced her with a look; and then, in clipped tones, addressed Denham. 'Sir, allow me to congratulate you upon your sleight of hand.'

Denham smiled grimly. 'Adam must take his share of that. 'Twas he who secreted the pistol in the cloak. An old trick—but an effective one.'

'I must remember it. We will bid you adieu, Captain Denham, Mistress Cathie.' He bowed stiffly to them both. 'Come, Rachel. Somers—are you coming?'

Lord Somers, who had been staring as if mesmerised at Denham, gulped and turned. 'Of course!'

Rachel flung up her head, her green eyes glittering. She was in a furious temper. 'So you have the last word, Captain Denham! If I had had *my* way, you would not have lived to play that trick upon us!'

His gaze was rapier-sharp upon her. 'I am aware of it, Mistress Devereux. I wish you a safe journey to France.'

For a moment she held his gaze; then her own wavered and fell. She turned to Randolph. 'Let us go!'

Denham, pistol still cocked, strode the length of the hall after them, and waited until they had gone out into the moonlight. 'Close the door, Reuben,' he ordered, and the man did so with an air of relief.

Cathie, left alone with Adam for a moment, said: 'How did you manage to conceal the pistol while you were being watched?'

He grinned, his blue eyes twinkling down at her. 'Bless your heart, mistress, I'd already done it. As soon as I got wind of what was going on, I went upstairs and wrapped the Captain's cloak round the weapon, leaving it lying, casual-like, on the bed. 'Twas an easy matter to pick it up later and carry it downstairs.' He laughed.

She was unable to share his laughter. The events of the past few hours had left her feeling completely shattered. As he turned away to speak to Reuben, she sank down on the stool near the fire, trying to marshal her thoughts. All at once she felt a light touch on her shoulder. Denham was bending over her, his expression concerned.

'Did that knave hurt you?'

'No.' She drew a quivering breath. 'I—I thought they were going to *kill* you!'

'It's all over,' he said gently; and she nodded, and managed to give him a little shaky smile.

'All over—thank God!'

They were interrupted by Shag, who thrust his cold nose in between them with an anxious whine.

'He has been very quiet all this time,' Denham remarked, frowning.

'Yes.' Cathie glanced round, aware of a feeling of unease. 'I wonder what John is doing? He did not come out into the hall. . . . and neither did Mary!' She got to her feet, and Shag gave a short bark and leapt away, looking back as though expecting her to follow him. 'Something is wrong!' she exclaimed.

With Denham beside her she hurried to the dining-parlour, Shag bounding ahead of them. Mary was sitting there, all alone. Cathie took one look at her and then, her mouth suddenly dry, rushed to her side.

'Mary——!'

Mary's hands were clenched upon the table. She was gripped by a fierce spasm of pain. Her forehead was beaded with moisture, her face grey and drawn with agony. She waited until the pain had receded and then gasped, 'I asked John—when he went out—to fetch Betsy. That was—some time ago. Perhaps he—he did not hear me.'

'I'll go!' Denham strode out returning within a couple of minutes with Betsy, full of anxious concern, her coif awry and her apron-strings flying.

She took immediate command of the situation, and between them they managed to get Mary upstairs to her bedchamber, where Betsy, her sleeves rolled up above the elbow, issued a stream of orders to Jane and Susan. 'Hot water—we'll need plenty of it—and get Reuben to fetch up more logs at once. The room must be kept warm. Now, where's those old sheets that were put aside?'

'I'll fetch them.' Cathie scurried away.

Denham was busy replenishing the fire. He rose and dusted his hands together. 'Is there anything I can do?'

'No, sir, there is not,' Betsy informed him decisively, 'unless it so 'appens you be a doctor.' Her voice dropped. 'There's not one this side o' Torrington, and I 'eard this morning that the midwife in the village is down with the ague, so we're in a proper way. Ar, that be right, my dear——' This to Cathie, who had returned with the sheets. 'And now you'd best go and change out of that grand gown, for you'll be needed 'ere tonight. Annie's took to 'er bed with 'er cold, and Susan be the only one left, saving yourself, with a mort of sense in 'er 'ead. My eymers! When I saw 'er ladyship today so poorly, I knew in my bones something like this would 'appen. I up and told 'er—babes don't wait for nobody. They come when they've a mind to!'

'I'll go and change,' Cathie murmured, and with a glance at Denham went out.

Mary raised her head from the pillow. 'Captain Denham——?'

'Here I am.' He crossed to the bedside.

'I am worried about John,' she said weakly. 'I fear he may have done something foolish. Could you send someone to see if his horse——' She broke off as another spasm of pain took control of her, scarcely hearing his assurance that he would do so at once.

He looked helplessly at Betsy, who brushed him aside and bent over her mistress. 'We must get you undressed, my lady. Here comes Susan——'

Denham beat a hasty retreat.

He found Adam hovering anxiously in the hall and despatched him to the stables. He was back within a few minutes with the news that Mr Gifford's horse was missing. According to Joe, he had ridden away some time ago, but the groom was unable to say where he had gone; only that he had been in desperate haste.

'Do you suppose he's gone after Lord Randolph and the others?' queried Adam.

Denham frowned. 'I don't know. In his present mood he is capable of anything.'

'What will you do now, sir?'

'The only thing I can do, Adam—wait!'

There was a cheerful fire in the winter-parlour. Denham seated himself on the settle before it, making himself comfortable on the cushions, with a bottle of wine beside him, and a book on his knee: a copy of George Chapman's translation of the *Iliad*. It remained unopened as he sat frowning into the flames, deep in thought.

Where had John gone in such a hurry? *Had* he followed Randolph? If so, with what intention? He feared, as Mary had done, that the boy would perpetrate some act of folly which might have tragic consequences.

He groaned and reached out for his glass of wine, and in doing so he knocked his book to the floor. Bending down to retrieve it, his fingers touched something silky. He picked it up—it was the length of pink ribbon Mistress Cathie had worn in her hair. This, then, must be where Wyndham had brought her. His face hardened. He wished with all his heart he had not been prevented from teaching that insolent young gallant a lesson in swordplay.

He lifted the ribbon to his lips. It smelt faintly of lavender, reminding him of her hair, golden-brown and gleaming in the candlelight, satin-smooth to the touch; of her eyes, wide and wondering as they had looked into his; of her mouth, warm and tender, and infinitely sweet.

He knew now she had come to mean more to him than any other woman he had met. He longed to hold her in his arms, to know the joy of possessing her; above all, to have her there beside him for the rest of his days.

He sighed. Had the war not thrown them together, they would

never have met. When his wound was healed he would be riding away to take up arms again, to fight for the cause in which he believed so strongly. How could he expect her, a dedicated Royalist, to understand his feelings—with her own brother fighting for the King?

Even had they not been on opposing sides, there still remained the difference in age between them. She was but eighteen, he nearly thirty.

He gave a wry smile. Nearly thirty—and in love for the first time in his life!

CHAPTER
NINE

A CHARRED log fell on to the hearth. Denham jerked and opened his eyes, blinking round him for a moment, until he remembered where he was. He must have fallen asleep. His book lay open on the floor. Candles, burnt down to the last couple of inches, flickered and smoked, and the air was heavy with scented wax.

He yawned and stretched and then, wondering what the time was, took out his watch. A quarter past eleven.

The house was quiet. He rose and went over to the big windows. Drawing aside a curtain, he looked out. Nothing stirred in the moonlight. He let the curtain fall into place and as he did so heard, far off, the sound of hoofbeats, slow, weary, uneven. A lame horse returning to its stable. John was home.

Denham went out into the hall, lit only by a few wall sconces, where Shag lay stretched out before the dying fire. He raised his head as Denham approached, thumping his plumy tail upon the floor. Denham seated himself on a stool and waited for John.

The boy came at last, a dispirited droop to his shoulders, his step dragging, his clothes muddied. Shag went to meet him and he paused to fondle the dog, not seeing Denham until he was almost on top of him. Then he checked.

'Oh, it's you!' he said flatly.

Denham rose. 'I suggest we go into the winter-parlour. There is a better fire in there. We can talk over some wine.'

'Talk?'

Denham quirked an eyebrow at him. 'Isn't that what you want to do? Talk things over?'

'Well, I——' John hesitated, tapping his whip against the top of his boot; then he shrugged. 'I suppose so.'

They went into the winter-parlour, Shag at their heels. John flung his things on to a stool and went to stand in front of the fire, frowning heavily. Denham handed him a glass of wine, and returned to his seat on the settle. John sank wearily into the chair opposite him, Shag flopped down between them.

'It must be late,' John observed.

'Nearly half-past eleven.'

'They will have reached Bideford by now, with luck.'

'You did not follow them?'

'No.' John hesitated and then said defiantly, 'I went after the troopers.' He waited to see Denham's reaction.

'I rather thought you might,' the latter remarked drily. 'When I learned you had ridden away in such a hurry, I guessed your motive to be one of revenge. I am right, am I not?'

John shrugged wearily. 'Yes, you are. I intended to fetch the troopers back and send them after Randolph and—and the others.' He checked, and then burst out: 'It was the way she spoke to me, the way she behaved this evening—as though I were nothing but an—an addlepated yeanling of no account! I knew then she had never really cared for me.' His mouth twisted bitterly. 'She never cared for anyone save herself. All those things she said to me in the past—they meant nothing. Cathie was right—she was just amusing herself and I—I was too blind to see it.'

He looked down at the glass in his hand, tossed back the contents, and held it out wordlessly to Denham, who refilled it.

'So,' the latter said quietly, 'you went to fetch the troopers back. What happened?'

'I took a short cut over the moor which would have brought me out on the Chulmleigh road. The moonlight was bright, everything was clear. I should have managed well enough, had my horse not stumbled and thrown me. I wasn't hurt, just shaken and bruised a bit; but I lamed Swallow again. Joe is vexed about that. He has been doctoring him for a week past for a sprain, now it seems he will have to start all over again. I should have taken another horse, I suppose. I didn't stop to think.'

'You were going too fast over the uneven ground,' Denham murmured.

'I was in a hurry!'

'You walked him home?'

'Yes, after a while. When I had picked myself up and taken a look at Swallow I didn't feel like coming home straight away. I wanted to sit down and think things out. So—I did.' His voice died away.

Denham sipped his wine and regarded the boy's brooding face with a certain amount of sympathy, waiting in silence for him to continue. When he did so it was in a low, musing tone, as though he was talking to himself.

'She changed everything for me. Everything. I thought she was the most beautiful thing I had ever seen. I believed in her. What a fool I was!'

One by one the candles were dying, the room growing dimmer every minute. A log fell with a shower of sparks. John kicked it back again.

'I sat there and turned it over in my mind, and all at once it occurred to me—had I succeeded in accomplishing what I had set out to do, I should have been nothing but a traitor. I had been so intent upon avenging myself upon Rachel, I hadn't thought of that! I had completely overlooked the fact that Randolph and his friends were Royalists, my own brother's comrades-in-arms. And I had been about to betray them!' His voice shook. "Od's wounds, Captain! I would never have dared face James again, if I had! And all because of Rachel!'

'But you didn't do it.'

'No, but I should have done, had Swallow not stumbled and thrown me. There would have been nothing to stop me catching up with the troopers.' He broke off, running agitated fingers through his hair; and then, with a quick glance at Denham, said, 'I suppose you think I'm a fool, too?'

'No. You fell under the spell of a beautiful and dangerous woman, who used you for her own ends, as she would use any man if he were willing. You have seen the way moths hover round a flame. Even though they singe their wings they still return to it. It is as though they cannot help themselves.'

John considered this in silence. 'She tried to use *you*, didn't she?' he said slowly. 'She asked you to help her get to France. Why should she want you to do that, when she knew Randolph was returning for her?'

'She wanted me to procure a written pass from General Fairfax for them both, though not, I fancy, in Randolph's name. That would have given the game away.'

'Was that why you were in her room that night? Because she was trying to persuade you?'

'It was.'

'You refused.' It was a statement rather than a question. The shadow of a smile touched John's lips. 'You didn't singe *your* wings!'

'I refused point-blank to help her. I didn't trust her.'

'So that was her reason for urging them to kill you tonight. I wondered at the time why she should have betrayed you.' His expression was suddenly uncertain. 'I—I think I owe you an apology. I have behaved very badly towards you.'

'Shall we regard it as a closed chapter, and start afresh?'

'I should be glad to, if *you* would.'

'That's agreed, then,' said Denham briskly. 'I suggest we drink to it.'

They drank, solemnly.

'It is very late,' John observed. 'Perhaps we ought to go up to bed.' He rose.

'You can, if you like,' Denham replied. 'I think I will stay here, and wait.'

John eyed him in surprise. 'Wait?—For what?'

'When you rushed out of the dining-parlour this evening, I believe Lady Gifford asked you to fetch Betsy for her.'

John looked suddenly contrite. 'Oh yes—that's right. I'm sorry to say I forgot. I hope it was nothing important.'

'It would depend upon what you consider to be important. I imagine you were so intent upon your own affairs, it did not occur to you that Lady Gifford had been taken ill.'

'*Ill*! You don't mean—oh no!' John stared at him, his face draining of colour. He sat down again as though his legs had suddenly given way beneath him.

'But the baby isn't due for another month—not until April!' He looked stricken. 'It's *my* fault! If I hadn't behaved so badly—if I had only had more consideration for her——' He slumped forward, his hand over his eyes. 'If—if anything should happen to her or the baby, I will never forgive myself!'

'Nonsense,' Denham said crisply. He rose and stood over him, his hand on his shoulder. 'Nothing is going to happen to either of them.' He recalled Betsy's prophetic words and repeated them. 'Babies come when they've a mind to! And now, I suggest we find some more candles before we are plunged into total darkness.'

John raised his head. 'There should be some in the press,' he mumbled. 'I'll get them.'

With fresh candles lit, the room presented a more cheerful appearance. Denham replenished the fire.

'We may as well make ourselves as comfortable as we can. Would you care for a game of piquet, or would you rather talk?'

'I think I would rather talk, if you don't mind; but first of all, ought I to go upstairs and see how Mary does?'

'She was worried about you. It might be as well if you let her know you are back safely.'

John departed, to return shortly with the news that he had had a
few words with Cathie outside Mary's door. She had told him that
nothing had happened as yet.

'These things take time,' Denham murmured.

John looked at him. 'Are you married?'

'No, not yet. One day, perhaps.' Denham stooped and picked up
the fallen book. 'I was reading this before you came home. Have you
any other of Chapman's works? My father has collected several of
his plays—*The Gentleman Usher* and so forth. For my part I prefer
Ben Jonson, or Will Shakespeare.'

He went on to talk of them, while John listened gravely. It seemed
to him that Denham had changed the subject deliberately. From
plays they went on to discuss masques.

'I believe the Queen acted in one or two, did she not?' John asked.
'Much to the disapproval of the Puritans.' He glanced at Denham. 'I
suppose you agree with their views?'

'No, not particularly, though I do agree that the Court masques
were far too costly, and the money spent on them could have been
put to better use. Nevertheless, I greatly enjoyed those I saw. Mr
Inigo Jones used to devise some wonderful effects for them.' He
leaned forward, launching into an enthusiastic account of Mr Jones'
elaborate scenery and costumes, describing them with a wealth of
detail that captured John's interest and imagination.

When he had finished, John regarded him curiously. 'You fre-
quented the Court, you enjoyed masques and dancing and music,
and all the other pleasures Puritans frown upon, and yet you chose
to fight for the King's enemies. How can you justify that?'

'I suppose,' Denham returned slowly, 'it is all a question of
values.' He gave John a measuring look. Would he understand, as
Cathie had, the reasons for his decision? Choosing his words carefully, he began to explain.

Some time later Cathie came wearily downstairs to find them.
Hearing the low hum of voices, she opened the door of the winter-
parlour and stood on the threshold for a moment, staring at them in
bewilderment. Never in her wildest dreams had she pictured John
in animated conversation with the Captain; and yet, here he was,
expounding his views to him upon—of all things—husbandry! And
Denham was listening intently, nodding his head in agreement,
interposing a remark here and there.

They were so engrossed that neither of them noticed her. Slightly aggrieved, she went towards them, and broke in abruptly: 'Mary has given birth to a boy. She says she will name him James.'

They stared at her in startled surprise, then Denham exclaimed: 'A boy! That's wonderful!' Smiling broadly, he rose to his feet. 'How is Lady Gifford?'

'Very tired.' Her tone was colourless. She turned to John. 'Mary wishes to see you. You had better go up at once. She will want to sleep.'

'Yes, I will.' He plunged towards the door, spurs jingling, and went out.

Denham's gaze was on Cathie's wan face. 'You are tired, too,' he said gently.

She nodded. Her hair was tied back at the nape of her neck, her eyes smudged with weariness, her mouth drooping. She looked at him wordlessly, and all at once burst into tears.

In between sobs she tried to explain. So much had happened—Randolph and his companions—the Round-heads—Mary and the baby. . . .

'He's so small—so frail. I thought he was going to die. He was scarcely breathing. Betsy had to slap him.'

By this time he had drawn her down beside him on the settle, his arms strong about her. Cathie turned her face into his shoulder and wept unreservedly, sobbing out all her fears in a burst of reaction; only vaguely aware of his murmured words of solace, his tender endearments.

After a while she groped for her kerchief, mopped her streaming eyes and blew her nose. 'I'm sorry,' she said huskily. 'What must you think of me!'

One last tear coursed slowly down her cheek. Bending his head, Denham kissed it away, the salt taste of it lingering on his lips. Then, rising to his feet, he went to the table and poured wine for them both, returning with the two glasses, one of which he handed to her.

She drank thirstily, and made no demur when he refilled her glass. He was thankful to see a tinge of colour in her cheeks. He stirred the fire into life, adding another log to it.

'That's better!' He seated himself close beside her once more.

She stirred. 'I mustn't stay. Mary will be wondering where I am.'

'She will be asleep by now.'

'Betsy won't be!'

'A plague on Betsy!' He slipped an arm round her and drew her against him, half expecting her to resist, but she did not. Instead she let her head fall on his shoulder, and they sat there, relaxed and content, gazing into the fire.

For a while they remained silent. Then she said in a small, dreamy voice, 'I shouldn't be sitting here with you like this, should I?'

'Probably not,' he agreed, adding: 'Would you rather go to bed?'

Her head moved slightly. 'No. It's—very pleasant here.' She finished her wine, and he took the glass from her and put it down on the floor, beside his own.

'I wonder what time it is,' she murmured.

'Approaching dawn, I shouldn't wonder.'

'What were you and John talking about?'

'Various things—court masques and balls, Puritans and pleasures.'

'Did he tell you where he went tonight?'

'Yes.' He recounted John's tale, and she sighed.

'Poor John. How miserable he must be. He would never listen to a word against Rachel. She was the world to him. He was too blind to see her in her true colours.'

'Love makes us blind,' he said softly.

'Does it?' She looked up at him. 'I suppose you—you know a good deal about it.'

The corners of his mouth twitched. 'Probably more than you do.'

'You are not the first man to kiss me!' she retorted.

'I'm sure I am not! The Devonshire gallants would be wanting in their wits if they did not make every effort to further their acquaintance with you.'

She frowned. It seemed to her that he was laughing at her. 'I know I must seem very silly to you. Indeed, I expect we all do. After all, you are a—a man of experience, used to a vastly different kind of life than we lead here. C-court masques and balls, didn't you say? The sort of life that would appeal to Rachel.' She was talking wildly, she knew, but once started, she couldn't stop. 'She was beautiful, really beautiful.' She snatched a ragged breath, and then exclaimed passionately: 'Oh, I wish I was like her!'

'Thank God, you are not!' Denham declared. He was beginning to wonder whether he had been right in offering her so much wine. 'Don't you think you ought to go to bed?' he suggested carefully.

She flung him a quick, fierce look. 'You always treat me like a child! I'm nearly nineteen. Old enough to be married and have ch-children.'

'I know.' His mouth twisted in a wry smile.

'You never spoke to Rachel like that. She had only to—to look at you and you would——' She stopped.

'I would—what?' he asked in clipped tones.

His sudden coolness brought Cathie somewhat belatedly to her senses. She realised she had gone too far.

She sat up, and his arm fell away from her. 'I'm sorry.' Her voice shook. 'I—I don't know what made me say that. Only it always seemed that you had so much in common.' She did not look at him.

Her hair-ribbon had become loose, and he put out a hand and pulled it away. Her hair, thick and glossy, was silky to his touch. He wound a strand round his fingers.

'Shall we forget Rachel?' he asked, and she nodded.

'I suppose I was jealous of her, because she took John away from me, and then——' she hesitated.

'Tell me.'

She turned her head towards him, and gave him a quick sideways glance beneath her lashes. 'I thought she would win you, too. . . .'

He caught the wistfulness in her expression, the hint of tears valiantly kept in check, and with a smothered exclamation, pulled her roughly into his arms, and kissed her.

He had intended it to be merely a light, quick kiss, as before; nothing more than that. But the feel of her in his arms, her warm young body pressed against him, her lips parting beneath his, drove all thoughts of discretion from his mind.

And Cathie, held captive, was conscious of nothing save the mounting tide of excitement and desire which threatened to engulf her. Her free arm went round his neck, holding him closer, the other was crushed between them in the fierceness of his embrace. She felt his hand caress her breast and then move down her body, and quivered in ecstasy. When finally they drew apart, both were considerably shaken.

He looked down into her face. Her eyes were closed, the long lashes brushing cheeks that were burning; her rosy lips, bruised by his own, were still slightly parted, her hair tumbled in wild disarray over her neck and shoulders. He smoothed it gently back from her forehead, and she gave a tremulous sigh, and opening her eyes, gazed up at him.

'Piers——' His name came involuntarily to her lips. She touched his lean cheek, and he took her hand in his and kissed her fingers.

Her eyes were as bright as stars, the pupils dilated. Never before had she experienced such a clamour of emotions, or realised how potent a kiss could be, how deeply disturbing to her whole being.

She was conscious of the tumultuous beat of her heart, the fire of passion he had kindled into flame. She felt altogether different, with a strange, tingling awareness of herself. It was a rather frightening feeling, completely new to her. She did not know how to cope with it.

Suddenly shy of meeting Denham's gaze, she turned her head away, and a little to her surprise he loosed his hold on her. The silence lengthened between them. When she eventually glanced at him, she saw that his face was set in harsh lines.

'What is wrong?' she faltered.

He forced a smile. 'Nothing. I was thinking—I have kept you up far too late. You will be so tired——'

'I don't mind!' Her voice quivered a little.

'Nevertheless, I think you ought to go.' He avoided her troubled, pleading glance, and picking up the two empty glasses, took them over to the table, standing there with his back to her, head bent.

The sudden, inexplicable change in his manner cast a chill upon her. She felt rejected, spurned, and was overcome by a feeling of such wretchedness that she did not know what to do. What *was* wrong? She could only conclude that he was regretting the incident. Perhaps she had been too forward, too eager in her response to his kiss. And yet, how could she have remained indifferent to it?

With a quick, indrawn breath, she got to her feet, and he turned his head and looked at her, his expression veiled. For a brief second their eyes met. She waited for him to speak, and when he remained silent gave him an almost incoherent 'Goodnight!' and rushed from the room, leaving him gazing after her.

Starting up the stairs, heart heavy, she saw that the pale light of early morning was creeping in at the window. She paused there, staring out at the grey scene yet seeing nothing of it, so deep in thought was she, so filled with misery.

Why had he kissed her, if he hadn't really wanted to? Why was he angry with her? It had all been so wonderful—the long, intimate moments when she had been locked in his arms, the breathless rapture of his kiss. And afterwards, when she had looked up into his face, she had found him gazing down at her with such burning intensity that she had felt her whole being melt.

She had been certain, in that moment, that he loved her, and was on the point of declaring his love. If she had only remained in his arms, and not allowed herself to be overcome by her confused feelings, all might have been well. And yet, she reminded herself painfully, he had released her at once, and had not attempted to draw her back into his embrace as he surely would have done had her conclusions been correct.

She became aware that she was shivering. Moving away from the window, she went heavily up the remaining stairs, shoulders hunched, hugging herself against the chill air.

She crept past Mary's door, not wishing to be heard, but it seemed to her that every floorboard creaked protestingly beneath her tread, proclaiming to the silent house that she was stealing to her bed like a wanton.

It was a slow, tedious process disrobing herself without Susan's help, especially when it came to unlacing her bodice with fingers that had become so stiff and numb that she could barely move them.

The fire had gone out many hours ago, and the room was like an icy cavern. It was a relief to climb into bed and close the curtains against the draughts, but though she longed for the solace of sleep, she found that it was denied her. Instead she lay there, her body tense, her thoughts tormenting her.

Over and over again she relived those moments, asking herself what had gone wrong, convinced it was her own fault, that in some way she had displeased him. Her throat constricted. Tears gathered in her eyes and began to trickle down her cheeks. She felt as though her heart was breaking. Turning her face into the pillow, she wept.

Downstairs in the winter parlour, Denham sat on beside the dying fire, staring into space. His thoughts were no less bitter than Cathie's, his self-condemnation no less severe. Why, in heaven's name, had he allowed himself to be so carried away, instead of keeping a rein on his senses? He, who prided himself on his ability to remain in command of every situation, had lost his head completely the moment he had taken her in his arms.

Ever since his boyhood, women had been attracted to him. His conquests had come easily, too easily perhaps. As he had grown older his father had constantly reminded him of the necessity to take a wife and settle down. He was not a boy any longer, free to go his own way; he had reached an age when he should be facing up to his responsibilities—marriage to a suitable young woman, preferably an heiress, and in due course the begetting of an heir.

He had eventually agreed, albeit reluctantly, to consider the question of his marriage; and at his father's suggestion had approached the parents of a certain nubile and eminently suitable young woman, wishing he could summon up more enthusiasm at the prospect of making her his wife.

Matters had been progressing slowly but satisfactorily when the growing hostility between King and Parliament had flared into open conflict, and in time he himself had been drawn into the rebellion; but by throwing in his lot with the Parliamentarians, he had not only estranged himself from his father, but from the family of his future bride. As a consequence, the marriage contract had been torn up.

Denham's thoughts strayed once more to Cathie. His father would undoubtedly approve of her. Of gentle birth, she had looks and breeding, and there was no denying her Royalist affiliations. Though not an heiress, she would doubtless have a substantial dowry when the time came for her to marry.

His eyes narrowed. Cathie—his wife? Sharing his life, ordering his household, bearing his children. His alone, to love and to possess.

He had much to offer. His father's estate was equal to her brother's, and would one day be his. Apart from that he had a tidy income of his own, left him by a childless uncle. She would not come to a pauper if she married him. She could have all she wanted—fine clothes, jewels, a travelling coach. . . .

The longer he thought about it, the deeper became his conviction that here, at last, he had found the woman he wanted—Cathie. Looking back, it seemed to him that he had always known it.

He fell to pondering upon the strange workings of Fate that had brought them together. Had it not been for the war he would never have become a soldier. Nor would he have come to Devonshire, and been wounded in the ambush and left for dead. He owed a debt of thanks to the Royalist trooper who had fired the fateful shot that had all but ended his life, for without him he would never have met Cathie. Perhaps one day he would meet him. He might even be one of the men in her brother's command.

Denham checked. He had completely forgotten her brother—her guardian. The one he would have to apply to for permission to marry her.

His feeling of happiness evaporated abruptly. He would be a fool to hope that because he had been fortunate enough to win Cathie's love, and had succeeded in overcoming the natural hostility that had originally shadowed his relationship with John and Lady Gifford, he would find Sir James equally well-disposed towards him. Indeed, the reverse seemed likely.

Feelings still ran high between the opposing factions. Four years of conflict had left bitterness and smouldering resentment in their wake, especially among the officers commanding the King's forces, for it was they who, in defeat, stood to lose the most.

It would be an extremely forbearing man who would be willing to give his sister in marriage to his erstwhile enemy; and from what he had heard of Sir James, such a course would be most abhorrent to him. A Royalist through and through, he would return home with his pride in the dust, with nothing left but to gather up the pieces of his life and face the consequences of his loyalty to the King's cause. To be met with the information that Cathie had fallen in love with a Roundhead would in all probability prove to be the last straw, and he would refuse point-blank to give his consent.

And that, thought Denham bleakly, would be the end of it. He dared not contemplate the only alternative that would remain for them—elopement. That Cathie would readily agree, he had no doubt. With her determined spirit she would not shrink from such a course, even though it would mean defying her brother and estranging herself from him and from the rest of her family.

And supposing they did take such a step, would she not live to regret it? And would it not inevitably come between them in time, tarnishing the love they bore one another?

He took a long, drawn-out breath. He could not allow that to happen. There was only one thing to be done. He would have to remain silent. He must never let her know that he loved her. He must let her think that what had happened tonight meant nothing to him, that he had merely allowed himself a moment's distraction.

He closed his eyes. 'Slud, how tired he was! The wound in his side was nagging him. Confound it—it should have healed by now.

He became conscious that he was no longer alone, and opening his eyes with an effort, he found Adam standing anxiously beside him.

'Sir—are you not coming to bed? 'Tis long past cock-crow.'

'Yes, I'm coming. I was—just sitting here.' He got stiffly to his feet, with a barely-concealed grimace. 'I've been thinking.'

'Yes, sir?' said Adam hopefully.

'It's time I got into the saddle again. We can't stay here for ever. The sooner we leave, the better.'

Adam looked taken aback. 'Well, sir—if that's what you wish,' he answered.

Denham turned towards the door. 'It is, Adam. Make no mistake about it.'

Inevitably, Cathie slept late on the following morning. She was eventually awakened by Susan, who, having opened the bed-curtains, informed her that her ladyship had asked to see her as soon as she was dressed.

Cathie, pale and heavy-eyed, nodded. Susan gave her a troubled look.

'Bain't 'ee well this morning, mistress?' she asked.

'Just tired,' Cathie murmured.

Heaving a sigh, she sat up, pushed aside the bedclothes and swung her legs out of bed. Susan handed her her slippers, and then went across to the toilet table and poured warm water into the wide, shallow bowl.

'There now,' she said. 'You'll feel better once you've washed your face.'

'I hope so,' Cathie replied, without conviction.

She had slept but fitfully, troubled by despairing thoughts, unable to find relief in the deep, refreshing slumber for which her body craved. As a result, her head ached wretchedly, and her eyes felt hot and strained after so much weeping. She took a quick glance at her reflection in the hand-mirror, and grimaced.

Dressed in a clean gown, and with her hair neatly pinned back from her face, she went along to Mary's bedchamber, where she found her propped up against her pillows, looking pale and a little fragile. On a tray before her was a silver porringer containing a mash of bread, beaten egg and milk, sprinkled with sugar and grated nutmeg.

She was not eating this concoction with any show of enthusiasm, though Betsy, hovering nearby, was doing her best to induce her to do so, saying that she needed to build up her strength now that she had her baby to feed.

'How is he?' Cathie asked, when she had greeted them both and given Mary an affectionate kiss.

She peeped into the cradle. Little could be seen of Master Jamie save his tiny, wizened face. On his head he wore a bonnet-shaped cap of fine cambric, and his body was tightly bound with swaddling linen, over which he was wearing a long, lace-trimmed gown. Fast asleep he lay, warm and snug, beneath layers of blankets and an elaborately embroidered coverlet; his cradle placed close to the fire.

How small he was! Cathie felt sudden tears sting her eyes, and blinked them hastily back. Looking up, she saw them both watching her. Mary's expression was troubled, Betsy's, somewhat grim. The latter showed no signs of having been up for the better part of the night. Solid and protective, she stood beside her mistress and, as soon as Mary had swallowed the last mouthful of food, picked up the tray and moved towards the door.

'I'll take this back to the kitchen,' she said.

It seemed to Cathie that she gave Mary a significant look before she went out, closing the door firmly behind her.

'Come and sit down,' Mary said quietly. 'I want to talk to you.'

Something in her manner, coupled with Betsy's unwonted dourness, struck a chord of alarm in Cathie's heart. She knew at once what Mary was going to say.

'It's about last night, isn't it?' she said quickly. 'I expect you—you heard me going to my room.' She sat down on the stool beside Mary's bed, her expression wary, her fingers twisting nervously together in her lap.

'Yes, I did hear you,' Mary moved her head wearily against the pillows. 'I was awake, and so was Betsy. She went to the door and looked out to see who it was. She saw you go into your room——'

'I'm sorry, Mary! I hadn't realised it was so late. We—Captain Denham and I—we were talking and——' Her voice trailed away. Meeting Mary's level glance, she flushed, bit her lip, and made a helpless gesture. 'I'm sorry,' she mumbled.

Mary sighed. 'I had thought better of you, Cathie! To say that you lost count of the time is a poor excuse. You know very well that you behaved badly—and so did Captain Denham. I have always considered him to be an honourable man, but now——'

'You must not blame him! It was my fault for—for keeping him talking. It was he who said I—I must go to bed.'

'Then it is a pity he did not tell you before! You should have come up with John, instead of staying there, just the two of you, alone together.' Mary's voice was sharp. She could not miss the unhappiness in Cathie's face, any more than she could mistake the tell-tale signs of weeping. But she could feel no sympathy towards the girl. Indeed, she was too tired to feel anything but impatience and growing irritation.

Once again she could not help wishing that James was home, and then he could have been the one to deal with the problem. But no, he had gone off to the war, and left her to cope with everything. It wasn't fair!

For the first time she questioned his decision. Always before she had been quick to defend him, her loyalty to him being as selfless as his was to the King. But now she began to wonder—had he been right in leaving her, and his home and family, in order to fulfil what he considered to be his duty? Would it have made one scrap of difference to the outcome of the war, if he had refrained from throwing in his lot with the Royalist forces?

If only she did not feel so weak! All her strength seemed to have ebbed away with the birth of her son. Had she had her own way she would have let things ride for a day or two, but Betsy had been so insistent that she take Cathie to task at once, saying that otherwise matters might get out of hand and then where would they be, that to please her she had given in.

'What do you suppose James would say if he knew about this?' she asked.

Cathie's eyes widened in alarm. 'Will you tell him?'

'I don't know. It's not the first time I have had to speak to you concerning your association with Captain Denham, is it? I warned you then to take care. Apparently I wasted my breath——'

'Oh no, Mary!'

'I told you before, it is easy to be swept off one's feet at your age, especially by a man as experienced as Captain Denham. You have allowed yourself to become infatuated with him. It must stop, Cathie. Do you think I want to see you hurt, or come to harm because of this man?'

'How can you speak of him like that?' Cathie cried. 'He risked his life for our sakes!'

'I know—I know!' Mary moved her head wearily from side to side. 'But at the moment I am more concerned with *you*. Here I am, confined to my bed, and likely to remain here for some time, while you——' She drew a ragged breath. 'Do you suppose I shall know a moment's peace, wondering where you are, and what you are doing?'

'Are you implying that you don't trust me?' Cathie's voice trembled.

'I should feel a lot happier if I had your word that you will behave in a more circumspect manner in future!'

'Yes, I will. You—you may rest assured of that.'

'I hope so. For I warn you, Cathie, that if so much as a whisper reaches me that you and Captain Denham have been conducting yourselves in any way that oversteps the bounds of propriety, I shall order him out of the house at once. Is that clear?'

Cathie nodded, her heart thumping painfully. 'Yes, Mary.'

'Good.' Mary closed her eyes. 'You'd better go and have your breakfast.'

'Yes.' Cathie hesitated. She and Mary had been good friends ever since the latter had become her sister-in-law, and they had always had a close understanding. It upset her to think that Mary was now at odds with her. She longed to put things right, to win back her place in her esteem. Above all, she yearned to confide her troubles to her, as she had been wont to do in the past.

'Mary——' she began tentatively.

Mary stirred and opened her eyes. 'I thought you had gone.' She sounded displeased.

'I was wondering whether I—I could talk to you——'

Mary drew a quick breath. 'Haven't we talked enough? For goodness' sake go away and leave me in peace!'

Cathie got to her feet, startled and not a little dismayed by Mary's sudden and totally unexpected burst of temper. It was so unlike her that she felt she had come face to face with a stranger. Murmuring an apology, she turned, and leaving the room, went slowly and unhappily downstairs.

Mary, no less unhappy, but for a different reason, lay with her eyes half-closed and thought about James. She recalled his last brief visit to the house. He had known then she had not long to go before her confinement. He had known she had not felt well. Yet he had gone back to the war, leaving her to face her ordeal alone.

She reminded herself that he had given his word that he would fight to the end, and he had to keep that word, no matter what it cost him. She had always looked up to him, admiring his courage and his deep-rooted sense of honour. He had never been one to shelve his responsibilities, to take the easy way out. If he had chosen to remain by her side instead of keeping his vow, would she have felt quite the same about him? And wouldn't he, in time, have come to despise himself?

She pushed the thought away. She didn't want to acknowledge the truth, not at this moment, when she felt so tired and weak and miserable. A great wave of resentment and self-pity washed over her. What did he care if she lived or died, or if the baby thrived?

'He doesn't care,' she thought wildly, 'he doesn't love me. If he did he would have stayed with me.' She began to cry, helpless, bitter tears streaming unchecked down her cheeks.

Betsy, coming in at that moment, rushed to her side, to soothe and comfort her. ''Tis only natural for 'ee to be in low spirits after giving birth,' she told her. 'You'll be better when your strength comes back....'

CHAPTER
TEN

FOR a few days the baby's life hung in the balance. He lay in his cradle, small, weak, fragile, with scarcely enough strength to cry plaintively for sustenance; sounding, as Betsy remarked, very much like a new-born lamb. For most of the time he slept, awakening only when he was hungry.

It seemed to Mary that he was growing more frail. Holding him in her arms, she would gaze anxiously into his little puckered face and blink back the tears that pricked her eyes. She was still in a sadly weakened state herself. Betsy fussed over them both, and saw to it that Mary was provided with nourishing broths, tasty dishes of spiced meats, plenty of eggs and milk. When Mary expressed concern over the estate, Betsy told her firmly she was not to worry about it. Master John and Captain Denham between them were quite capable of dealing with anything that should arise.

'Captain Denham?' Mary queried in surprise.

'Seems like 'e wanted to 'elp, and Master John were glad to let 'im,' Betsy replied tersely. She was in two minds about the Captain. Granted, he had acted bravely on the night the cavaliers had come, but she could not overlook the fact that he was as much to blame as Mistress Cathie for causing her ladyship so much distress.

Denham had thrown himself thankfully into the task of helping John to run the estate, for it gave him something with which to occupy his mind. It also gave him the opportunity of becoming used to being in the saddle again, though he found he could only manage short distances at first, returning to the house aching in every limb and with a gnawing pain in his side.

Cathie, watching him and John riding away together, was painfully conscious that he was deliberately avoiding her, as he had been doing ever since the night they had been alone together in the winter-parlour. Indeed, apart from mealtimes they scarcely saw one another at all. If he was not out with John, he was closeted with him in the book-room or in Mr Henty's old room, where the estate books were kept. The rest of the time, he apparently remained in his bed-chamber.

She herself was much occupied with household affairs, having taken over this responsibility from Mary while the latter was recovering from her *accouchement*. Though they were more or less on good terms again, there was still a slight coolness between them. They were both conscious of it and both regretted it, but they could not bring themselves to broach the subject and put matters right.

Mary noticed that Cathie never brought Captain Denham's name into the conversation unless she herself spoke of him; and then the girl would answer quickly and go on to something else in the next breath. Betsy vouchsafed the information that they seemed to be avoiding each other. Mary felt she should have been relieved to hear this, but paradoxically she wasn't; she had only to look at Cathie to know that she was unhappy, for all that she did her best to pretend that nothing was wrong.

'She'll soon be 'erself again,' Betsy said comfortably. Lady Gifford was her main concern. If Mistress Cathie was heart-sick, it was her own fault and she must get over it as best she could.

Upon the day following that fateful night, Cathie's horse had been returned to her. The man who had brought him back had also brought a hastily-penned note from Lord George Randolph in which he said that all had gone well with them and they were about to embark upon the ship Wilmot had managed to hire on their behalf. He trusted their voluntary exile would be of short duration.

'I wonder if we'll ever hear from them again,' John remarked. He was thankful to have plenty to do, for it gave him less time to brood over Rachel.

As the days went by, news began to trickle through from Cornwall. The Prince of Wales had been taken to the Scilly Isles, out of reach of the advancing Parliamentarian troops, though whether he would be able to remain there in safety for very long seemed doubtful.

Lord Hopton's army was being driven farther and farther back into the Cornish peninsula, its size rapidly diminishing as it went, for men were deserting every day. Fairfax had made it generally known that he would treat all those who laid down their arms with the utmost clemency. The Cornish people, sick to death of the war that had bereft them not only of their finest leaders but of so many of their own husbands and sons, were greeting him and his army with relief. They saw in their victorious progress an end to hostilities in the West.

From James, however, there was no word.

Mary fretted for news of him, and Betsy scolded her. It would harm the baby, she warned, and that would be a mortal shame now he was showing signs of making progress. She placed the hungry infant in his mother's arms with a complacent smile on her broad face. It was true—he was at last gaining in weight and strength; still small, but no longer giving cause for anxiety. His cries of hunger had lost their plaintive note, were now positively demanding.

'Bless 'im!' Betsy cooed, as his groping mouth found what he was seeking, and his cries ceased abruptly. Some time later, replete, winded, changed, and at peace with the world, Master Jamie lay fast asleep once more in his cradle, one tiny dimpled hand lying against his rosy cheek.

Rain tapped upon the window panes.

''Ark at that, now,' Betsy exclaimed as she moved about the room. 'And the Captain intending to go out riding this morning! Ah well, 'e'll just 'ave to bide within doors until it stops.'

'He seems to be riding nearly every day,' Mary said dubiously. 'Surely he has not yet recovered sufficiently to do much?'

''E thinks 'e 'as. Seems to me 'e's in a ter'ble 'urry, but maybe 'e's fretting to get back to the war afore it's all over. Or maybe———' She stopped.

Mary eyed her enquiringly. 'Yes? What were you going to say?'

''Twas just that I were wondering whether 'e might think it were time 'e went on account of Mistress Cathie. For all we know 'e might be married, and 'e don't want 'er to get too fond of 'im.'

'Married?' Mary had not thought of that. 'Yes, he may very well be.'

The next time John came to her room to report upon affairs in the village, she brought the subject up, as casually as she could.

'No, he's not married,' said John, giving only half his mind to the question. 'I remember him telling me so.'

'Betsy tells me they seem to be avoiding one another,' Mary remarked.

John gave her a blank look. 'Who are?'

'Cathie and Captain Denham.'

'Are they? I hadn't noticed. He's with me most of the time. I must admit, he's been a tremendous help. He knows all there is to know about managing an estate, and it gives him something to do while he's regaining his strength.'

'And Cathie?'

'Oh, well—she's busy too, isn't she? Come to think of it, she is rather quiet these days.' John looked thoughtful for a moment. Then he grinned. 'I expect it's the responsibility of having to run the house.' Clearly he saw nothing to worry about.

Reflecting that men could be infuriatingly blind at times, Mary said: 'I have not yet thanked the Captain properly for what he did on the night Lord George and his friends descended upon us. Had it not been for him, there might have been serious trouble here. Would you tell him I should like to see him? Perhaps he could spare me a few minutes after breakfast tomorrow?'

When Betsy admitted the Captain next morning, Mary, sitting up in bed against a mound of pillows, was holding her son in her arms. Tendrils of fair hair escaped from beneath the confines of her lace cap, and her cheeks were touched with soft colour. She wore a cape-like lace tippet over her lawn smock.

He was glad to see that she was recovering from the rigours of her confinement. Indeed, he thought that she and her baby made a delightful picture, and he told her so.

She smiled. 'Do you like babies, Captain Denham?'

'To tell the truth, I have not been acquainted with many of them.' At a sign from Mary, he seated himself beside the bed and leaned forward to tickle Jamie beneath the chin. The latter, fixing him with an opaque stare, promptly gripped his finger in his own tiny hand.

Mary, watching the Captain's face, caught the tenderness in his expression as he studied her son. 'I think you would make a good father,' she pronounced.

He looked at once surprised and amused. ''Slud! Do you? My respected sire has long given up hope that I shall bow to his wishes and enter the marriage stakes, with a view to presenting him with a grandson.'

Mary saw her chance. A quick glance showed her that Betsy was busying herself discreetly at the other side of the room, presumably out of earshot. 'It seems a pity,' she said quietly. 'Have you never wanted to marry?'

'I came near to it once.' He told her the circumstances.

She listened attentively. 'So you are still free,' she commented. 'Have you never met anyone else you would wish to lead to the altar?'

'I have been far too busy for the past few years to give the matter serious thought,' he countered lightly, smiling down at the baby.

'And in the past few weeks?'

His gaze lifted to hers. 'Ah!' he said. 'I thought you might be leading to that.' He withdrew his finger gently from Jamie's grasp, and sat back. 'I cannot deny that Cathie has come to mean—a good deal to me.'

'Do you love her?'

His eyes burned suddenly. 'I could.'

'Enough to want to marry her?'

He looked away from her. It was difficult to read his expression. She sensed that he had himself under tight control. 'That is an entirely different matter, isn't it?' He was giving nothing away.

Mary glanced down at Jamie. He had fallen asleep. 'Yes,' she said quietly, 'I suppose it is. I'm sorry. I have no right to probe into your affairs.'

'On the contrary!' He gave her an understanding smile. 'You have every right where Cathie is concerned. After all, Sir James is her guardian, and during his absence you are acting on his behalf.'

'Yes, that is so.'

'You may rest assured I shall not be here much longer to plague you. I've no doubt that John has told you I ride out with him nearly every day, accustoming myself to being in the saddle again.'

'You must not be in too much of a hurry to go! We shall all miss you.'

'You are very kind, but I have made up my mind to leave.'

As he was speaking, Cathie walked into the room, and her gaze went straight to Denham. Her eyes held a look at once questioning and stricken.

'She heard,' Mary thought, and felt a rush of pity for her.

Denham took himself off shortly afterwards. When Cathie went downstairs again, some time later, she found that he and John had gone out. On impulse she decided to follow their example, and sent word to the stables to have her horse, Dickon, saddled.

On the moor the March wind tore at her hat and cloak, tumbling her curls and whipping colour into her cheeks. She took Dickon for a brisk canter over the springy turf, rejoicing in the sense of freedom and movement. When she finally reined in, she was at the highest point of the Moor. From here she could see the whole valley spread out below, the village clustered round the church, the thin ribbon that was the river, the bridge spanning it.

Fern Place stood a short distance away, sheltered by trees, so that she could see very little of it from this angle, save for a glimpse of a red roof and a group of tall, twisted chimneys.

She turned her gaze in the opposite direction. There was the Chulmleigh road, winding away into the distance; the road the Parliamentarian troopers had taken. What had happened to them? When had they discovered that Captain Denham had sent them off on a wild goose chase? Or had they merely assumed that they had lost their quarry in the dark?

Upon reflection, she was inclined to the latter belief. Otherwise they would surely have returned to the house to demand the truth. It suddenly occurred to her that if the truth did become known, the Captain might be in very serious trouble indeed. The thought chilled her. He had never spoken about it, but then, he had hardly spoken to her at all since that night.

Dickon suddenly pricked his ears and turned his head with a soft whinny. She glanced round. Captain Denham was riding towards her.

He reined in beside her, smiling slightly. 'I did not expect to find *you* here.'

'Nor I you!' she returned stiffly. 'I thought you had gone into the village with John.'

'He went to pay a call upon the parson, so I left him there and decided to take a ride on the moor.' He looked about him appreciatively. 'I have never come as far as this before.'

He might have been addressing a casual acquaintance, she thought, and was overcome by a wave of despair. Had it meant so little to him—to have held her in his arms and awoken her heart to the meaning of love?

She said dully, 'It's one of my favourite spots.'

'I'm not surprised,' he remarked conversationally. 'It's a splendid view.'

He saw that her gaze was directed upon the valley below. As though becoming aware of his glance, she said, 'That's the Chulmleigh road,' pointing with her whip.

'I thought it might be.'

'It seems strange that no one has called at the house to find out what happened to Lord George Randolph and his friends.'

'It will be common knowledge by this time that they got away.'

'Then your people must know what part *you* played in their escape, yet they have not bothered to come and ask you.'

'They are probably too busy with more important matters.'

'Do you think so?' Without waiting for a reply she turned her

horse and began to move away. After a moment, he followed her.
They rode for a while in silence, he a little behind her. She rode well,
he thought, a light hand on the bridle, her body in complete accord
with the rhythm of her mount.

She glanced back, and their eyes met. He increased his pace and
caught up with her.

'You—you're leaving, aren't you?' she said abruptly.

'Yes.' He kept his tone light. 'I think it's time I went.'

'Why?' Despite herself her voice broke, and the eyes that looked
into his were filled with such anguish that he felt his resolve
crumble.

But he must not go back on his decision. He turned his head away.
'I have stayed here too long.'

She swallowed hard, and then cried wildly, 'In that case, the
sooner you go, the better!' And, wrenching Dickon's head round,
she careered away from him before he could utter another word.

He watched her go, a bitter twist to his mouth.

When he eventually arrived back at the house, he was met by
Adam, who informed him that a messenger from Torrington had
arrived a few minutes earlier. 'He brought a letter for you, sir,'
Adam informed him, adding: 'He's waiting in the kitchen for the
reply.'

The letter was from Jack Dowd. While he was reading it, John
came into the hall, followed more slowly by Cathie. He saw that she
had changed out of her riding dress, and was clad once more in the
neat blue gown she had worn earlier that morning, when he had seen
her in Lady Gifford's room. She glanced at the letter in his hand, but
said nothing. It was John who asked the question that was uppermost in both their minds.

'Is there any news from Cornwall?'

'Yes.' Denham's voice was grave. 'Captain Dowd writes that
Hopton has been pushed back to Truro. Fairfax is hard on his heels.
He has written to him, requesting him to surrender. His terms are
fair—all who wish to do so may leave the country and join their
comrades who have already fled to France and the Low Countries.
Cavalrymen who surrender their horses and arms are to be given
twenty shillings apiece. He also gives his word to Hopton that he will
intercede on his behalf with Parliament. He is now awaiting Hopton's reply—or he was, when this letter was written.'

There was a sudden stillness. It seemed to him that John and
Cathie had drawn closer together.

'They are good terms,' he told them quietly.

John found his voice. 'Do you suppose Hopton will agree?'

'He has no choice but to do so.' Denham tapped the sheet of paper. 'Jack says he has a mere remnant of his army left to him; so many have deserted, both officers and men. To refuse to sign would only lead to unnecessary bloodshed.' He paused, and then continued carefully, 'It might also lead to a wholesale mutiny among Hopton's remaining troops if they learned of the terms. Dowd says it is the general opinion that within a few days it will all be over.'

'The Royalists still hold Pendennis and Exeter!' John flashed.

'True, but I think even you will agree that they will find it impossible to hold out against the full weight of a besieging army, when all communications have been cut and no supplies or reinforcements are able to get through.'

They gazed at him in silence. Although they had been expecting to hear something of the sort, it had still come as a shock to have their fears confirmed. The war was nearly at an end, and the King was facing defeat.

'It doesn't seem possible!' Cathie whispered.

John took a ragged breath. 'No——' he passed a hand over his forehead, then forced a smile. 'At least James can now come home for good.'

'Mary will be glad.' Cathie's glance flickered towards the Captain. He was watching her, his expression one of sympathetic understanding. It was too much. Feeling that she couldn't bear it, she turned and hurried away.

Had she given herself time for rational thought, she would have gone straight upstairs to impart the news to Mary, but, conscious only of the need to escape, she went blindly through the screens and found herself halfway along the kitchen passage before she realised where her steps had taken her.

The kitchen door stood open, and from within came the sound of voices. She looked into the big, low-ceilinged room, her gaze alighting on the trooper who had brought Captain Denham's letter. He was seated on a stool at the huge, scrubbed table, eating a pasty with obvious enjoyment, a tankard and blackjack of ale before him.

Annie and the maidservants were clustered about him, voluble and lively. It took only a second for her to realise that they were discussing the eventful night when Lord Randolph and his companions had escaped from the Roundheads. Cathie paused inside the doorway, unnoticed by any of them, as they described in derisive terms the manner in which the Captain had put the pursuing Roundheads off the scent. She saw the man put down his half-eaten pasty, an odd look on his face.

'I don't believe you,' he said flatly. 'You're trying to cozen me. I was with Captain Tindall's troop that night. I heard Captain Denham say the malignants were on the road to Exeter. Why should he lie? He's one of *us*.'

'Maybe he bain't, any more!' Susan retorted saucily, arms akimbo.

Thinking it was time she intervened, Cathie stepped forward, and the little group dispersed. A moment later Adam came into the kitchen. Captain Denham had written a brief reply to his friend's letter: the trooper took it, and put it carefully away inside his coat. He then finished the remainder of the pasty, drained his tankard, and wiped his mouth with the back of his hand. Having given gruff thanks to Annie for her hospitality, he departed with Adam for the stable-yard.

Cathie watched him go with foreboding, wishing devoutly that the servants had not spoken so freely to him. It seemed highly unlikely he would keep the information to himself. Supposing it reached the ears of his commanding officer? The latter would be bound to investigate the story, and the consequences would be extremely serious as far as the Captain was concerned.

She would have to warn him. Going reluctantly to find him, she ran him to earth in the book-room with John. From their grave faces, she gathered that they were still discussing the momentous events in Cornwall. They broke off as she entered, and she wasted no time in coming to the point.

They heard her out in silence. Denham thanked her for the warning, but it seemed to her he treated the matter lightly; and John, taking his cue from the older man, said carelessly that she was probably making a mountain out of a molehill. Who would believe the boastings of a pack of silly serving wenches?

'Very well,' she said, gazing stonily at Denham, 'on your own head be it!' And she went upstairs to Mary, to tell her that the war would soon be over, and James would then be free to return home.

The next few days passed uneventfully, and she began to think that John was right, and that she had attached too much importance to the incident. They had heard by now that Lord Hopton had accepted the surrender terms, albeit with reluctance. It was the end of his army; the end of all Royalist hopes in the West.

Then came the morning when Denham announced to John and Cathie that he would be leaving on the following day. They were at breakfast, and John, about to toss Shag a tasty mouthful of mutton collop, arrested his hand.

'Tomorrow! So soon!'

'Your brother will be home any day now. He will not want to find me still here.'

'Yes, but——' John's glance strayed to Cathie. She was staring down at her trencher, lips tightly compressed.

'I did mention to you before that I intended to leave soon,' Denham reminded him quietly.

Cathie put down her knife, rose to her feet and went quickly from the room, John's gaze followed her. Then he looked at Denham. 'She's upset.' His tone was accusing.

Denham's brows contracted. 'Yes, I feared she might be.'

'You *have* been avoiding each other, haven't you? Mary spoke about it, the other day. What's wrong? You seemed to be such good friends a short while ago.'

Denham hesitated, and then answered constrainedly, 'I think the least said about it, the better. Are you going to give Shag that piece of meat? He'll be helping himself in a moment.'

Clearly he had no intention of satisfying John's curiosity. The latter turned the matter over in his mind, and decided to tackle Cathie, but all she would say was: 'If you must know, I made a fool of myself. I don't want to talk about it.'

He looked at her pale, set face. 'You can tell *me*, surely? I hate to see you looking so miserable.'

She smiled faintly. 'I'll get over it. I just wish that——' Her voice faltered, and then steadied again with an effort. 'I wish I could talk to him—but I can't. Not any more.'

They were standing by the fire in the winter-parlour, so engrossed in their conversation that they were totally unaware of anything else. When Susan burst in upon them, they stared at her uncomprehendingly. Eyes wide with alarm, she gasped, ''Tis they Roundheads come back!'

Cathie's hand went to her throat. Once again she was visited by that sense of foreboding.

They heard someone hammering upon the outer door.

'Do they have to make that din!' John exclaimed. 'I'd better go and see what they want.'

By the time he reached the hall, Reuben had opened the door. Outside stood two officers of the New Model Army, behind them a small but nonetheless formidable troop of men.

Cathie, who had followed close on John's heels, heard the name 'Captain Denham'. It was enough. Picking up her wide skirts, she took to her heels and sped to the book-room. The Captain was sitting behind the heavy oak table, poring over the household accounts. Without looking up, he said, 'You could economise on candles——'

'Captain Denham!' she cried. 'They're here!'

He got quickly to his feet. 'I thought you were John. Who are here?'

She did not have to answer. The expression on her face told him.

'I see.' He put down the account book he was holding and then, with an air of finality, closed it, as though he knew it would be for the last time.

'I did try to warn you!' Cathie's voice held a note of despair.

'I know.' He moved away from the table without looking at her, aware that if he did so, he would want to take her in his arms; and that was something he must not do. 'Don't worry,' he said lightly, 'I promise you, all will be well.' He went out.

She hastened after him as he strode towards the hall. Some of the troopers were standing stiffly inside the screens, and the two officers were talking to John. As the Captain approached they turned their heads and looked at him, unsmiling and hostile.

Cathie, trying to make herself as inconspicuous as possible in the shadows at the back of the hall, heard them exchange a few crisp words with him, and then the more senior of the two said something to John, who nodded.

She saw the Captain turn and, followed by the two officers, walk back the way he had come. A trooper brought up the rear. When the others had gone into the book-room, he remained on guard outside the door.

Cathie glanced at John. He shook his head helplessly. 'There's nothing we can do. You'd best go and warn Mary.'

'Yes.' She went slowly away, wishing with all her heart that she could be in the book-room, could know what was happening.

'Sit down, Captain,' said Colonel Merrick. He had seated himself behind the table, in the chair that Denham had recently vacated. His glance falling upon the book of household accounts, he moved it aside and then, removing his gloves, laid them down on top of it. He chose not to remove his hat.

The younger man, Captain Tindall, placed a chair for Denham in front of the table, and then seated himself on a stool at one end of it. Businesslike and alert, he had already arranged a sheaf of paper, an ink bottle and quill pens ready for use. Having tested the point of one of the pens, he proceeded to write the date at the top of the first sheet—'17th March, 1646.'

Denham watched him and then looked across the table at Merrick. He had met him several times before, during the councils called by Fairfax and Cromwell with their senior officers. He was one of the blunt, God-fearing kind with whom General Cromwell chose to surround himself. He wore no adornment, his dress being plain, his greying hair uncurled. He had never made any secret of the fact that he strongly disapproved of Denham, sharing his commander's opinion that the Parliamentary army would be the better without him.

He began the proceedings by informing Denham that he had been sent at the express wish of Cromwell himself, when the latter had received the report concerning the escape of Lord George Randolph and his fellow malignants. The General had ordered an immediate and thorough investigation to be made.

'He regards the matter as one of extreme seriousness,' Merrick continued, fixing Denham with a cold and distant eye, 'as well he might, considering Lord George Randolph's importance to the Royalist cause. You are doubtless aware, Captain Denham, that his father is an honoured member of the King's council.'

Denham inclined his head. 'I am aware of it, sir.'

Merrick gave him a sharp look beneath his heavy brows. 'Yet you deliberately connived at his escape. Why?'

Denham returned the look steadily, feeling the weight of the other's disapproval and disparagement. Merrick was a conscientious officer and would doubtless obey his orders to the letter, sifting all the facts he managed to unearth. Nevertheless, Denham felt his judgment would never be impartial, for he was already biased in his opinion against him.

'Well, Captain? We are waiting for your explanation.'

'You shall have it.' To the scratching accompaniment of Tindall's pen, Denham launched into a brief account of the evening in question, choosing his words carefully, omitting everything he considered irrelevant. Merrick cross-questioned him keenly, but was unable to shake his story: that Randolph and the other Royalists had secreted themselves when Captain Tindall and his troop had arrived, using Mistress Cathie as a hostage.

'Do you seriously believe they would have carried out their threat against her?' Merrick demanded.

'Yes, I do.' Denham's eyes darkened at the scepticism in the other's tone. 'They were desperate men, determined at all costs to evade capture. They would have stopped at nothing.'

Captain Tindall, hunched over his notes, raised his head. Clearing his throat, he said: 'I find that difficult to believe, Captain Denham. I do not think they would have deliberately harmed a woman, especially one known to favour their cause.'

'Exactly!' Merrick exclaimed. 'Shall I tell you, Captain, what conclusion I have come to? You were influenced in your actions not so much because you considered the woman's life to be in jeopardy, but because your own life was threatened. You have told us they were all armed, Lord George himself was close at hand and had his pistol trained upon you, whilst the rest were within earshot. I put it to you, Captain, that you deliberately gave false information to Captain Tindall in order to save your own skin!'

Denham reacted at once. 'Sir, are you accusing me——'

'Of cowardice? Yes!' There was a note of finality in Merrick's contemptuous tones.

Denham controlled his rising anger with some difficulty. 'That, sir, is completely without foundation, as you should know, having campaigned with me since Winceby! Have I ever, during that time, acted in a cowardly manner?'

Merrick's gaze wavered, but he was not prepared to concede the point. 'There is only one other possible explanation for your conduct, which is that you have, during your stay in this house, become sympathetic towards the views held by the members of the household, and have transferred your allegiance from Parliament to the King.'

For a moment Denham stared at him in blank astonishment, and then demanded: 'Is that your honest opinion?'

'I can come to no other. You deny acting the coward; therefore I must conclude you helped the malignants from choice.'

'That being so,' Denham said sardonically, 'why did I not accompany them to Bideford and join them on the ship to France? May I remind you, sir, that I turned a pistol on them in order to prevent them forcing me to go with them as a hostage? My servant will bear me out in that.'

'He will be questioned in due course. Have you anything further to add to your account?'

'Nothing.'

'Very well, Captain. I must inform you that you will not be allowed to leave the house. You will be placed in your room, under guard. When I have completed my enquiries here, I must ask you to accompany us to Torrington. I shall then take my report to General Cromwell. He will decide——'

'Sir, is it not for General Fairfax to decide? I am under *his* command.'

Merrick permitted himself a thin smile. 'General Fairfax is far too occupied with more pressing matters at the moment to be troubled by this affair.'

'I see,' said Denham slowly.

So Cromwell was to be his judge. And what of Fairfax? Was he being deliberately kept in the dark until his, Denham's, fate had been decided?

At a word from the Colonel, Tindall went to the door and called the guard into the room. Within a few minutes Denham found himself incarcerated in his bedchamber whilst Adam was marched downstairs to the winter-parlour. When the latter returned to him some time later, it was with an unusually grave expression on his rubicund face. He had received orders, he said, to pack their gear at once. Whilst he did so, he gave his master a full account of all that had transpired between him and the officers.

'I told them the truth, but——' he paused, and then, regarding Denham with a troubled frown, added '——it seems to me, sir, that Colonel Merrick has already made up his mind to believe the worst of you.'

'Yes.' Denham turned away and went slowly across to the window, staring unseeingly out. When he had assured Cathie that all would be well, he had presumed that the report of the incident had been sent to Fairfax. He had not feared the enquiry, thinking that Tom would dismiss any charges that might be made against him, knowing them to be without foundation.

But Fairfax, it seemed, knew nothing of the affair, and Merrick was doubtless under orders to ensure that he, Denham, was prevented from sending word to him. The future looked black indeed.

He and Adam were given their dinner in the bedchamber. Susan brought it to them on a tray, accompanied by a trooper who followed her in and watched while she set out the things on the table. She gave Adam an anxious glance, and he grinned cheerfully at her.

'You'll soon be rid of me, my dear! We're off to Torrington shortly.'

'I know.' She shot a swift look at the trooper, standing near the door. 'They're questioning all of us; wanting to know everything that 'appened that night. Oh, Adam——' she moved closer '——what'll they do to 'ee?'

'What's it to you?' he teased. 'I didn't think you cared, one way or another.'

She blinked, her cheeks reddening. 'Well, I do, then!' And with this admission, she turned on her heel and scurried out of the room, her hand pressed over her mouth; brushed past the trooper on guard outside and disappeared, leaving Adam staring after her, his eyes round with surprise.

The trooper who had accompanied her made as if to leave, but Denham detained him for a moment.

'Is Colonel Merrick questioning everyone in the house?' he asked.

'Yes, sir. Except for Lady Gifford, that is.'

'I see. Thank you.'

The man, thus dismissed, went out, leaving Denham gazing into space. By 'everyone' he had meant Cathie. He had not wanted her to be dragged into it; it seemed she was, willy-nilly. He wished he knew what she had said to Merrick, whether the man had treated her courteously, or in his usual brusque fashion.

Behind him, Adam coughed. 'Sir, shall we eat our dinner? There's venison steaks, and I see Annie has baked a trout.'

It was late afternoon when Merrick had finished his enquiries and gave orders for departure.

John and Cathie stood together in the hall as Denham descended the stairs, unfamiliar to them in his blood-stained buff coat. He seemed all at once a stranger. He crossed the hall towards them, aware of Merrick and Tindall watching him, of the servants peeping nervously round the screens, one or two of the maids crying into their aprons, of the troopers guarding the entrance.

His gaze came to rest on Cathie's face, and for one aching moment his stern resolve almost cracked. He loved her as he had never loved any other woman in his life, and never would. And yet, for her sake, he must leave her without once betraying his true feelings, must let her believe she meant nothing to him.

'So it is "goodbye",' he said lightly. 'Thank you—both—for all you have done for me; and will you kindly convey my gratitude to Lady Gifford? I shall never forget——'

Merrick stepped officiously. 'Come, Captain. We are waiting. Time is pressing.'

John glared at him. 'Goodbye, Captain Denham. And good luck!'

'Thank you.' Denham shook hands with him, and turned for the last time to Cathie.

Her hand was cold in his. Pressing a swift kiss upon it, he then turned away and strode out without a backward glance.

CHAPTER
ELEVEN

THE next day James was home, bringing with him the men from the estate who had survived the years of fighting.

He was given a warm welcome by John and Cathie, and after a few minutes' conversation with them, hastened upstairs to see Mary and the new son of whose existence he had hitherto been unaware. He remained with them until the dinner hour, and then joined the others in the dining-parlour.

Upon his arrival at the house he had worn an air of strain and fatigue. This had lessened somewhat, but the toll of the past few weeks had left its mark upon him. He was much thinner, and there were lines of weariness carved into his face, a dour look that had never been there before.

'What is this I hear about Captain Denham?' he asked.

John looked at Cathie, but her gaze was fixed on her trencher, and as she seemed unwilling to speak he took it upon himself to reply to his brother's query.

James dismissed the matter with the words, 'Utter nonsense! If he and Fairfax are such close friends, Denham will soon be released again.'

He found Cathie gazing at him earnestly. 'Do you really think that? You don't suppose he will—he will be severely punished?' Her voice trembled.

He looked at her in surprise. 'Why should you concern yourself? He is only a Roundhead——'

'He is not! He——' With a choking sob, Cathie flung down her napkin, and rushed out, leaving James staring after her with raised brows.

'What in heaven's name is amiss?' he demanded.

'She is in love with him,' said John.

'What! Cathie?' His tone was incredulous. 'In love with a Roundhead? She cannot possibly—I never heard anything so preposterous!' He resolved to speak to Cathie at the earliest opportunity and have it out with her.

When he did so, however, it seemed to him that his arguments were falling upon deaf ears. She refused to listen to reason and was, in his view, behaving in an unnecessarily stubborn and capricious manner. He told her so, in no uncertain terms.

'Listen to me, Cathie. You are to forget this man. You are merely infatuated with him, that is all. If he spoke of love to you, he had no right——'

'He did not!' She reflected bitterly how true that was. He had never once mentioned the word, and since the night he had kissed her had scarcely spoken to her at all. Could it be that she had allowed herself to be carried away, and had exaggerated the whole incident in her mind? She found it hard to believe she had imagined that burning look in his eyes, and yet it was possible. She only knew that it made no difference to her own feelings. She loved him with all her heart, and always would.

James said: 'What do we know of him, save that he turned against the King—which says little for his integrity!'

'He gave me his reasons for that. It cost him much heart-searching before he came to his decision to fight for Parliament.' Her voice was strained, her eyes red-rimmed and deeply shadowed. She had slept little on the previous night.

'No doubt.' James was fast losing his patience. 'Mary tells me she has had to speak to you on more than one occasion concerning your behaviour with him.'

'I have done nothing of which I am ashamed.'

'It should not have been necessary for her to have had to speak at all. He has left this house, and will not be returning. Kindly oblige me by not mentioning his name again. As far as I am concerned, he is an enemy and a traitor!'

Her face whitened. 'You are being utterly unreasonable! You forget how much he has done to help us, how he has advised John——'

'It was the least he could do, considering the way he was cared for and nursed back to health.'

'What would you have us do—leave him to die?'

'You are being childish! I do not want to hear another word on the subject. God's teeth! Have I not enough on my mind without having to bother with the silly vagaries of a besotted female!'

With this parting shot he left her, spending what remained of the afternoon riding round the estate with John, to whom he confided much of what had happened during the last few weeks—those weeks which had seen the slow disintegration of Hopton's army.

He spoke of the hostility of the country people which had added to the difficulties in obtaining supplies for the men and forage for the horses; of the two days and nights spent on the open moor near St Columb while Hopton hesitated to negotiate the surrender terms, and the Parliamentary troops continually harassed them.

He then went on to speak of the final Council of War, when Hopton's officers, himself included, had urged him to yield and the General had at last unwillingly agreed; of the heartfelt relief when the news was made known—relief tinged with bitter regret.

They rode over High Moor and James looked keenly about him, his expression forbidding. John had already told him about the sheep.

'You have the receipt for them?' James demanded. 'I am determined to get full payment from Fairfax. That will be one of the first things I intend to do. I told you, did I not, that I have to compound for the estate with Parliament, under the surrender terms? I presume they will be sending some of their confounded Commissioners here to poke their noses into everything and assess the amount of my fine. What a'pity Captain Denham is no longer with us. I am sure he would have been only too pleased to advise me!'

John caught the sarcasm in his tone, and remained silent. James had already made his opinion of the Captain clear to him. *He* thought it somewhat unfair. After all, as James had never actually met him, how could he possibly tell what manner of man he was? It was not like him to prejudge anyone. His attitude must be due to the extreme strain he had been undergoing. As time went by he would recover, and be his old self again.

He ventured to speak of the Captain as they rode homeward, saying: 'I hope all goes well with him. I must admit I had my differences with him at one time, but I have realised since I was in the wrong.' He glanced at his brother's set face. 'He has been extremely helpful to us.'

'So Cathie told me.'

'It is hard to think of him as—as an enemy.'

'Nevertheless, he *is* one. Did you say the stable roof is leaking? We must have it repaired.' James went on to speak of other matters, making it clear he had no desire to discuss Captain Denham.

As the days passed, however, it became apparent to him that no one else shared his views. Even the servants spoke well of the Captain, for he had completely won their allegiance by the part he had played on the night of the Royalists' escape, and they were full of praise for him. 'A right proper gentleman,' was Reuben's estimation of him.

Cathie, forbidden by her brother to mention his name, moved about the house like a ghost, grieving inwardly, yearning for news of him; growing more and more convinced that she would never see him again. She could not forget her interview with Colonel Merrick, the way in which he had snapped questions at her as though trying to trick her into admitting some conspiracy between herself and the Captain. John had told her that Merrick had acted in exactly the same forceful manner with him.

It was from John she had learned that Merrick was taking the Captain to Torrington under guard, and was then reporting, not to Lord Fairfax but to Cromwell himself, the result of his investigation. She recalled only too well Captain Denham telling her that Cromwell had a poor opinion of him, and would be only too happy to have him removed. Supposing he succeeded? If he did decide that the Captain was a traitor, what was to stop him from ordering him to be hanged? Fairfax would never know until it was too late.

Her heart seemed to stand still, and she felt as though her blood had turned to ice in her veins.

'Oh no!' she thought wildly. 'I can't let that happen to him—I can't!'

Yet what could she do? It would be useless going to Torrington to appeal to the garrison commander there. He could do nothing. There was only one person who was in a position to help, and that was Fairfax himself, who, according to James, was going to Pendennis once the surrender terms had come into force, to see what could be done to capture the castle. Pendennis—that was at Falmouth, miles and miles away.

'If only I were a man!' she thought desperately. 'I would ride there, and no one would stop me.'

Her mind fastened upon the thought, enlarged upon it. In the book-room she found a map of Devon and Cornwall and pored over it, trying to memorise the route between Great Torrington and Falmouth. She was not ready to admit to herself the reason why she was doing this, but somewhere inside her the resolve was growing—by some means or other she would make her way to Pendennis, and appeal personally to Lord Fairfax to save the Captain's life.

Lost in thought, she became suddenly aware that John had come into the room. He glanced at the map, and then at her, brows raised enquiringly.

'Why are you looking at that? It wouldn't have anything to do with Captain Denham, would it?'

'Why should it?' she countered swiftly.

He surveyed her wary expression, and seated himself on the edge of the table, one leg swinging. 'You'd better tell me, Cathie.'

'There's nothing to tell.'

'Then let me guess. You're going to write to Lord Fairfax concerning the Captain.'

She looked down at the map. 'Do you think it would do any good?'

'It's worth a try, if the letter reaches him.' He paused, then added 'To make sure of that you would have to take it yourself, wouldn't you?' She looked up, startled, to find him grinning at her. 'You didn't think you could fool me, did you? Directly I saw you with that map, I knew very well what was in your mind.'

'You won't say anything to James, will you?'

He regarded her thoughtfully. 'You're not really serious, are you? You couldn't possibly go all that way on your own—I presume you were contemplating going on your own?'

'Yes.'

'Sneaking out of the house at the crack of dawn? Stealing away to the stables, saddling Dickon, and then galloping off, hell for leather, all the way to Cornwall?'

Her chin lifted. 'Why not?'

'Because, you zany, you couldn't possibly do it! Have you any idea of what such a journey would entail, the dangers you might encounter on the way—an unprotected female——?'

'I should keep to the main highways. I have money enough to meet expenses——'

He shook his head firmly. 'No, Cathie. I'm sorry, but I can't let you do it. It would be madness.'

'You can't stop me!'

'I could. And so could James! He'd probably lock you in your room for a week, with nothing but bread and water for sustenance. Be sensible. Write a letter to Lord Fairfax by all means. I'll see that someone takes it for you, and try to keep James from finding out about it. But put the other idea right out of your head!'

She looked at him without speaking. He could tell by the expression on her face that she had no intention of taking his advice.

The men had started the repairs on the stable roof. James went to see what progress had been made, and expressed himself as satisfied; he wished other matters could be as easily resolved. Cathie, for instance, for ever mooning after that pernicious Roundhead. Since the day he had reprimanded her she had withdrawn even further into herself, scarcely speaking unless spoken to, avoiding his glance and doing her best to keep out of his way.

Her attitude engendered a feeling of growing irritation within him, which was by no means mitigated by the fact that she and John appeared to be on the best of terms. He was always coming across them, heads together, deep in conversation, or catching a glimpse of them riding away towards the moor. There was nothing new in this, of course. Since childhood days there had been a close bond between them. But now there was something more than that. He had the distinct impression that they had ranged themselves against him.

Captain Denham's name was never mentioned by either of them in his presence, but he knew very well that they discussed the man when they were alone together. So did the servants, much to his annoyance.

Damn the man! He seemed to have cast some sort of spell over the household. Even Mary spoke well of him, saying how kind he had been, how considerate.

'Considerate!' he had exploded. 'He had a fine way of showing it—doing his best to seduce an innocent young girl!'

Mary had flown to the Captain's defence. 'I'm sure he did no such thing! He was a gentleman——'

'I've met a good many so-called gentlemen! I wouldn't trust my sister with any of them. Look at the way Cathie is behaving now—convinced she is in love with the fellow! She would never have become so infatuated with him had he not encouraged her. No, Mary, he is to blame. It was extremely unfortunate that the two were thrown together so much, and left to their own devices—oh, I'm not saying it was your fault. I know how difficult things have been for you while I've been away.'

'Thank you.'

Struck by the unusual note of bitterness in Mary's quiet tones, he had shot her a quick, questioning glance, but her head had been bent over her sewing, so that he had been unable to read her expression.

He was thinking of that incident now, as he walked back from the stables, and it occurred to him, not for the first time, that Mary had changed. True, her love for him seemed as deep and constant as ever, but for all that, he sensed a depth of reserve in her that had not been there before he had gone away to the war.

There was no question that she was happy to have him back, happy and relieved. So what was wrong? Was she not well? He did not have to be told that she had suffered during her confinement. All women did at such times. It was to be expected.

He wished with all his heart that he could have been with her when her time had come. Instead he had been many miles away, enduring the misery of those final days on the rainswept Cornish moor, with Hopton keeping them all in suspense while he had slowly come to terms with the fact that surrender was inevitable.

If only the war had ended sooner, or the baby had gone the full term, then he and Mary would have been together. James' step faltered and slowed. Was that the crux of the matter—that she had wanted him there, and considered he had failed her? Surely not! Mary was not given to such illogical fancies; but then, he reminded himself, the pangs of childbirth had a strange effect upon the most sensible of women.

He would go and talk to her at once.

Having come to this decision, he found that while he had been lost in thought he had walked round to the front of the house, instead of going in by the garden entrance at the back. About to retrace his steps, he became aware of the sound of a horseman approaching along the avenue. He paused, and then frowned as his gaze alighted upon the rider—a trooper of the New Model Army.

He waited for the man to alight, nodding briefly as the latter greeted him and, producing a sealed letter, asked if he were Sir James Gifford.

'I am,' James said coldly.

'Then, sir, may I give this to you? It is for Mistress Catherine Gifford.'

'Thank you.' Thrusting the letter into his pocket, James turned on his heel and strode back the way he had come, leaving the trooper to climb back onto his horse and ride away again.

When James entered the big bedchamber, he found Mary seated by the fire, wrapped in a warm nightgown, her feet in their little slippers resting upon a stool.

'My dear!' The sight of her momentarily dispelled his annoyance. Crossing to her side, he bent over her and kissed her. 'How are you?' Since his return home he had slept in the adjoining room, in consideration for her, and being an early riser, did not disturb her until after she had breakfasted and attended to the baby's wants.

'I'm feeling better every day,' she assured him. 'I shall soon come downstairs again.'

'Not too soon, I hope. Good morning, Betsy.'

The latter had come into the room with a pile of small garments, washed and aired ready for Master Jamie to wear. She gave James a smiling curtsey. It was good to have the master home at last.

'Good den to 'ee, sir!' She lumbered to the press and put the clothes away, while James took a look at his sleeping son.

'I do believe he's grown since I came back,' he remarked, laying his finger for a moment against the baby's soft round cheek.

Betsy beamed at him. 'Why, to be sure 'e 'as, sir! 'E be growing so fast, 'e'll soon be too big for 'is cradle!' She went out again, leaving them alone together. They would talk more freely on their own, and she could go back later to attend to the rest of her tasks.

'What have you been doing?' Mary asked.

James flung himself down in a chair. 'I went to take a look at the stable roof. Another day's work, and the men should be finished. What's that you're making?'

She held up her piece of sewing. 'It's a petticoat for Jamie.' She glanced towards the cradle. 'He really *is* growing, isn't he?'

He leaned towards her, and pressed her hand. 'You don't have to worry about him any more.' He had heard from Betsy how she had fretted over the baby in the early days of his life, and remembering this, felt a sudden upsurge of tenderness towards her. 'I wish I could have been here with you.'

She gave him a strange look. 'Do you? You couldn't have done anything. At such times men only get in the way.'

'Nevertheless, I should have liked to be here. To—to know how you fared.'

She smiled slightly but said nothing, the needle moving briskly in and out as she continued her hemming. He watched her, conscious that she was once again shutting him out of her thoughts. He wanted to take the sewing from her and toss it aside, make her look at him, listen to him. He wanted to say, 'What's wrong, Mary? Why have you changed towards me? What have I done?' But something in her calm, composed face stopped him, and the words remained unspoken.

He stirred restlessly, and the letter crackled in his pocket. He drew it out, and looked at it, at the name written in a firm sloping hand: 'Mistress Catherine Gifford.'

'A letter?' Mary suspended her sewing.

'Yes.' He turned it over, eying the thick blob of red wax that sealed the paper, trying to decipher the impression. It had been done hastily, as though the writer had been in a hurry. Two initials intertwined. One was too blurred to read clearly, the other was a 'D'. Of course it was. He had known it would be.

'Who is it from?' Mary asked. 'Are you not going to open it?'

For the space of a few seconds James stared down at that smudged monogram and then, with a quick movement, thrust the letter back, unopened, into his pocket.

'It's not important. It can wait.'

The sudden darkening of his expression had not escaped Mary. Clearly the letter had upset him. Who could it be from? Cudgelling her brains, she recalled him mentioning that he was expecting a visit from the Parliamentary Commissioners. Could they have written to him, reminding him of their impending visit? It seemed to her the most likely solution, and the more she thought about it, the more convinced she became that she was right.

But why had he not told her? He had always confided in her in the past. Hurt by his silence, she took up her sewing again and in a little while he left her, and went downstairs to the book-room, seating himself at the table. Taking the letter out of his pocket once more, he stared at it, turning it over to re-examine the seal.

Should he give it to Cathie and let her read it? Or should he destroy it and say nothing? His instinct favoured the latter course. He would throw it on the fire, unread.

Having come to this decision, he tore it across, and was about to get up and go over to the fireplace when he heard someone approaching the door. Acting on impulse, he pulled open a drawer, thrust the pieces inside and closed the drawer again just as his brother entered the room.

'Ah, there you are!' John exclaimed. 'The horses are ready.'

'The horses?' It took James a moment to remember that he had arranged with John to ride over to the Pridhams'. He rose to his feet. 'Sorry! Have I kept you waiting?' He would deal with the letter when he got back.

While they were out, Cathie paid Mary her customary morning visit. Having seen James going into the bedchamber earlier, she had waited until he had gone before presenting herself to her sister-in-law.

She and Mary sat together, discussing various household matters, mostly appertaining to the kitchen and still-room, and then Cathie got up to take her leave.

Mary stopped her. 'Could you not stay a little longer? I should like to talk to you.'

Cathie flashed her an uncertain look. Since the morning when she had provoked Mary into that rare show of temper, she had been conscious that they had never managed to regain the bond of intimacy that had previously existed between them. But now it seemed that Mary intended to make amends.

She sat down again, folding her hands in her lap.

Mary looked at her aloof face. 'Cathie, you must know what I want to say. It's something that should have been said before. I'm sorry I lost my temper with you. I should have listened, instead of cutting you short. Indeed, I would have done had I not been feeling so wretched at the time. The truth of the matter was that I just wanted to be left alone. You don't know how often I've wished since that I had called you back——'

'Oh, Mary, I wish you had!'

They looked at each other, torn between laughter and tears, and then Cathie sprang to her feet, and giving Mary a fierce hug, kissed her.

Mary returned the kiss. 'So you've forgiven me?'

'I was the one at fault! I should have had sense enough to see that you were not well enough to be bothered with my silly little troubles.'

'Silly? Were they?' Mary gave her a shrewd look. 'Come, sit down and tell me. I've a notion they concern Captain Denham. Am I right?'

'Yes.' For a moment Cathie hesitated, wondering how much, or how little, she ought to confide to Mary; and then, taking a deep breath, launched into the whole story, finishing, 'So you see how foolish it is of me to feel the way I do about him, when he—he doesn't care for me at all——'

'Are you sure?'

Cathie gave a despairing gesture. 'Oh yes! He made that perfectly clear. But——' she swallowed a sudden lump in her throat '——I can't help it—I love him, and—and if anything should happen to him, I don't know how I could go on living!'

'James said——'

Cathie's head went up. 'I know what James said! That there was no need to worry about him, because he was Lord Fairfax's friend, and *he* would ensure that he came to no harm. James doesn't understand! He looks upon Captain Denham as an enemy, a—a traitor to the King!'

'I know.' Mary's tone was sympathetic. 'But then, how else would you expect him to think of the Captain? He's only been home a few days. It will take him time to adjust, to take up the threads of his old life again.'

'He'll never think any differently about Piers! He won't even discuss him.' Cathie sprang to her feet and took a few agitated steps towards the window. Then she whirled about and said in a low, intense tone: 'I've *got* to find out what's happening!'

Mary stared at her. 'How can you possibly do that?'

Cathie returned swiftly to her side. 'There's only one way—to go to Lord Fairfax at Pendennis and appeal to him. Don't you see? General Cromwell hates Piers. He's quite likely to—to condemn him to death for what he did; and Lord Fairfax will be none the wiser until it is too late. I must stop that happening!'

Mary, feeling that the situation was getting out of control, asked firmly, 'And how do you propose to go about it?'

The light of battle died in Cathie's eyes, and she sank into her chair. 'I don't know! Oh, if only I had been born a boy! The days are going by—it's nearly a week since—since he went. For all I know, he may already be——' Her voice broke. She turned her head away, biting her lip.

Mary leaned towards her, putting her hand over hers. 'I'll speak to James, and see if I can persuade him to do something. Try not to worry.' She recalled the occasion when she had quizzed the Captain concerning Cathie, and added, 'And I think you are mistaken if you believe Captain Denham doesn't love you. I'm pretty sure he does.'

Cathie gave her a dubious look. 'Then why did he lead me to suppose otherwise?'

'I expect he had his reasons.'

After Cathie had gone, Mary sat on by the fire with her sewing. Her mind was not on her work, however, and after a minute or two she let it drop into her lap while she considered Cathie's problem.

With all her heart she wanted to help the girl; but how? James was set adamantly against any liaison between his sister and Captain Denham. He would do all he could to keep them apart, and certainly had no intention of finding out what had happened to the captain since that dreadful day when the latter had been taken from the house under guard.

She had told Cathie she would speak to James, but she had little hope of persuading him to adopt a more lenient attitude. The war had changed him. As she had said, it would take him time to adjust; but time, so far as Cathie and Captain Denham were concerned, was fast running out.

There must be some way in which she could help! Cathie's whole future was at stake, though James appeared to be too blind to see it. He had a stubborn streak in him. She thought that it seemed to be present in all the Gifford family. His father had been exactly the same, and his father's elder sister, Lucy, who lived just outside Tavistock, had her own share of the family trait, absolutely refusing to move out of her rambling old house even though she could no longer afford to keep it up and had had to let most of her servants go.

Mary remembered having written to her, inviting her to come and live at Fern Place, and the polite but firm letter she had received in reply, to the effect that Lucy's old bones would not permit her to journey so far, but if any of the family would care to visit her, they would always be welcome.

Mary stiffened. Of course! That was the answer. Cathie could go to Aunt Lucy, ostensibly on a visit, and could then travel on to Pendennis from there. It would be out of the question, of course, for her to make such a journey alone, but John could accompany her—and James need never know the true purpose of the visit.

She felt a momentary qualm. She had never deceived her husband before, and she hated the idea of doing so now. To salve her conscience, she decided that she would speak to him on his return from the Pridhams', asking him to get in touch with Lord Fairfax; and only if he refused would she go on with her plan.

John and James stayed to dinner with the Pridhams, arriving home during the afternoon. Both were in good spirits, and full of their visit. Hal's arm was healing well, his parents had given them a warm welcome, they had partaken of a splendid meal and drunk a fair quantity of wine. All in all, they had thoroughly enjoyed themselves.

James regaled Mary with a long and detailed account of the proceedings, exuding goodwill and contentment, sprawled in a chair in front of the fire.

Mary let him talk on for a while and then, when he had exhausted the subject, said tentatively, 'Cathie kept me company for a while.

She seems very dispirited.'

'Oh, she'll soon forget it!' James said carelessly.

'It worries me to see her so unhappy. I was wondering whether——'

'No, I will not interfere! The fellow's gone, and there's an end to it.'

How quick he was to read her thoughts!

'But, James——'

'No, Mary! We've been over it all before. There's nothing more to be said.'

'Very well.' Mary hesitated, and then said, 'In my opinion she should have a change of scene—somewhere right away from home, where she will no longer be reminded of—what has happened.'

He considered the suggestion, and then nodded. 'Yes, I think you may be right. What have you in mind?'

'I believe I told you I had received a letter from your aunt at Tavistock a week or two before you came home?' Giving him no chance to reply, she went briskly on: 'She wrote to say how much she longed to see us, but she is too old to make the journey here. I was thinking, John could escort Cathie to her, and they could stay with her for a while. It would take Cathie's mind off her troubles, and you know how fond Aunt Lucy is of her. It would make a change for John as well. He has had little opportunity of travelling far from home recently.'

'A good idea!' James agreed warmly. 'I can manage without John, if you don't mind losing Cathie for a week or so.'

Mary smiled faintly. 'Then that's settled. I'll write a letter to Aunt Lucy this evening. One of the men can take it tomorrow.'

She told Cathie the news that evening, explaining that she had written to Aunt Lucy suggesting that she and John paid her a visit. The old lady would welcome them at any time. They could probably go on the day after tomorrow. Then she added quietly, 'It occurred to me that once you were away from home, there would be nothing to stop you and John going to Pendennis. You could tell Aunt Lucy that you have to go there on some errand for James——'

Cathie caught her breath. Her whole face lit up. 'Oh, Mary! What a wonderful idea! But supposing James finds out?'

'He is in favour of the visit to Aunt Lucy, so you don't have to worry about that.'

'But what if he should discover that we're cozening him? He'll be terribly angry with you, and I don't want that to happen. Perhaps it would be better if we didn't go.'

'I'll deal with James when the time comes,' Mary said firmly.

Waving John and Cathie off on their journey, two mornings later, she turned back into the house with a feeling that the die had been cast. When James came up behind her and said, 'You're looking very serious, my love,' she jumped.

'Serious?—Am I?' she countered quickly, striving to keep a nervous tremor out of her voice. She took a steadying breath. 'What are your plans for the day?'

'I thought I'd take a look at the woods. There's a lot of old stuff that ought to come down.' Busy with his own thoughts, he appeared not to have noticed her confusion, but she was nonetheless thankful to see him ride away, shortly afterwards.

It was strange to be downstairs again. As Mary wandered through the rooms, she felt that she was seeing everything for the first time. Old, familiar pieces of furniture looked somehow different. Shag, left behind by John, followed her about, and she was glad of his company.

She went into the book-room; James's favourite room. Wandering over to the big table, she seated herself in his high-backed elbow chair. Then she saw that something was protruding from one of the drawers; James had evidently closed it in a hurry. She opened the drawer, and then checked.

It was a letter—or, to be exact, half a letter. The other half lay beneath it. She took them both out. The name 'Mistress Catherine Gifford' seemed to leap up at her. A letter for Cathie, torn across, unopened.

This, then, was the letter James had had in his pocket. He must have intercepted it, and for reasons of his own decided to destroy it instead of handing it to Cathie. He had guessed that Captain Denham had sent it, and he would make sure that Cathie never knew.

Presumably he had been interrupted before he could burn it, so he had dropped it in the drawer, intending to deal with it later. Had he not forgotten about it, no one would have been any the wiser. A shadow of pain crossed Mary's face. How could he be so blind, so bigoted?

The day wore on. James returned for the midday meal, full of plans for selling some of the timber.

'We used to do so in the old days, if you remember,' he said. 'Most of the trees we felled went for ship-building, and I don't see why we should not do the same now. Damn it all, the country will still need ships, whether the King is in power, or Parliament. And it will bring in some money to help pay my confounded fine.'

'A good idea,' Mary said quietly.

She let him talk on, contributing little to the conversation herself. He noticed her reticence, but put it down to her state of health. When they rose from the table, he walked to the door with her, his arm round her shoulders.

'Go and rest, my dear,' he advised gently, and kissed her on the cheek. She did not return the kiss, but merely smiled slightly and walked away, leaving him standing there with the strange, uncomfortable feeling that a door had been shut against him.

At supper-time, with the candles lit, the curtains shutting out the night, and the great logs crackling cheerfully in the wide fireplace, James hoped that Mary would be more talkative and forthcoming, but he was doomed to disappointment. After a while he too fell silent.

As soon as the servants had departed, closing the door behind them, he burst out: 'Mary, what is wrong? What is troubling you?'

For a moment he thought she was not going to reply; then she raised her head and looked at him across the table. He was startled by the expression of condemnation in her grey eyes.

''Sblood!' He essayed a light laugh. 'What have I done?'

For answer she took something from her lap, and threw it on to the table between them. The letter. He stared at it, his wits momentarily scattered, then he looked up at her.

'When did you find this?' His voice was strained.

'This morning, in the drawer in the book-room table, where you put it the other day. Why, James? *Why*?'

'For God's sake, Mary! I have every right to——'

'You have no right at all!' She spoke in a tone he had never heard from her before, a fierce, controlled anger.

'I am Cathie's guardian.'

'That doesn't give you the power to ruin her life!'

'What do you mean?'

'You know very well! You have never met Captain Denham, yet you condemn him out of hand. It does not matter to you that he is fundamentally decent and honourable; that he risked his life in order to prevent bloodshed in this house. Oh, no! Because he chose to support Parliament, he is the blackest traitor that ever lived. If he were here now, you wouldn't even give him a hearing. Yet, if Lord George Randolph and his—his drunken cronies came, you'd condone their insults and their vile behaviour because *they* happened to fight for the King!'

'You never mentioned this to me before. What insults?'

'I didn't mention it because I knew you wouldn't listen! They acted abominably, and so did Rachel. She wanted to kill the Captain because he refused to help her.'

James frowned. 'John said something about that. I think you had better tell me the whole story.'

She did so, and his face darkened. 'I wish to heaven I had been here when all this happened!'

'So do I! But you weren't, were you? You were miles away, following the dictates of your conscience, while we had to fend for ourselves as best we could.'

The shaft struck home. 'I never realised you felt that way about it. Why did you not tell me?'

'Would it have made any difference? You were determined to go.'

'I thought you understood,' he said slowly. 'I had to go. I should never have held my head up again if I had failed in my duty to the King.'

She sighed. 'I do understand. I might feel a little less bitter if the war had not changed you so much. You used not to be so hard, so—unjust.'

His gaze dropped to the torn letter. 'You think I should have given this to Cathie?'

'Of course you should! It would have made all the difference to her. You know how desperate she has been, waiting for news of him, not knowing whether he is alive or dead. I presume you were going to burn it?'

He nodded. 'Yes.'

'Hoping, I suppose, that she would never know he had written to her; that she would come to believe in time that he had been executed. And then you would have married her off to someone of your own choosing, without giving a thought to her feelings in the matter. Well, I warn you, if that is still your intention, I shall fight you every inch of the way!'

'Mary!'

'I mean it, James. I will not stand by and see you destroy Cathie's happiness.'

He got up and went slowly across to the fireplace, standing there with his back to her, gazing down unseeingly into the flames. Mary watched him, sensing his inner conflict, longing to fly to him and put her arms round him, yet hardening her heart, knowing she must not weaken now.

When finally he turned and came back to the table, she saw that his expression was troubled and uncertain.

'You are right, of course. I have allowed myself to be blinded by prejudice instead of keeping an open mind.' He gave a rueful smile. 'And I have always prided myself on being a tolerant man! As you say, I have never met Captain Denham. Perhaps if I did so, I would see his true worth.' He touched the letter. 'Do you suppose Cathie would object if we opened this and read it? It might provide some news of his present whereabouts.'

They read it together, James peering over Mary's shoulder. 'So he has been released,' he commented.

' "——Thanks to the intervention of Lord Fairfax," ' Mary read aloud. ' "I am to report to him at Pendennis at once, so I fear I shall not be able to bring my good tidings to you in person, however much I long to do so——" ' She looked up at James. 'He does love her! I told her I thought he did.'

'Humph,' said James. 'What else does he say?'

' "One day soon, please God, this war will end, and then I hope to see you again. Remember me to Lady Gifford and your brother, John. I trust Sir James has returned safely. Pray excuse this brief letter. You are always in my thoughts. I remain, your humble and devoted servant, Piers Denham." '

'Pendennis,' he said thoughtfully. 'A pity it is so far away. Had he been at Torrington I might have ridden in to see him.'

Mary's heart fluttered nervously. Now was the time to confess. 'Cathie and John will be going to Pendennis from Tavistock,' she said, her gaze fixed anxiously on his face. 'Oh, James—don't be cross——' She poured out the whole story, finishing, 'If only you had given her the letter! Then we should never have deceived you.'

He nodded heavily. 'I was in the wrong. I admit it.' He ruminated for a moment, and then said, 'I think the best course would be for me to follow them. I will set out for Tavistock at first light tomorrow.'

CHAPTER
TWELVE

AUNT LUCY was exactly as John and Cathie remembered her, save that she was thinner and more frail. But her eyes were as sharp as ever, and there was nothing wrong with her hearing, as she proudly informed them while they sat with her in her parlour before supper.

They had reached Tavistock in the late afternoon, having stopped at an inn in Okehampton for their dinner. Joe was with them. James had suggested that Susan should accompany them as Cathie's tiring-maid, but the latter had said hastily that there would be no need for her to do so; there would surely be someone at Aunt Lucy's who could act in that capacity.

James had agreed, and she had breathed a sigh of relief, thankful that he had not insisted. Joe would be returning to Fern Place on the following day, but Susan's presence would have made it difficult for them to have carried out their plan.

James had announced his intention of coming to Tavistock when their visit ended. He would stay the night, and then ride home with them next day. He was hopeful that he might succeed in persuading his aunt to change her mind and come to them on a protracted visit. This idea, however, was roundly pooh-poohed by that determined lady when John mentioned it to her.

'No, no, I shall stay here until the Lord thinks fit to take me. I'm too old to go gallivanting about. And now, child——' this to Cathie '——tell me all your news. I declare, you've grown quite a beauty. I'll warrant you'll have plenty of suitors now the men are back from the war!' She cackled in high good humour.

At supper, John broached the subject of their pending trip into Cornwall, giving a plausible account of the fictitious business matter that James had supposedly requested him to attend to in Falmouth, and saying that they would be staying overnight with friends.

Aunt Lucy heard him out in silence while she tackled her small portion of jugged hare. She had but little appetite, and had some difficulty in masticating her food. Her eyes and ears might be as good as ever, but her teeth certainly weren't. Most of them were missing, and those that were left were loose and yellowing.

She appeared to accept John's explanation, merely remarking that she had heard that John Arundell was still holding Pendennis for the King, though how long he would continue to do so against the besieging Roundheads was a moot point.

'Yes, we heard that too,' said Cathie. 'They say that—that Lord Fairfax is personally taking charge of the siege.'

Aunt Lucy wiped her mouth with her napkin. 'Oh no,' she said, in her thin clear voice. 'He merely went there to view the situation and to call upon Arundell to surrender—which he didn't, God save him for a brave soul. After that Fairfax went away again, without wasting any more time.'

She caught the quick, dismayed glance that passed between brother and sister, and immediately her suspicions were alerted.

John said quickly: 'Do you know where he has gone?'

'To be sure. He's taken most of his troops to Plymouth, to raise the siege there, leaving a sufficient number of men to deal with Pendennis——'

'Plymouth!' Cathie exclaimed. She looked at John; Aunt Lucy looked at her.

'Why this sudden interest in Lord Fairfax, pray?'

Cathie stared at her, the picture of guilt. The old lady's face was severe. 'Come—you'd best tell me. The pair of you are plotting some mischief, I'll be bound! Well? Have you pledged yourselves to put a bullet through Lord Fairfax's head, or are you merely going to kidnap him and hold him to ransom?'

Severe or not, there was a twinkle in her eye, and it was this that decided Cathie to confide the truth to her.

She listened with great interest, remarking when Cathie had finished that she had not heard anything so entertaining for years, and of course they must go to plead for the Captain's life. Roundhead he might be, but he sounded a most remarkable young man, and James was a fool if he failed to appreciate the fact.

Next morning, they could scarcely wait for Joe to leave before making their own departure. Aunt Lucy had recommended an inn in Plymouth to them, the Drake's Head, saying she was sure they would be able to bespeak rooms there for the night, if need be.

'I wonder if Lord Fairfax has succeeded in raising the siege yet?' Cathie remarked as they rode along.

They were not to learn the answer to that question until they came within a few miles of the town a couple of hours later, when they caught up with a farm cart loaded with produce, drawn by two slow-moving oxen.

'Aye,' said the farmer in response to their enquiry, 'the General entered the town yesterday, with never a shot fired save for those that were discharged by the garrison in their joy at being relieved. 'Twas a rare old noise. Did 'ee not 'ear it?'

John shook his head. 'We were too far away.'

'Ar, well, when I 'eard un, I gave thanks. Now us can go about our daily business with no more trouble from they pesky Royalists!'

' "Pesky Royalists", indeed!' John exclaimed, as they rode on, leaving the farm cart behind. 'If we had not been in such haste, I would have taken that fellow to task!'

Cathie gave him an anxious look. 'Oh John, please try and guard your tongue when we reach Plymouth! It's bound to be full of Roundheads, and we don't want to fall foul of them, do we?'

He grinned. 'Don't worry. I know better than to provoke one of those runyons.'

'I'm relieved to hear it. Oh, look!'

They reined in their horses. Before them the ground sloped down towards the distant cliffs, with the sea sparkling in the spring sunshine; and there, encircled by its battered walls, stood Plymouth, between its two rivers, the Plym and the Tamar.

Outside the town was a vast encampment, with smoke from a myriad cooking fires rising into the air. Cathie's bemused gaze wandered over the scene, taking in the seemingly endless number of wagons, carts, even coaches, that were drawn up on the outskirts; the horse-lines, where troopers were busy grooming their mounts; the huge cart-horses which were necessary to drag the cumbersome, canvas-tilted commissary wagons and the heavy field guns.

The whole place seemed to be a seething mass of activity. Musket drill was taking place, pikemen were being put through their paces. They were being watched at a respectful distance by groups of citizens who had wandered out from the town.

There were women in the camp, as well as men; gossiping together over the wash-tubs, mending shirts and stockings, preparing food. Cathie drew John's attention to them, and he remarked with a grin that they surely could not be the usual run of camp-followers—the stern disciplinarians of the New Model Army would have had them turned out long ago—so they must all be virtuous wives following their husbands from one place to the next.

Banners streamed in the breeze, some captured from the Royalist army, all making a brave and colourful show.

Ringing the town stood the Royalist forts, abandoned by them when the surrender terms had come into force, and now taken over by the Roundheads.

There were a good many officers in the camp, and it was one of these whom John and Cathie approached in their quest for General Fairfax. A somewhat harassed-looking young man, he paused just long enough to inform them that the General could be found within the town, whither he had gone with General Cromwell and their senior officers, before hurrying away again.

The narrow cobbled streets of the town were thronged with people, market carts moving among them with some difficulty. Cathie saw that men, women and children alike wore the pinched, hollow-eyed look of those forced to subsist upon the barest rations of food for far too long. Many had an air of bewilderment, as though even now they could not quite grasp the fact that their ordeal was over, that deliverance had come at last.

But it had, and to the citizens the two men chiefly responsible for that feat were Fairfax and Cromwell. Cathie and John heard their names mentioned on all sides, saw little groups of soldiers cheered and applauded, and given cans of ale from the barrels that had been brought into the town that very day to replenish the empty cellars of the taverns and inns.

They found the Drake's Head, and as Aunt Lucy had prophesied, were able to bespeak the accommodation they sought for the night. Having arranged to return for dinner they went out again, leaving their horses in the inn's stables.

People were streaming in the direction of the Guildhall and John and Cathie went with them, having learned that this was where they would find General Fairfax and the equally popular General Cromwell. The Guildhall was an imposing Jacobean building, the main hall being on the first floor above an area enclosed by open arches, which was used as a market for corn, meat and vegetables.

Cathie, standing with John at the back of the crowd, could see very little, but John informed her that she need not worry, for there was little to see save some pikemen on guard outside the hall, and a body of troopers who had taken their mounts into the covered market and were now lounging at ease there, beneath the eye of a moustachioed Cornet of Horse.

A man standing next to them broke in upon their conversation to say that the troopers were the Lord General's bodyguard, and what a fine sight it had been to see them all come ariding through the streets—the Lord General, with General Cromwell by his side, and their brave officers following in their train.

'''Tis a shame you missed it,' he observed, having learned that they had only entered the town themselves but a short while ago. 'They were received by the Mayor and the members of the Committee of Defence—and a brave show *they* made, too.' He went on to tell them that they would now be partaking of a celebratory dinner, where there would be speech-making and much rejoicing.

'No doubt,' said John, 'but how long will it be before we can expect to see them come out again?'

Their informant stroked his beard and looked thoughtful. 'They've been in there nigh on two hours. I'd say they'll be out soon.'

The crowd was shifting all the time as people came and went and John and Cathie found themselves gradually moving forward, until they were close to the front. Time passed slowly, and they were both beginning to wish that something would happen when all at once a messenger emerged from the Guildhall and spoke to the moustachioed Cornet. He immediately barked an order to his men, and with a sudden flurry of activity they filed out, leading their horses.

A ripple of excitement ran through the crowd. Standing on tiptoe, Cathie saw a tall, thin figure in black, who could be none other than General Fairfax. His appearance was greeted with wild enthusiasm. Cathie, seeing her chance, began to work her way through the press of people. She must speak to the General. She *must*!

Alas, her efforts were of no avail. By the time she had managed to reach the front of the crowd he was already mounted, and with General Cromwell beside him was moving away, with his bodyguard falling in behind him.

Without thinking, she ran after them, but had covered only a few yards before she was seized by a soldier.

'Let me go!' she cried wildly. 'I must speak to Lord Fairfax!'

'Not now, you won't!' he retorted brusquely. 'And hold still, you jade!' His grip on her arm tightened, as she endeavoured vainly to free herself.

Another voice broke in. 'What's the matter, soldier?'

An officer had reined in beside them. Cathie looked up, eyes swimming with tears. 'I must talk to Lord Fairfax. It's a matter of life and death!'

She heard the officer utter a sharp exclamation. 'It's Mistress

Gifford, isn't it?—Release her, man!'

The soldier promptly did so. Cathie blinked rapidly, and as her vision cleared, found herself gazing up into the harsh, angular face of Major Dowd.

'Did you say—a matter of life and death?' he demanded, and she nodded.

'Yes! It concerns C-Captain Denham! He's going to be court-martialled—if he hasn't already been—and I'm so afraid he will be—be sentenced to death!'

He looked astounded. 'Court-martialled? But——' He broke off, sent a quick glance after the departing cavalcade, and then said hurriedly: 'Leave this to me. Are you staying in Plymouth?'

'Yes, I'm here with my brother.' She gave him the address of the inn.

'I will see what I can do, and will send word to you later.'

'Oh, *thank* you!'

He smiled, an odd look in his eyes. 'When it concerns Piers Denham, nothing is too much trouble. Good day to you!' He rode away.

A moment later, John reached her side. 'Was that Major Dowd?'

'Yes. He offered to find out what has happened to Piers.' She recounted the brief conversation to him, her eyes alight with hope.

'So our wait was not in vain.' John slipped a hand beneath her arm. 'I suggest we go back to the inn for our dinner. It's long past midday.'

The innkeeper's wife had their meal ready for them, and told them how delighted she was to be able to restock her larder shelves at last. They sat down to roast chicken and apple dumplings, falling to with a will, for they had eaten nothing since breakfast, many hours before. When they had finished, John went out to the stables to ensure that the horses were comfortable. While she waited for his return, Cathie wandered over to the window overlooking the street.

People were passing and re-passing all the time, and she watched them with interest. Unused as she was to the busy life of a town, she found the panorama wholly fascinating. So many people! Where had they all come from? What was their business here?

The inn was situated in one of the streets leading down to Sutton harbour. Had their visit to the town been purely for pleasure she would have asked John to take her there, but uppermost in her mind was the thought of Piers and the news of him that Major Dowd might be able to glean for her. If only the messenger would come! If only she knew that Piers was safe!

She sighed, the familiar knot of anxiety heavy in her breast. To take her mind off it, she fixed her gaze upon the passing throng once more. All at once her attention was caught by a trooper riding by. As she glanced at him she gave a startled gasp, scarcely able to believe her eyes. It was Adam Potter!

Snatching up her cloak, she made for the door, dashing into the lobby, and out into the street. The landlord, emerging from the tap-room, stared after her in some surprise, then, shaking his head, he went along to the kitchen, and informed his wife that the young lady had run out without so much as a word of explanation. Queer things, women. There was no accounting for what they'd do next.

Cathie was beginning to find that it was no easy matter to keep Adam in sight. Try as she might, it was impossible for her to draw any closer to him, for every time she attempted to increase her pace someone would step in front of her, or jostle her out of the way. She had gone some distance from the inn when she realised, with a sinking heart, that he had disappeared. Somehow she had lost him.

She halted, and was immediately cannoned into by a man who had been walking behind her. Aplogising to him, she stood there for a moment deep in thought. If Adam was in Plymouth, then Piers must be there too! In that case, why had Major Dowd not told her? Unless he intended to send Piers to her, as a surprise. . . .

Her heart suddenly lightened. She must go back to the inn straight away, and wait for Piers: apart from that, John would be wondering where she had gone. It was easier said, than done, however, for in her anxiety to catch up with Adam she had taken no heed of direction, and had not the slightest notion where she was, or how far she had come from the inn. She only knew she had been going uphill for most of the time; therefore she must go down again, towards the harbour.

She set off, but after a while, acknowledging to herself that she was still lost, she stopped a freckle-faced urchin in order to enquire the way to the Drake's Head.

He pointed with a grubby finger. She must go down the street as far as the ship's chandlers, and then along the 'ope'. When she reached the next street she must turn to the right and take the next 'ope' on the left, which would bring her into the street where the Drake's Head stood. She gathered that 'ope' was the local name for an alley.

She thanked him, rewarded him with a penny, which he received with a delighted grin, and started off again. She must have been away from the inn for over half an hour. John would be terribly worried about her. Not only that, but Piers might have arrived in her absence! At the thought, she began to run.

The area, in the vicinity of the harbour, was a maze of narrow streets lined with old dark houses and taverns. The broken cobbles were slippery with all manner of filth, and Cathie, in her haste, stepped on some rotting cabbage leaves, all but measuring her length. After that she went more carefully.

She came to the ship's chandlers, which stood at the corner of a dingy 'ope'. This must be the one the boy had mentioned. It ran between high, dank walls which seemed to close in upon her, and the stench which permeated the atmosphere made her bury her nose hastily in her kerchief.

Picking her way along, she became suddenly aware that she was no longer alone. Two men were coming towards her, clad in the rough garments of seamen, battered old hats pulled well down so that their faces were in shadow.

As they drew near she stopped instinctively, a sick feeling in the pit of her stomach, ready to turn and run. What if they should accost her? In a place like this, would anyone bother to come to her rescue? Her fears were groundless, however, for they stood politely aside to give her room to pass.

Murmuring her thanks, she glanced up at them; and then her heart gave a sudden lurch. Despite the rough clothes and unshaven faces, she recognised them at once.

'Sir Harry Wyndham! And—and Mr Porteous!'

'Ecod!' Sir Harry exclaimed softly. ''Tis Mistress Turncoat!' He exchanged a swift look with his friend. 'All alone?'

Conscious of a prickling of danger, she said quickly, 'John is waiting for me at the inn. I must go.'

'Oh, I think not!' said Mr Porteous, and before she could move his hand closed round her arm. 'You'd better come with us.'

'No!' She started to struggle, and as she did so, her kerchief fell, unnoticed, into the mud.

She heard Sir Harry say 'Leave her to me!', and the next moment something struck her a violent blow on the head. The world went black, and she knew no more.

As Cathie struggled back to consciousness, she heard someone say, 'She's coming round.'

The voice sounded a long way off. She moved her head a little, and felt a sharp stabbing pain above her right temple. She gave a moan, and forced her eyes open. Someone was standing over her. When her gaze cleared, she saw that it was Sir Harry Wyndham.

She seemed to be lying on a bed of some sort, covered by her own cloak. The room was not very warm, neither did it appear to be particularly large. The ceiling sloped; there was a damp patch in one corner.

'Am I—am I at the inn?' she asked faintly.

'The inn?' Sir Harry gave a short, derisive laugh. 'No, my sweet, you are not. What particular one had you in mind?'

'The—the Drake's Head. John will be waiting——' Her voice trailed away. It was almost too much of an effort to speak.

'Then he'll have to continue to wait. How did you come to be in Plymouth?'

'We—we went to see Aunt Lucy, at Tavistock, and then came on here this morning.'

'What brought you to Plymouth?'

Cathie put a hand to her head. 'Plymouth?' She winced as her fingers touched the swelling on her forehead, a little below the hairline.

'Yes—Plymouth! God's teeth! Do I have to repeat everything to you?'

Someone laughed nearby. 'Patience, Harry! Give her this. It may help to loosen her tongue.'

'This' proved to be brandy in a small glass. Cathie took it thankfully, though not being used to it, could not help spluttering and gasping as the fiery spirit slid down her throat.

'Better?' asked Sir Harry brusquely.

'Yes, thank you.'

He had removed his hat and Cathie saw that his hair, which she remembered as being worn in long Cavalier curls, had been shorn to within a few inches of his head. What with this, and the unkempt appearance he presented with his unshaven face and old, stained garments, it would have been difficult to associate him with the dashing young gentleman who had sat beside her at supper that night at Fern Place.

Mr Porteous came to stand beside him, regarding her with a sardonic look of amusement in his green eyes. He looked very much the same as his friend, his red hair straggling round his ears, his homespun shirt sweatstained beneath the old leather jerkin he wore over it.

'I can see you consider we make a fine picture,' he remarked.

She said nothing to that, but transferred her gaze to Sir Harry, who had pulled up a joint-stool and seated himself upon it.

'Now,' he said, 'perhaps you will be good enough to collect your thoughts and answer a few questions. First of all, why have you and your brother come to Plymouth?'

The brandy was taking effect, clearing her head, and bringing warmth and strength back to her body. She sat up carefully and put her feet to the floor, moving her cloak aside. The floor, which was bare of rugs, was none too clean. She saw that her couch was a shabby day-bed, drawn up before a small fire of smoking wood.

'Well?' said Sir Harry sharply.

Something warned her that it would be better to keep the truth hidden. 'I believe I told you we went on a visit to Aunt Lucy—my father's sister? Well, she asked us to come to Plymouth in order to—to find an old friend of hers, with whom she had lost touch because of the siege. She wanted her to go and stay with her for a while.'

Was the explanation plausible enough to convince them? She saw that they were both watching her intently.

'And have you found this friend?' Mr Porteous enquired.

'Not yet. We only arrived here this morning.'

'What is her name?—I presume it is a woman.'

'Yes.' Cathie paused, and then gave the first name that came into her head. 'Bassett. Mrs Bassett.'

'Where does she live?'

'John knows the address. I believe it is somewhere on the other side of the town. We are going there this afternoon. That is to say——' She broke off uncertainly.

Sir Harry smiled thinly. 'That is to say—you *were* going there this afternoon. I fear your brother will have to go without you.'

She took his meaning at once. 'You cannot keep me here against my will!'

'Unfortunately we have no choice. You recognised us, and we cannot run the risk of allowing you to leave. What is to stop you informing against us?'

'I shouldn't do that!'

'No? You have already shown that your sympathies lie with the Parliamentarian cause—or at least, with one particular advocate of that cause. Let me see, what was his name?'

Her heart began to thump painfully. 'Captain Denham.'

'Ah yes! The gallant Captain.' His voice was edged with malice. 'Do tell me—did he bed you that night? I have often wondered.'

Cathie felt her colour rise. 'No, he did not!'

'How disappointing for you. And there you were, positively palpitating for him! He must be a very dull fellow not to take advantage of such an opportunity.'

She said cuttingly, 'He is a gentleman, sir—which is more than can be said for some!'

Mr Porteous chuckled. 'Tit for tat! You asked for that, Harry!'

Sir Harry shrugged. 'What happened to him? I assume his wound has healed by this time?'

'Yes. He—he left a short while ago.' Not for the world would she tell them the truth—that as far as she knew he had been court-martialled as a result of the action he had been forced to take on their behalf. She would not give them the satisfaction of jeering at what, to them, would be the downfall of their enemy. Nor would she tell them that he might very well be in Plymouth at that very moment.

'Is Sir James home yet?' asked Sir Harry.

'Yes, he returned a few days ago.'

'I trust he is well?'

'Yes.' She paused, and then said quickly, 'I have answered all your questions. Pray give me leave to ask some of you!'

'Ask away.'

'How did *you* come to be here? We thought you would all be safely in France by this time.'

His face darkened. 'So we should have been, but for a series of mishaps. First of all the ship Wilmot procured for us was nought but a leaky old tub, and we had been at sea for less than twenty-four hours when she began to take in water like a sieve. Consequently we were forced to put back and find another vessel. While we waited, Somers and one or two of the others decided to try to reach the King at Oxford, so our party was a trifle depleted by the time we set sail again.'

'Was Rachel still with you?'

'No, she went with Somers.' He caught her look of surprise, and grinned. 'She decided she'd had enough of being tossed about on the sea. Apart from that, she'd quarrelled violently with George. I fancy the parting was a relief to both of them.' Getting to his feet, he kicked at the sulky fire, succeeding only in causing it to belch smoke into the room. He retreated, cursing.

'The wood's wet,' Mr Porteous observed.

'What happened when you set sail again?' Cathie asked.

'We made good progress until we rounded the Scilly Isles, when we had the misfortune to run into bad weather. 'Od rot me, I thought our end had come! Such waves! You never saw the like!' Sir Harry grimaced at the memory. 'However, the gale finally blew itself out, and we were able to get back on our course.'

'And then'—Mr Porteous took over the narrative—'as we were sailing up the Channel, we had the confounded ill luck to be sighted by a Parliamentarian man-of-war. Her captain ordered us to heave to. Ours said he'd be damned if he would!' He grinned. 'He gave the crop-ears a run for their money!'

'What happened?'

'They opened fire on us; and, damme, scored a hit! The ball struck the mainmast and down it came, with most of the sails.'

'Good heavens! Was anyone hurt?'

'No one was killed, but some of the crew were injured. The enemy ship promptly ceased firing. Their captain must have thought our capture was a foregone conclusion, but he was wrong. It had been misty for most of the day and then, with evening approaching, the mist thickened, thus enabling us to slip away like some lame duck, making use of the few sails that were left. Early the following morning our captain put into a small inlet, a mile or so to the west of Mount Edgcumbe.' He paused, regarding Cathie enquiringly. 'You've heard of Mount Edgcumbe, no doubt?'

'Yes. Colonel Edgcumbe has been holding it for the Royalists, hasn't he?'

James had remarked that the house was in an ideal position, situated as it was above the entrance to the Tamar overlooking Plymouth, so that the garrison there was able not only to harass the town, but also any shipping bold enough to venture into the Sound.

'We hoped he would be able to help us, but unfortunately on the day before our arrival he had begun negotiating with Fairfax for surrender terms. However, he did find someone willing to hide us for a few days, until another ship could be found to take us to France.'

'But before that could happen, we were betrayed!' Sir Harry put in, scowling. 'We had to make a run for it.'

'Harry and I escaped. George didn't.' Mr Porteous pulled a face. 'Poor George! He'll be on his way to the Tower by now.'

'The Tower of London?'

'They won't be taking any chances with him. He's far too important to them.'

Sir Harry nodded agreement, and they both fell silent, their thoughts doubtless with their captured colleague.

Cathie moved a little. 'But you managed to reach Plymouth safely?'

'As you see,' Sir Harry replied laconically.

'And you are still waiting for a ship?'

They exchanged a quick glance. 'We should soon be leaving,' said Sir Harry.

He turned, and went to stand at the grimy window, looking down at the street below. Cathie glanced round, and saw that the room was a bedchamber; the bed itself was of carved oak, hung with limp curtains of faded damask. There was little else in the room save for a closet, a table, a heavy oak chest and one or two stools. Wherever she looked there was evidence of neglect. The linen on the unmade bed was none too clean; cobwebs hung from the ceiling, and the floorboards were ingrained with dirt. There was an overall smell of damp and decay. She moved her shoulders in a gesture of distaste.

'Not what one would choose, is it?' asked Mr Porteous, watching her.

'How long have you been here?'

'A couple of days.'

Sir Harry called him over to the window. 'That boy, loitering about down there. See him? He's watching the house. Wait here, I'm going to have a word with Bodman.' He strode to the door, and went out.

Cathie heard him clatter down the stairs. She stood up and approached the window, but before she could look out Mr Porteous stepped in front of her.

'Sorry, my sweet, but I cannot allow you to show yourself at the window. You'd best go and sit down again.'

'Nobody is likely to recognise me!' she protested.

'Perhaps not, but they might wonder who you were, and what you were doing here.'

'They might think the same about you and Sir Harry!'

He smiled. 'I doubt it. Seamen come and go all the time, and this is well-known as a sailors' lodging-house. No one is likely to give us a second look in these clothes, whereas your appearance is far too elegant for such humble surroundings.'

'I didn't ask to be brought here!' she flashed, and returned with ill grace to the day-bed.

On the way she cast a measuring look towards the door, which did not go unnoticed by Mr Porteous. He shook his head at her.

'I wouldn't advise you to try to escape! There's always someone downstairs—Bodman, or his servant.'

'Bodman?'

'The landlord of this salubrious property.'

Sir Harry came back into the room, frowning. 'The boy has disappeared. Bodman sent his man out to look for him, but he drew a blank. A pity——' He picked up his battered old hat. 'Bodman wants us to go with him now.' He turned to Cathie. 'This way, mistress.' He gestured for her to precede him out of the door.

She took her cloak off the day-bed. 'Am I to accompany you?' she asked in surprise.

'Yes; as far as the back room!' Taking her arm, he led her swiftly across the small landing to a door opposite. Opening it, he thrust her inside, and before she had recovered her breath slammed the door shut and turned the key in the lock. A moment later she heard the two men descending the stairs. There was a rumble of voices, a door closed; then there was silence.

Cathie looked about her. The room was a small bedchamber, furnished even more meanly than the other, with a truckle bed, a stool and a chest. On the chest stood a cracked earthenware pitcher and a dirty pewter bowl. Evidently the seamen who came to lodge here were not fussy about their surroundings.

She went to the window and, finding it difficult to see anything clearly through the film of dirt on the diamond panes, gave one of them a vigorous rub with the corner of her cloak. She was then able to see that there was a small walled garden below, with a gate in the far wall. It appeared to open on to an alleyway.

The garden itself was nothing but a patch of earth with two gnarled apple trees in it. Half a dozen hens were scratching away beneath them, in a dispirited fashion. She was about to turn away from the window when her gaze was caught by a swift movement at the top of the far wall. Someone had climbed up on the outside.

First she saw a pair of hands, followed by a face crowned by a thatch of tow-coloured hair. Her heart gave a sudden leap. From this distance she could not see his freckles, but she knew at once who he was—the boy who had given her the directions to the Drake's Head!

She tried frantically to open the window, intending to call out to him, but it was too stiff to move. Instead she banged upon it with her knuckles, and to her relief, saw that she had succeeded in attracting his attention. He lifted one hand and waved, then he disappeared, as swiftly as he had come.

No sooner had he done so than a man emerged from the house and came out into the garden, staring suspiciously about him. Cathie guessed he must have heard her banging on the window. He looked quickly up at her. Too late to draw back out of sight, she stood there, holding herself still, gazing disdainfully down at him.

Short and squat, he was muscularly built, with a distinctly unprepossessing appearance. The thought flashed through her mind that she would not care to be molested by him. His weather-beaten face creased into an evil smile, and before returning into the house he gave her a low, mocking bow.

She went slowly over to the bed and sat down upon it, pulling her cloak round her. She was alone in the house with him, locked in this room, with the key still in the door. He only had to unlock it. . . .

She gave a shudder and then deliberately switched her thoughts to the boy. He must have been the one Sir Harry had seen watching the front of the house. For some reason he had been looking for her: he knew now that she was here. But what would he do? Could she rely on him to fetch help? She heard the man moving about downstairs, singing lustily.

She sat very still, her gaze fixed upon the door.

CHAPTER
THIRTEEN

THE landlord said for the third time, 'She ran out without a word, sir.' He rubbed his chin. 'That's all I can tell 'ee.'

He and John were standing on the steps leading up to the inn door, and John was scanning the street with growing anxiety.

'Soon after I went round to the stables, you say?'

'Aye, sir.'

'That would be about a quarter of an hour ago. Where the devil can she be?'

'Ah well, sir, as to that, I don't rightly know. 'Er went away up the street as though she'd seen someone she knew and wanted to talk to 'im. Don't 'ee fret, sir. 'Er's bound to be back soon.'

'I hope so.' John gave another look along the street. Then he said, 'I think I'll go and see if I can find her.'

'Ar. You do that, sir.'

The landlord watched John stride away, and then turned and went back inside the inn. He was not a man given to fanciful notions, but he had to admit to himself that he would feel a lot happier if the young gentleman returned with his sister, safe and secure. There were too many soldiers about for his liking, and though they might be better disciplined than those whoring Cavalier rakehells, they were soldiers for all that, and there was no accounting for what they might do with a bellyful of ale inside them.

But when John did return, some time later, he was alone; and he looked more anxious than ever when he found that Cathie had not come back.

'If she went after someone, sir, mebbe she's with 'im,' the landlord suggested.

'But we don't know anyone in Plymouth, except——' John stopped. 'I wonder if it could have been Major Dowd?'

'The officer you was expecting to 'ear some news from? Aye, well it could be.' He looked at John's worried face and said bracingly, "E'll be bringing 'er back any minute, you'll see!'

With these hopeful words he went back to the tap-room, leaving

John to his troubled thoughts. Going over to the window in the little parlour, John stood there, gazing out, hoping against hope that he would suddenly see Cathie hurrying back to the inn.

Time dragged by, and there was still no sign of her. He sank down wearily on the window-seat, shoulders hunched, head bent, turning over all the possible explanations in his mind. He did not heed the clatter of hooves on the cobbles outside, did not hear a voice call to the landlord, or the door open. It was not until his name was spoken that he became aware that someone had entered the room.

He started, and looked up, then his eyes widened. Standing before him, a broad smile on his face, was the last person he had expected to see—Captain Denham.

John got hurriedly to his feet. 'Thank God you've come!'

Denham's smile faded. 'John—what is it? What's wrong?'

'It's Cathie! She's—she's missing.' He told him what he knew—that Cathie had run out, without any explanation, and had not come back.

'If she followed someone, it certainly wasn't Jack Dowd,' Denham declared. 'He has been waiting for me for the past couple of hours or so. I've been out with a patrol, searching the harbour.'

A wry smile touched John's lips. 'Looking for escaped Royalists?'

'In point of fact, yes. When I got back and Jack told me you and Cathie were here, and your reason for coming, I could scarcely believe it. Did she not receive my letter?'

'No!'

'I wrote some days ago, to tell her I had been freed and was about to rejoin the army at Pendennis.'

'So there was no court-martial?'

'No, I have Jack to thank for that. When he heard what had happened, he went straight to Tom—Lord Fairfax—and put the matter before him. Tom intervened on my behalf, and so—' he shrugged—'here I am.'

'If only Cathie had had your letter! She was terribly worried.' John paused, then said diffidently, 'She loves you, you know.'

Something burned for a moment in Denham's eyes. 'Yes, I do know.'

John's gaze searched his face. 'And you love her, don't you? What I cannot understand is why you didn't tell her! You don't seem to understand how unhappy she's been——'

Denham's mouth tightened. 'Do you suppose I *wanted* to hurt her? I acted the way I did for her sake. I thought at the time it would be better for her if we did not become too involved with one another.'

'In heaven's name, why?'

Denham gave a twisted smile. 'Tell me—what is your brother's opinion of me?'

John looked momentarily disconcerted. Then, choosing his words carefully, he replied, 'He hasn't been back long. I suppose it's only natural that he should feel antagonistic towards you.' He stopped, frowning. 'Was that the reason why you—because of James?'

'He's Cathie's guardian. I considered it would be totally wrong for us to marry without his consent.'

'It won't come to that! Mary is on your side, and so am I! Between us, we ought to manage to persuade him to change his mind before long.'

'I'm delighted to hear it! I must tell you that since leaving Fern Place I have come to realise I am not prepared to give Cathie up—not for any man!'

'Good!' John approved. Then he sighed. 'If only we knew where she was!'

Denham appeared to be turning something over in his mind. 'You say she might have seen someone she knew? I think you could be right. I should tell you that the men we were looking for earlier today were among Lord George Randolph's party.'

'What!'

'We received word a couple of days ago that their ship had been forced to put in along the coast, and that they were to be found hiding in a house not far from Mount Edgcumbe. Lord George was captured, but the other two—Sir Harry Wyndham and Mr Porteous—escaped.'

'That's only three of them! What happened to the others?'

'His lordship informed us that when they reached Bideford they decided to go their own way.'

'And—and Rachel?' Despite himself, John's voice was not quite steady.

'I understand that she remained with Lord Somers. There seems to have been a difference of opinion between herself and Lord George.'

'I see.' John stared fixedly at the floor. He roused himself to say, 'What happened to—to Sir Harry and Mr Porteous?'

'As I told you, we believe them to be in Plymouth.' Denham's face hardened. 'I fear Cathie may have fallen in with them.'

John's face paled. 'Oh God! I hope not! Not after the way they behaved towards her when they were at Fern Place!'

'We have searched every ship in the harbour and every tavern and alehouse in the vicinity, and found nothing. A description of the two men has been circulated, but so far no one has come forward with any information.' He struck his clenched fist on the table. 'Dammit—they must be here somewhere! If they have Cathie, I'll tear the whole place apart to find her!'

'And I'll help you do it!' John declared.

'Someone is hiding them, there's no doubt of that. They've probably disguised their appearance in order to escape detection.'

'Where do you think they can be?'

'Somewhere near the harbour, waiting for a ship to take them to France or the Low Countries.'

'If they have got Cathie, do you suppose they intend to use her as a hostage?'

'They're desperate men. They'll seize upon any chance to remain free.'

Sick at heart, John turned away and went over to the window. Behind him he heard the door open and swung quickly round, to find that the landlord had entered.

'Beg pardon, sirs! There's a lad outside asking for a young lady. It sounds to me as though it could be Mistress Gifford——'

'Bring him in!' Denham commanded.

He came, staring in awe at the two gentlemen, and apparently so overcome by the sight of them that he was momentarily rendered speechless. The landlord prodded him in the back and adjured him to 'speak up, and be sharp about it!'

The boy gulped, and began at a great rate. 'If you please, the young lady asked me the way 'ere, and I told 'un and she give me a penny, and I thought she might get lost again and I went after 'er, and there was two men and they took 'er away——' He snatched a much-needed breath.

'Where did they take her?' Denham asked quickly, before he could launch forth again.

'To Bodman's. 'E keeps a lodging-house for seamen.'

'You're sure the men took her there?'

The boy nodded vigorously. 'I seen 'er at the window. An' I found 'er kerchief.' He produced it from inside his grubby shirt and handed it to Denham, who examined the embroidered initials.

'Yes, it's Cathie's,' he said, giving it to John. He looked down at the diminutive figure before him. 'What is your name?'

'Toby, sir.'

'Very well, Toby. Can you take us to Bodman's?'

'Aye, than I can, sir. Bain't far from 'ere.'

'I know the place, sir,' said the landlord. 'That Bodman—'e bain't partic'lar what 'e does, so long as there be money in it.'

'Is there only the one entrance to the house?'

'No, sir,' said Toby eagerly, 'there's a gate at the back. I climbed the wall—that's 'ow I come to see the young lady——'

'In a back room?'

'Ar. Upstairs, 'twere. The others 'ad gone out—Bodman and the men that took 'er. I saw 'em. But there's another man there, Jud Hawkins, 'im what works fur Bodman. 'E's there still.'

John picked up his hat. 'We'd better go at once.'

Denham was already turning towards the door. 'Adam is outside, I'll send him back with a message for Jack Dowd. A few more men will not come amiss.' He caught John's questioning glance. 'Once we have Cathie safely out of the house, I want you to bring her straight back here.'

'And you?'

'I shall stay there until my men arrive, and then—we shall see.'

They went out, John reflecting that it was an odd business when he, a Royalist, should be assisting a Parliamentarian officer to capture two men who had fought for the King; and yet what other course had he? Cathie's safety depended upon it, and he reminded himself that both Sir Harry and Mr Porteous had shown themselves to be men with little principle, capable of the most callous and reckless actions in order to gain their own ends.

It did not take them long to reach the alleyway behind the house. They looked up at the back window, but it remained blank. Denham, taller than John, craned his neck to peer over the top of the wall.

'There's no one about. Toby'—he beckoned the boy closer—'I want you to run round to the front of the house and bang as loudly as you can on the street door. While Hawkins is answering it, we shall go in at the back. Off you go!'

'Yessir!' Toby made off along the alleyway as fast as he could, and disappeared round the corner. Denham waited until he judged that the boy had reached the front of the house, and then opened the gate and strode quickly up the path, scattering the hens as he went. In his hand was a pistol.

John, hard on his heels, followed him into the kitchen. On the table were the remains of a meal, together with a black-jack and a pewter ale-can, both empty. At the same moment, they heard a furious thumping on the street door.

Opening off the kitchen was another room, sparsely furnished with a table and stools, and a dilapidated court cupboard. They passed through it and into the dark passage leading to the foot of the stairs. There was no sign of Hawkins.

'Odd,' Denham muttered. 'Where has the man gone?'

'Listen!' John clutched at his arm.

From above came the sound of a scuffle, a man's triumphant laugh, a sobbing cry. Denham took the rickety stairs two at a time, arriving in the open doorway of the back room to see Cathie doing her best to fend off the advances of the brutish Hawkins who, with a gloating smile on his ugly face, had her pinned against the wall.

Denham rushed forward, and before the man could move, struck him on the back of the head with his pistol-butt. Hawkins uttered a surprised grunt, staggered and crashed to the floor, where he lay still.

'Piers!' Cathie was staring at him incredulously. The next moment, she was in his arms. He held her trembling body tightly against him, soothing her with murmured endearments, and gently stroking the side of her face and neck.

He became aware that John was standing hesitantly in the doorway and lifting his head, said quietly, 'Go and tell Toby to stop battering the door down, will you? Oh—and ask him to keep watch. If he sees Bodman and the others returning, he's to come in the back way and warn us.'

John nodded in reply, and went.

'Was that John?' Cathie asked, somewhat incoherently. She added, 'Is he very angry with me?' She moved a little, so that she could look up into his face. 'I saw Adam. I wanted to ask him about you, but I lost him.—Oh, Piers! You're free! I can't believe it!' Tears of joy hung upon her lashes.

He bent his head and kissed her; and then, with sudden hunger, kissed her again, his mouth on hers fiercely demanding. Her lips clung to his, her arms went round his neck. Time lost its meaning. His hand moved over her back, pressing her even closer against him. She felt the masculine hardness of his body, and her own instant response to it.

When he had kissed her before he had awakened her to the meaning of love, now her body longed for fulfilment.

He drew his mouth away from hers, and looked searchingly into her face, then he gave a little shake of the head.

'I think it is time to stop,' he said softly. 'Don't you?'

Her pulses were racing, but she gave a long-drawn-out sigh. 'If you say so——'

'There will be all the time in the world after we're married.'

'Married?'

'Does the idea not appeal to you?'

'Oh yes! But you never said anything before. I thought you—you didn't care for me.'

'And all the time I was longing to tell you I loved you! Do you know why I remained silent?'

He told her, and she listened and nodded gravely. 'Mary said we must give James time to—to adjust.'

'How long do you suppose that will take?—For I am not prepared to wait for ever! I intend to claim you directly the war is over and I am free of my obligation to Tom and the Parliamentary cause!'

She sighed, her eyes misty. 'Oh, Piers! I do love you!'

He brushed her forehead with his lips, and to his surprise, felt her wince. Lifting the hair back from her face, he exposed the bruise on her temple. ''Od's wounds!' he exclaimed. 'Who did this to you?'

'Sir Harry.'

His face darkened. 'That's another score I have to settle with him! And the sooner the better.' Still frowning, he looked towards the door. 'John is very quiet down there. Perhaps he's in the garden. Come, I'll take you to him, and then he can escort you back to the inn.'

He led her to the door, and they descended the stairs together.

'Are you not coming?' she asked.

'Not yet. I shall wait here, until——'

He broke off. As they reached the passage, someone came out of the shadows, and they found themselves facing Sir Harry Wyndham, pistol in hand.

He smiled mockingly. 'Well met, Captain Denham! I hear you have been searching the harbour for us. Ah, allow me to relieve you of your weapon.' He held out his free hand. Denham hesitated and then, seeing he had no choice, relinquished his pistol.

'What have you done with Mr Gifford?' he asked curtly.

'He's in the kitchen, tied up and gagged, together with that grubby little urchin who I gather is your informant. You will be joining them shortly, but we have other plans for Mistress Cathie.'

Cathie felt a tremor of fear. 'What do you mean?'

He transferred his mocking gaze to her. 'Had the Captain not come to your rescue, we would have left you here, safe and sound, and Bodman would have released you in due course. As it is, we are forced to take you with us——'

'Safe and sound!' Denham expostulated. 'You left her here to the mercy of that vile ruffian upstairs! Had we not arrived when we did, God knows what he might have done to her!'

There came a sudden exclamation of shocked disbelief. Mr Porteous was standing in the doorway of the ill-furnished parlour, a sharp-featured, middle-aged man peering over his shoulder.

Mr Porteous looked at Sir Harry. 'I told you I didn't trust him!'

Sir Harry gave an irritable shrug and slid a glance towards Cathie. 'I'm sorry. Pray accept my apology. This way, please.' He indicated that they were to precede him into the parlour.

Denham took up his stance in the middle of the floor, his arm round Cathie. 'I trust you have apologised for striking her?' he asked curtly.

'That was—that was necessary.'

'To save your miserable skin?' Denham saw Sir Harry's colour rise, and went on deliberately, 'You are nothing but a loathsome bully; a cowardly braggart, full of fire and empty words!'

Sir Harry's eyes flashed. 'Have a care what you say!'

'I seem to remember you were all for running me through with your sword! Why don't you try it? Or are you only brave when you're drunk? A pot-valiant hero——'

With a furious oath, Sir Harry cried, 'No one insults me and goes unpunished! Den, fetch my sword!'

Mr Porteous stared at him in consternation. 'No, Harry! Think what you're about. There isn't time. We have to be at the ship by dusk——'

'There's time enough to teach this upstart a lesson! My sword, if you please!'

Mr Porteous groaned. 'Oh, very well! It's wrapped in your cloak.' He dived into the kitchen and reappeared a few seconds later, handing the sheathed sword to Sir Harry.

The middle-aged man, who had hitherto been a silent onlooker, said anxiously, 'The light's fading already, sir!'

'Be damned to you, Bodman!' Sir Harry retorted. 'Stop whining!

This won't take long.'

Bodman looked from him to Mr Porteous, muttered something and retreated into the kitchen, apparently washing his hands of the whole affair.

Cathie looked up beseechingly into Denham's face. 'Piers——' she whispered.

He gave her a reassuring smile. 'I know what I'm doing,' he said quietly.

The table and stools were moved hastily out of the way, leaving a clear space in the centre of the room. Denham's sword rasped as he drew it from the scabbard; Sir Harry's was already drawn. He gave Denham a swift, measuring look, and then lunged forward. Denham, ice-cool and purposeful, parried the thrust. Cathie shrank back, white-faced, into the kitchen doorway, where she was joined by Mr Porteous, who was holding Sir Harry's pistol.

Through the clash of sword-blades, she was vaguely aware of other sounds, as of someone moving hurriedly about, opening and closing cupboards and drawers. Mr Porteous muttered, 'Bodman is deserting us. If I had a ha'porth of sense, I'd follow him.'

'Then why don't you?' Cathie snapped in low, fierce tones.

He shrugged, his gaze on the duellists. 'I'll stay with Harry.'

It was apparent to him, if not to Cathie, that his friend was going to be hard put to it to make good his boast. Excellent swordsman though he was, the Captain was more than a match for him. Again and again Sir Harry attempted to pass his guard, but each time the Captain's sword met his, turning the blade aside.

The furious energy with which Sir Harry had begun the duel was beginning to drain away, his breathing becoming increasingly irregular. His swordplay had acquired an element of desperation. He felt himself sweating. Confound it! He would not be beaten by this scurvy runyon!

Summoning up his strength, he rushed in once more with a lightning thrust aimed at the Captain's heart, only to find once again that Denham had parried the blow with masterly skill.

He ground his teeth in fury, and Denham smiled. Hitherto he had been content to allow Sir Harry to take the initiative, biding his time and conserving his own energy. He considered that the moment had now arrived for him to turn the tables upon his flagging opponent, and proceeded to do so with a dazzling display of swordsmanship that brought a gasp of admiration from Mr Porteous, even while he cocked the pistol in readiness. If it came to it he would stop the

Captain with a bullet in order to save his friend, not only from defeat but possible death.

That moment came swiftly and suddenly. Forced to retreat, Sir Harry lost his head and attempted a wild riposte. Denham parried the blow with ease and then, with Sir Harry off guard, struck. The latter fell back with a gasp of pain, blood trickling down his sword-arm.

Mr Porteous raised the pistol and Cathie, becoming aware of his intention, uttered a cry of warning as she turned upon him, her hand going out to grasp his wrist. He thrust her aside, knocking her to the floor. At the same moment she heard a sudden shout, a rush of heavy footsteps, and in a trice the room seemed to be full of buff-coated soldiers.

She scrambled to her feet in time to see Mr Porteous overwhelmed before he had the chance to fire his weapon. Sir Harry had collapsed upon a stool, holding his arm, his face ashen.

Denham, having confiscated his sword, gave it into the keeping of the red-faced sergeant who was in charge of the men, and made his way swiftly to Cathie's side.

'Did that blackguard hurt you?'

She shook her head. Her eyes shone. 'How splendid you were! Oh, I'm so glad you taught him a lesson!'

'That was my intention.'

She caught the steely note in his voice. 'Would you have killed him?'

'Remembering the way he treated you, I would have run him through with the greatest of pleasure. However, my orders were to take both malignants alive, if possible.'

'What will happen to them now?'

'A spell of imprisonment. They'll probably be released on payment of a heavy fine; perhaps banished from the country.' A sardonic smile touched his lips. 'They'll reach France, after all.'

The room was emptying. The soldiers marched their prisoners outside, and John and Toby had been released from their bonds. Denham gave the latter a broadpiece for his help and, speechless with delight, he scampered homewards, doubtless to regale his family with an account of his adventures.

Hawkins, coming groggily down the stairs at this moment, was chased out by John, who helped him on his way with a well-placed kick.

They went back to the inn, to find James there.

He was standing before the fireplace in the little parlour, a certain air of challenge in the tilt of his head that reminded Denham at once of Cathie and John. These Giffords, he reflected with wry amusement, were very much alike. Then he reminded himself that James was the head of the family, and as such had power over his future.

The introductions were made by Cathie, a faintly troubled look in her eyes. The two men shook hands, appraising one another.

'James, what are you doing here?' John demanded. 'We were not expecting to see you for at least another week.'

'I would not have come, had it not been for this.' James produced the letter in its two halves, which he handed to Cathie. In quick, incisive tones he explained what had happened—that his intention had been to destroy it. 'I was entirely in the wrong, I know that now. I can only ask your forgiveness, Cathie—and yours, Captain Denham. Mary took me to task in no uncertain terms.'

He gave a rueful smile. 'As you see, we broke the seal and read the letter, and when we discovered that you had been released and were on your way to Pendennis, Mary told me that it was Cathie's intention to seek out Lord Fairfax there, and beg him to save your life——'

'I know.' Denham spoke quietly. His expression, as he gazed at Cathie, held such a depth of feeling that James was left in no doubt that he loved her with all his heart. Glancing quickly at Cathie, he saw the same luminous look reflected in her own eyes.

He felt a stab of remorse, remembering his efforts to part them, which but for Mary's intervention might well have succeeded. He and Mary had sat up late last night, talking things over and unburdening their hearts to one another, until all bitterness, all misunderstandings, had gone.

'So you followed us?' John's voice broke the spell.

'Yes, we thought it was the best thing to do. Aunt Lucy sent me on here.' James turned to Denham. 'She and Mary were both of the opinion that the sooner I met you, the better it would be for all concerned. Would it be possible for you to join us for supper, Captain?'

'Thank you,' Denham said promptly. 'I accept with pleasure, though I must first return to headquarters and make my report——'

'Ah yes! What happened this afternoon? The landlord told me that Cathie had been abducted, and you had gone to her rescue. Is that right?'

They recounted the story between them, and he listened with furrowed brow and growing anger. "Slud!' he exclaimed. 'What kind of men are they, to act in such a fashion? Mary spoke to me of the way they, and the others, behaved on the night they came to Fern Place. I am ashamed to own them as comrades in arms, though I fear there were many like them in the King's armies.' He glanced at Denham. 'I owe you a debt of gratitude for rescuing Cathie from their clutches. Had you not done so, I dread to think what might have happened to her.'

Supper was a convivial occasion, and as they talked, James found that he and Denham had more in common than he would have been prepared to acknowledge at one time. John joined in the conversation, but Cathie was content for the most part to sit and listen, her gaze turning from one to the other, a glow of happiness warming her heart.

James said, 'How long do you expect to remain in Plymouth, Captain?'

'A few days only. Lord Fairfax intends to march upon Exeter and summon the Royalist garrison to surrender.'

'A matter of form, I should have thought. Sir John Berkeley is hardly likely to put up a show of resistance.' Once James would have returned a harsh answer; now the matter seemed almost unimportant. 'And after that—what?'

'Oh—Oxford and the King.'

James nodded. 'And when the war is over?'

Denham's glance strayed to Cathie. 'I hope to come back to Devon.'

James twirled the stem of his wine glass. 'May I ask your intentions concerning my sister?'

Denham smiled. 'I want to marry her,' he said simply.

Again James nodded. 'Very well, Captain. When you are free of your obligations, I shall be happy to welcome you at Fern Place as Cathie's future husband.'

They said their goodbyes a few days later, on the eve of the departure of the New Model Army for Exeter. Cathie would also be leaving in the morning, riding home with John and James.

'You'll write to me?' she said.

'I'll bombard you with letters!'

'And I shall reply to every one.' She stirred in Denham's arms, and he kissed her, his lips moving across her cheek and covering her mouth, so that her bones seemed to melt.

'My love, my love,' Denham said achingly. One last kiss; and then he released her. Turning to Rom, he swung himself up into the saddle, waved a hand in salute, and rode away over the cobbles. The darkness swallowed him up.

Cathie sighed, and someone came out of the inn behind her.

'He'll be back,' said John.

Masquerade
Historical Romances

Intrigue excitement romance

Don't miss
September's
other enthralling Historical Romance title

HOUSE OF SATAN
by Gina Veronese

In 1785, Vienna's gaiety has been curbed by the
Emperor who has closed all public amusements.
The nobility, led by the elegant Count Anton von
Arnheim, refuse to have their pleasures curtailed.
The Count's home is called the House of Satan, for
the gambling, dancing and flirtation so beloved by
the Viennese continues there undisturbed. And
into this notorious mansion comes Eloise, his
innocently beautiful ward.

How can so unscrupulous a rake become the
guardian of such a young and unworldly girl? And
how can the spirited Eloise, thrilled to be
introduced to the sophisticated pursuits of the
Count, go on living in the House of Satan with the
man who threatens to own her body and soul?

You can obtain this title today from your local paperback
retailer

Masquerade
Historical Romances

Intrigue excitement romance

TARRISBROKE HALL
by Jasmine Cresswell

Utter ruin confronted the Earl of Tarrisbroke. Faced with discharging his father's mountainous gambling debts, what could he do but marry for money? But the wife he chose, the wealthy young widow Marianne Johnson, was not at all the vulgar title-hunting woman he expected!

ZULU SUNSET
by Christina Laffeaty

Cassandra Hudson wanted to be a missionary's wife — more particularly, her cousin Martin's wife. So she travelled to Zululand to visit him, confident that her new fortune would smooth her way. Unfortunately she found herself in the midst of an impending war between whites and Zulus, and the only man who could help her reach Martin was the odious, arrogant Saul Parnell . . .

Look out for these titles in your local paperback shop from 10th October 1980